Sonia wiped sauce from her chin and licked her fingers. She approached Marina and ogled her breasts under the black bodice. "How about you and I have a little fun, sister?" she suggested coyly.

As Sonia raised her hand to touch, Marina grabbed her wrist and nearly broke it. "Touch me and I'll rip your heart out, *sister*."

Marina whirled, and placed the barrel of her pulse pistol against Sonia's forehead. "Do that again and I'll put a hole in that bubble head of yours," she warned.

Balthus opened the flat cedar box on his desk and depressed a button inside. The trap floor sprang open in front of the desk and Marina dropped to a holding cell below.

PRINCESS PAIN

by Michael D'Ambrosio

A BlackWyrm Book
Louisville, Kentucky

PRINCESS PAIN

A BlackWyrm Book
BlackWyrm Publishing
10307 Chimney Ridge Ct, Louisville, KY 40299

Printed in the United States of America.

ISBN: 978-1-61318-157-7
Cover design by Andy Rector
Edited by Ian Harac

First edition: March 2014
Second edition: December 2014

Dedicated to my wife, MaryJane
Without her support, I could not have come this far.

Chapter 1

Just Another Job

The Stanton District, twenty miles outside the palace area on the Planet Yord, was once a bustling city with a massive transportation hub that supported spacecraft coming and going all day and night from across the galaxy. When the war broke out due to the greed of several of the lords, the Human League of Kingdoms was broken into a hodgepodge group of thugs and militias. As a result, alien races shunned the once-buzzing metropolis and the loss of commerce transformed it to only a dying memory of what it once was.

Thirty years of neglect turned the once mighty kingdom of Yord into ruins. Many of its people fled the planet in search of more economically viable locations to avoid the scarcities of resources that ensued.

Moonlight shone randomly through passing clouds, landing on a wet cobblestone street in Stanton. A wooden sign in front of a blacksmith's shop creaked in the evening breeze.

A cloaked woman, Marina, hid in the doorway of a vacant shop as two men unknowingly walked past her with pulse pistols in hand. When they disappeared from sight, she stepped into the street and removed her hood.

Marina, thirty years old, tall with a long dreadlock wig and flash grenades shaped like silver balls attached to the locks, crossed the street, approaching the wooden door to an old warehouse. She knocked twice and waited.

A long-haired, mustached man opened the door slightly and peeked out at her. He was dressed in black denim jeans and a white shirt with a pulse pistol attached to his belt. "What do you want?" he asked impatiently as he pointed his pistol in her face.

"I have something for Balthus," she replied in a low monotone voice.

The man stepped aside and allowed her to enter. As soon as she cleared the doorway, he closed and latched the door. Marina knew what was coming next.

Two torches provided the only light in the hall and the flames left eerie shadows along the rutted walls. The wooden floor creaked as Marina stepped away from the man and stood by one of the torches.

"You must be Marina," he remarked in mild surprise. "Balthus didn't think you'd make it."

"I'm sure he was betting on it as well," she retorted. "Let's keep this brief, shall we?"

The man didn't appreciate her sarcasm. "Any weapons you have need to come off now," he ordered.

"Of course," Marina replied irritably as she removed her cloak. He was immediately distracted by her shapely form, well-displayed in the tight leather bodice and pants. Marina took advantage of his lapse of attention and tossed the cloak to him.

Instinctively he dropped his guard and reached for it. As he did, she lunged and punched him in the bridge of his nose. Falling into unconsciousness from the blow, he slid down the wall, ending at a sitting position with his head tilted down. Blood streamed from his nose, staining the front of his shirt.

Marina took her cloak from him and folded it over her arm. She picked the man's pistol up off the floor and stepped lightly across the hall. An office door squeaked as she turned the knob and pushed it open.

Inside the dilapidated chamber behind a steel desk, sat a grossly obese man, Balthus, with a scraggily beard and a long, ugly scar across his left cheek. He wore a red plaid kilt, boots and no shirt. On the desk to his left was a cedar box. To his right, a pail of chicken legs and a pitcher of dark ale

A blonde harlot, Sonia, sat on his lap. She was very petite, middle-aged, and dressed scantily in a partially unbuttoned blouse and a tattered mini-skirt. Without a bra, her perky breasts were quite visible, one through the blouse and the other displayed for Balthus' pleasure.

The two gorged sloppily on the chicken, drenched in a spicy sauce that filled the air with its aroma. Sonia licked blotches of sauce off of Balthus' chin and savored the taste with a lick of her lips.

Marina pushed the door open further and stepped inside, the pistol hidden under the folded cloak on her arm. She noticed the moth-eaten carpet tossed over the wooden-planked floor. The worn cloth extended from the door to about four feet short of Balthus' desk, which made her all the more suspicious.

Candles on either end of the desk dimly lit the room. Electricity was expensive and lights at night tended to attract soldiers and thugs.

When she saw Balthus and his young slut gorging themselves like gluttons, she felt nauseated and disgusted by their very presence. Most of her customers were pathetic degenerates but Balthus, by far, was the worst.

Balthus and Sonia stopped eating and looked up at Marina with amused expressions.

Sonia smiled coyly at Marina, revealing three missing teeth. She lapped at her lips seductively with her tongue and leered at their guest.

Marina ignored her and maintained eye contact with Balthus. She often countered the initial intimidation of a customer with a cold, unflinching stare; an effective deterrent that earned her respect from those clients.

"I'm surprised to see you, Marina," Balthus remarked pleasantly. "I sent my men to ensure you made it here safely with my merchandise."

"No worries. I handled them."

Balthus set his chicken leg down on the table and became concerned. "I hope you didn't kill Jerrold. If you did, you'll be doing his chores for me and, I promise, you won't like them very much," he warned as he reached under his kilt and stroked himself. "Get my point?" He and Sonia cackled giddily.

Marina ignored his crude gesture and remained focused. The very thought of physical contact with this grotesque slob made her want to vomit. "Jerrold is taking a little nap," she informed him. "Now, let's get down to business."

Balthus gently pushed Sonia off his lap. He brushed bits of chicken off his chest onto the floor and stood.

Sonia wiped sauce from her chin and licked her fingers. She approached Marina and ogled her breasts under the black bodice. "How about you and I have a little fun, sister?" she suggested coyly.

As Sonia raised her hand to touch her, Marina grabbed her wrist and nearly broke it. "Touch me and I'll rip your heart out, *sister*."

Balthus laughed hysterically at them.

Sonia stepped back defensively and rubbed her wrist tenderly. She glanced at Balthus and commented, "She looks good enough to eat, Honey."

Balthus ignored her and guzzled from the pitcher of ale. He leaned with both hands on the desk and inquired, "You have something that belongs to me, Marina?"

"Perhaps. And you have payment for delivery of that something?" she responded arrogantly.

"Let me see it first."

Marina pulled a data chip on a plastic cord from under her bodice and dangled it in the air for Balthus to see. Like Jerrold, he was distracted by her breasts, grinning perversely.

Sonia found her competition annoying and unbuttoned the rest of her blouse. She placed her hands on her hips and gazed at Marina, proudly showing off her perky assets.

Marina, still disinterested, stowed the chip under her bodice. "Now it's your turn, Balthus," she ordered. "Show me payment."

Balthus chuckled and mimicked her voice, "Show me payment."

Marina slid the cloak back on her arm, displaying the pistol. Balthus wasn't the least bit concerned that she was armed and that bothered her. She knew he was not to be trusted.

"So you want what's coming to you, huh?" taunted Balthus as he placed his hand on the cedar box.

Marina stepped toward the desk, forgetting about the shorted carpet and aimed the pistol at Balthus' head. Balthus found her aggression amusing.

"Give me any reason to pull this trigger and I will gladly do so."

Balthus held his hands out innocently and replied, "I'm happy to give you what you want."

Marina grew tense, sensing a trap. Sonia belched and startled her.

Marina whirled, and placed the barrel of her pulse pistol against Sonia's forehead. "Do that again and I'll put a hole in that bubble head of yours," she warned.

Balthus opened the flat cedar box on his desk and depressed a button inside. The trap floor sprang open in front of the desk and Marina dropped to a holding cell below. She landed face down against the concrete floor and lay unconscious. The trap floor closed as quickly as it opened.

Balthus and Sonia laughed hysterically.

"And they warned me not to mess with her!" Balthus proclaimed triumphantly. "This is like taking candy from a baby."

Jerrold opened the door and staggered in with a swollen nose and blood-stained shirt.

Balthus ceased laughing and scolded him, "She humiliated you like a fool."

"I'm sorry, Balthus," Jerrold answered humbly. "I underestimated her."

"Would you like to redeem yourself?"

"Yes, I would."

"She's down in the holding cell. Have fun with her."

Jerrold bowed before Balthus. "Thank you, boss. I'll make the most of our time together, I promise."

"Just bring me the data chip when you're finished and leave a little something for Sonia."

"Yes, Balthus," Jerrold replied and left the office.

Sonia rushed to Balthus and leaped on his lap. "Can we play with her when Jerrold is done?" she asked giddily.

"Oh, yes. We can play all day with her," Balthus promised. "Let's finish eating first."

The two grabbed chicken legs from the bucket and continued to gorge.

***

Marina's head spun and pain shot throughout her body. Jerrold had placed her on a stained lounge chair. Her cloak lay on the table along with her pistol and her two leather belts, each with two knives. As Jerrold slid his fingers under her bodice and massaged her breasts, Marina peeked through one eye slightly open. With his eyes closed, he breathed deeply and savored the experience. She was disgusted by his touch but refrained from any action yet.

The cinderblock basement had a walk-in freezer, located to her left. The holding cell was straight ahead of her, the door barred. At the far left end of the basement was a stairwell. Between her and the stairs were six gurneys; each with a tray of rusted instruments and grimy power tools, no doubt used for torture. The cement floor was grungy and marked with blood stains. The smell of raw meat made her queasy as she wondered how many fools fell victim to Balthus' sick pleasures.

Jerrold's fingers ran across the chip and lifted it from under her bodice. Marina again peeked, but this time she took advantage of Jerrold's lapse of attention, kicking him in the crotch. He froze with bulged eyes. Before he could retreat, Marina head-butted him and chopped him in the throat. Jerrold fell to the floor, writhing in pain and gasping for air.

Jerrold wheezed and struggled to breathe through his collapsed throat. Marina glanced at the instruments on the tray next to her chair. She chose a metal tube and grabbed Jerrold by his long locks. His eyes widened with fear as she tilted his head back and stabbed him in the throat. "You sound like a seal," she complained. "This should help."

Jerrold fell to the floor, horror-stricken by the turn of events. Marina dragged him by his legs to the walk-in freezer and left him inside. Shelves of meat lined the freezer box and four human shapes hung by their ankles, wrapped in plastic. At that point, Marina realized Balthus was more dangerous than she imagined.

Jerrold lay on the frosty floor, still clutching at his throat. A whistling sound came from the tube each time he breathed.

Marina stood by the door and quipped, "Until next time, my friend." He became frantic when the door closed and he was immersed in darkness inside the freezer.

The door slammed at the top of the stairwell and Marina recognized Sonia's soft steps on the wooden stairs. She hurried back to the chair and feigned unconsciousness.

Sonia approached and was quite pleased to see her in a seemingly helpless state. She grew anxious, thinking that Jerrold finished with her and left. Marina was hers to play alone with. She sat on Marina's lap and massaged her breasts under the bodice. Feeling aroused, Sonia reached under her own skirt with one hand and panted excitedly. Her mouth gaped and she began to climax.

Marina's hand slowly reached behind her head and yanked one of the silver balls free from a dreadlock. She grabbed Sonia by the back of the neck and shoved the ball into her mouth with the hole facing out until it became lodged. Four of Sonia's teeth were knocked in and blood trickled down her chin from her busted gums.

Marina stood and flung Sonia into the chair. Sonia was frantic and tried desperately to remove the ball from her mouth. Marina punched her in the forehead, stunning her. With her arms dangling limply by her side, Sonia stared back at her with tears in her eyes for a brief second and then her face was engulfed in heat and a bright light from the flash grenade. When the flash dissipated, Sonia had no flesh on her jaw or nose and her face was burnt severely. She lay motionless in the chair in shock.

Marina strapped the belts with the knives around her thighs. She stowed the pistol in a small holster behind her back. A brief whimper from Sonia caught her attention.

"Did you have something to say, Sweetie?" Marina mocked her.

Sonia's jaw dropped open and nearly fell off. She had no tongue left and her throat was charred like burnt bacon.

"Don't worry, dear, you still have your tits." Marina donned her cloak and walked to the stairs feeling satisfied that Sonia was properly dealt with. She looked back at Sonia and licked her lips seductively in mock fashion. "Next time stick to the slob, Honey," she taunted. "I'm much too hot for you."

Sonia stared blankly at her, with teary eyes as Marina disappeared up the stairs. The excruciating pain from her burns nearly drove her insane but she had no way to express herself.

Marina peered from the basement door, looking down the hall. Balthus stood outside his office as two men entered the warehouse. "Do you have the data chip, Balthus?" asked one of the men anxiously.

"Of course I do, Rock. In fact, it's downstairs with the courier who brought it."

Marina slid past the door and ducked into a closet across the hall without being noticed.

"You know, I could offer Victor a chance to up his bid," Balthus suggested.

"And we'll terminate more than our business relationship," warned Rock. "Victor will start a war with this technology if he gets it."

"What of the courier?" asked Rock's partner, Tulley.

Balthus responded proudly, "Just another trinket in my collection."

"I warned you not to screw with the woman," Rock chastised. "We don't need her meddling in our affairs."

Balthus laughed giddily, annoying the men. "She's just a woman," he remarked cynically. "Come and I'll show you how meddling she *really* is."

The two men glanced uneasily at each other and followed Balthus down the hall to the stairwell door.

"My little sex toys are down there now with her, priming her for a little Q&A time with me," he boasted.

"You're a fool," Tulley retorted. "She's dangerous."

Balthus led them down the stairs. "You guys worry too much," he replied wryly.

Marina exited the closet and hurried down the hall to the main entrance.

A burly, bearded man stood guard at the doorway this time. Marina took a coin from her pocket and rolled it across the floor to him. The man instinctively drew his pistol and focused for a second on the coin. Just as he looked up, Marina kicked his jaw. The stunned man fell to the ground. She retrieved the coin and slipped it into her pocket.

The man attempted to stand but she lifted his head and kneed him in the forehead. Satisfied with the impact, she released him. He dropped to the floor with a thud and was out cold.

Marina slipped into Balthus' empty chamber and rifled through the desk drawers until she reached one which was locked.

Annoyed by the smell of the chicken, she pushed it aside and opened the cedar box, searching for the key. To her surprise, she also discovered the red button that opened the trap floor in front of the desk, a key and a Taser. Marina stowed the Taser under her cloak, then took the key. She unlocked the drawer and opened it.

Inside was a small velvet box, an envelope with a wad of currency and a loaded pistol. She opened the box and found six perfectly cut diamonds spread evenly across a tiny satin pillow.

"Looks like sufficient payment for services rendered," she commented cynically to herself.

Marina closed the box and tucked it under her bodice. She removed the data chip from around her neck and set it on the table. Something bothered her about the importance of the chip to these criminals. The fact that Victor and two agents for an unknown agency were involved with the same dealer for stolen Fleet technology made her wary of their intentions. A war could be bad for business in her line of work.

After a moment of hesitation, she took back the data chip and swapped it with another from her pocket. Despite the risk she took in keeping the chip, she considered that the alternative could be much worse and she resolved to do some investigative work before turning it over to anyone.

Balthus entered the basement and was horrified to see Sonia so grotesquely disfigured in the chair in a nearly comatose state. Suddenly incensed, he searched frantically about the room for some indication of where Marina went.

Rock and Tulley crossed their arms and waited impatiently for an explanation. They were not surprised by the outcome and were eager to complete their transaction.

Balthus knelt by Sonia and wailed, "Oh, my kitten! Look what she did to you." He stood up in a rage and stormed to the freezer where he found Jerrold inside, unconscious and wheezing through the tube in his throat.

Balthus dragged him out of the freezer and left him on the floor.

"I guess this means you don't have the data chip, Balthus," Rock commented irritably.

"I'll get the chip and that bitch's head as well!" he shouted angrily.

Tulley took out a small calculator and pressed several buttons. He pondered for a moment at the sum.

Balthus watched nervously and waited for an explanation.

"It seems to me, Balthus, that you've already cost us a significant amount of money with this delay."

Rock added, "Time is money in our business. I'm sure you understand."

"I'll get the chip for you! She can't be far." Balthus plodded up the stairs. The men glanced at each other in disgust and followed him.

In the top drawer of Balthus' desk was a pad of paper and a pen. Marina took them out and jotted a quick note: "Paid in full. Thank you for your patronage." She placed the note in the center of the desk with the chip containing a record of the maintenance on her ship on top of it.

Just as she stood, Balthus burst through the door. Rock and Tulley stood in the doorway behind him and watched curiously.

"I'm gonna' kill you, you bitch!" screamed Balthus.

"I don't think so," Marina replied confidently. She slid her hand under her cloak, withdrew the Taser and aimed it at Balthus' face.

"It will take more than one Taser to stop me," he warned. "Before you can count to five, I'll have ripped your head off!"

Marina set the Taser on the table. "And I hoped you would use that time to take a shower," she mocked. "I guess I was mistaken."

Rock and Tulley chuckled at her remark.

Balthus snarled and charged at her. Marina pressed the button in the cedar box and watched as Balthus dropped through the trap door. He clung desperately to the floor boards and wailed for help. The spring-loaded trap floor slapped at him repeatedly in an attempt to close. Marina stepped out from behind the desk and gloated.

"Please help me," he pleaded. "I'll let you go, I promise."

"Nice doing business with you, Balthus," Marina responded with a note of pleasure in her voice. "Don't worry, Sonia will keep you company down there. She seems quite chatty."

"I hate you!" he cried.

Marina took the Taser and shoved it in Balthus' mouth. She blocked the trigger with a wad of paper and taunted, "Smile, asshole."

Balthus shuddered violently and fell to the holding cell below with the Taser still discharging in his mouth. The floor sprung closed and the chamber grew quiet.

Marina turned to the men at the door and aimed her pulse pistol at them.

"Is that the data chip on the desk?" inquired Rock.

"Yes, it is."

Then by all means pass," he replied. "We have no quarrel with you."

Tulley added, "Your discretion would be appreciated."

Marina nodded to him in agreement. She inched warily to the door as Rock and Tulley sidled past her cautiously to the desk.

"Have a good evening, gentlemen," Marina replied and exited the office. She unlatched the front door and stepped into the dark street.

The sound of boots on the cobblestone street caught her attention. She hurried across the street and disappeared down an alley.

Twelve soldiers led by a man in a Lieutenant's uniform from the Space Fleet stopped in front of Balthus' door. The Lieutenant, followed by six of the young guards, entered to investigate. The other six spread out in the surrounding alleys.

Marina pulled herself onto a fire escape above the alley and watched. She touched her swollen eye delicately and cringed from the pain. A few moments later, Balthus' shouts caught her attention.

A transport vehicle with barred windows arrived and parked in front of the warehouse. The soldiers dragged a handcuffed Balthus out of the building and shoved his large frame into the rear of the vehicle. One soldier waved to the driver and the vehicle raced away.

There was no sign of Rock or Tulley outside the building. Marina found that interesting and watched as the soldiers departed down the street. She climbed three stories up the fire escape to the top floor and reached for the edge of the roof. As she did, a gloved hand grabbed her wrist. She was startled by another's presence, and caught at a disadvantage.

A handsome man in a militia uniform looked down at her. He was in his mid-thirties with black shoulder-length hair. "My name is Britt and I have some questions for you, Ma'am," he informed her. "I'd appreciate your cooperation."

"Does the Fleet know you're out here?" she asked sarcastically.

"That's not your problem. Where is the data chip?"

"I delivered it to Balthus. Talk to him."

"My commander will be very unhappy if we don't return with it," he warned. "And that can be a painful experience for you."

"My job was to deliver it to him and I did that."

"I'm not stupid. We can do this here or at the palace," he warned.

Marina relented and reached up with her other hand. Britt gripped it and hoisted her onto the roof.

"I'm not going anywhere with you," she declared defiantly.

"I don't think you have a choice," he answered as he maintained a hold on her wrists.

"Then join me!" Marina exclaimed. She leaned off the roof and shoved away with her feet. When Britt couldn't hold her back anymore, she yanked him with her to the fire escape stairs below. They crashed onto the grating and tumbled apart, both stunned from the fall.

Marina scurried to her feet and leaped across the alley onto another fire escape. The impact of her weight broke the rusted supports of the platform and sent her flying against the wall of the building. The bulk of the structure broke away from the wall and fell across the alley to the opposite wall underneath Britt. She rolled off the grating and fell.

Britt looked down frantically from his perch as she landed on a trash dumpster with a loud bang.

Marina groaned and fell onto the street. "I really hate this place," she muttered to herself.

When she looked up at the roof, she saw the outline of Britt in the moonlight. He stared down at her for a moment and disappeared. The sound of approaching soldiers' boots on the street again echoed in the night.

Marina hobbled down the alley with a sprained knee and turned the corner. The old transportation hub was four blocks away but between her and the hub were a dozen militia soldiers. She hurried into another alley and up the next street. As she passed the intersection, more soldiers approached.

"Halt or we'll fire!" ordered one of the men. "We have orders to detain you."

Marina drew her pulse pistol and fired at the street in front of them. Killing militia or Fleet soldiers was bad business for someone like her. It created a lot of unwanted attention and usually resulted in a bounty on one's head.

The militia spread out on either side of the street and took cover behind empty crates and trash cans.

Marina turned to run but was surrounded by more soldiers. One of the men approached and held a gun to her temple.

"Please don't make me use this," he said politely.

Marina reached toward him to surrender her pistol. "You win. Take the damn gun."

"Keep it. The Captain only wishes to interrogate you, not arrest you."

Marina was stumped by his reply. She cautiously stowed the pistol under her cloak.

"Where is your Captain?" she asked impatiently. "I have a schedule to keep."

"He'll be here in a moment."

Britt arrived and pushed his way through the men. His black jacket was torn at the shoulder from the fall and his lower lip bled slightly. He forced a smile and offered his hand to Marina. "Can we try this again without the theatrics?"

Marina folded her arms and frowned at the inconvenience he presented her.

"I'm Britt, Captain of the 1st Militia Group," he informed her.

Marina shook his hand warily. "Look, I'm just a courier. What do you want from me?"

"Who has the data chip?"

"I can't divulge client information. It's bad for business."

"So you don't have it and Balthus doesn't have it. Who does?"

"Check with the two civilians. They might know."

"Are you sure they have it?" Britt pressed her, aware that she may have misled Rock and Tulley as well.

"You could say that."

Britt became impatient with her game. "Forget the damn chip. Who the hell are you?"

"And if I refuse to tell you?"

Britt's frustration showed as he became annoyed. "Please don't make this any harder than it has to be."

"Then how about some privacy?" she requested.

"Very well," Britt relented and, as a sign of trust, waved the other men away. They reluctantly backed off to the corner and left the two to speak alone.

"Let me help you out, Captain Britt: Who are you really looking for?"

"I see where this is going," he replied disappointedly with his hands on his hips. "You fit the bill of two individuals that I am searching for. One is a rebel leader and the other, I believe, is a princess."

"Well, I am not the rebel leader you seek. I don't play well in groups and I certainly don't look like a princess."

Britt studied her facial expression and her eyes. "But you are the Princess of Yord, aren't you?" he asked in hope of establishing one shred of evidence from their discussion.

"I'm just a courier. What makes you think this princess even exists?" she questioned him playfully.

"I need to know if she exists before it's too late. There are threats to all our safety that started with her family."

Marina stared at the ground in a daze, recalling a memory of her childhood inside the palace. She sat on her mother's lap and listened as she sang songs to her in a sweet voice. Next to them sat her father, twirling her hair in his fingers. Then something happened and both her parents rushed off. They left and never returned.

Britt noticed the faraway look in her eyes. "Did I hit a nerve?" he asked respectfully.

Ignoring his question, Marina sat on an empty crate and looked up sadly. "I have no family."

"Are you helping the rebels?" he asked adamantly.

Marina became annoyed, exclaiming, "I don't even know who the rebels are! I haven't been to this forsaken planet in over ten years and I'm only here to deliver a package. It's a stinkin' slum here!"

"It's still a kingdom and its people rely on its rulers to provide leadership and protection. Right now they have neither."

Marina laughed cynically. "Listen to you! Aren't you part of the contingent that's controlling this pathetic world?"

"I don't have to be and neither do my men. War with the other militias or the Fleet is bad for everyone. Only if the Princess comes forward to claim her birthright to the throne can we unite everyone."

Marina stood nose-to-nose with him. "Maybe it's you who needs to find out who you really are. Conversation's over," she declared and walked away from him.

Britt glared at her, fists clenched. "The next time we meet, I will arrest you for smuggling," he warned. "I gave you your chance."

Marina flipped her middle finger at him and turned the corner. Britt punched the trash dumpster in anger and stormed away.

Marina reached the abandoned depot without further incident and crept past broken spacecraft, stepping around parts and motors scattered across the ground. Water dripped from the ruined rooftop and echoed eerily when it struck the cement floor.

At the last dock on the left, her ship was hidden behind the rusted hulk of an abandoned freighter. Rats scurried across the oily floor and startled her. She drew her pistol and checked frequently over her shoulder as she passed the remains of the cargo ship.

To her surprise, the hatch to her ship was open. She peered around the depot but saw no one. When she cautiously boarded the ship, she found another of the captains from the militia, Meloche, waiting inside.

The man was tall and muscular with shabby, black hair, about fifty-five in Earth years. He reminded Marina of an old-world barbarian. She recognized that his rank was equal to Britt's. "Geez, how many captains does your militia have?" inquired Marina with a note of sarcasm in her voice.

"Only four," he replied icily. "We have some things to discuss and you will answer me."

Marina stood her ground and informed him, "As I told your buddy Britt, the conversation's over."

"You don't understand, Missy. If you are neither of the two women we seek, then you are a high profile criminal who was in possession of stolen designs for the Fleet's advanced weaponry. That would be treason, a crime which carries a penalty of death."

Meloche's revelation of the designs shocked Marina. "You can't prove I knew what was on that data chip! I'm just a courier."

"I don't need to. In fact, I'm thinking of a nice reward for turning you in to the Space Fleet as a traitor. You see, they don't appreciate smugglers arming their enemies."

"Then you'll have to earn that reward," she challenged.

Meloche grinned through broken teeth and reached for her throat. Marina raised her arm and deflected his hand. She latched onto his arm and flung him against the hull next to the hatch.

"You bitch!" He groaned and jabbed at her head wildly with an elbow.

Marina ducked and punched him in the gut with her other hand, followed by a kick to the stomach. Meloche lost his balance and fell out of the spaceship.

Marina pressed the 'close' knob next to the hatch and hurried to the pilot's seat. She started the ship's engines and lifted off.

The alarm panel warbled. She looked up and saw two illuminated message windows reading 'Imbalanced Load – Right Side" and "Hatch Open."

Marina steadied the ship and inspected the hatch. It was barely open and Meloche dangled from the side of the ship with his fingers wedged between the hatch and the hull. She looked at the gauge and piston on the wall next to the opening. The pressure to the door piston was set at fifty percent. Marina adjusted it up to its maximum force and the hatch slammed shut.

Meloche's scream pierced the silent night air. The hatch sealed and six bloody fingers severed at the knuckles lay on the floor. Marina reset the pressure to fifty percent and pressed the 'Open' knob. The hatch slid open and she peered out. Thirty feet below, Meloche writhed in pain on top of the broken crates, with only his thumb and forefinger remaining on each hand and six bloody knuckles.

Marina kicked the severed fingers out the hatch and closed it. The alarms cleared immediately. She returned to the controls and set a course for Magnus, a space station near the center of the sector. The ship eased through a hole in the roof and vanished into the night.

After the ship left Yord's atmosphere and entered space, Marina activated the auto-pilot system. With a fourteen hour journey ahead of her, she indulged in a bottle of whiskey until she passed out.

Chapter 2

Spellbound

The auto-pilot system alarm sounded when Marina's ship arrived in close proximity to Magnus. After two minutes, the auto-pilot turned itself off and the ship automatically reverted to 'manual.' Marina acknowledged the alarm and reduced speed. She searched one of her lockers opposite the hatch. Her head pounded and her body ached from the earlier fall in Stanton. She opened a small cardboard box of six syringes of adrenalin and removed one.

The ship shuddered briefly and another alarm shrieked, startling her. She glanced up front at the control console and saw 'Hi-Engine Temp Left Side' illuminated on the panel.

"Damn that friggin' cooling system!" Marina grumbled. "I've gotta' get a new ship soon." She stowed the case in the locker and injected herself in the neck with the contents of the syringe. Her heart raced and she felt renewed vigor.

Magnus was a small space station, handling about twenty ships, where smugglers and traffickers could do business without fear of reprisal from the Space Fleet's Law Enforcement Division. The station was half the size of Glomus-5, where Marina's handler, Dix, operated from.

The facility was controlled by a mysterious woman named Kat. Very few people ever met her in person and those who did, never spoke about it. She was rumored to be gifted in the black arts – a witch with many talents. Marina had apprehensions about this assignment but Dix assured her that she wouldn't have any problems.

Marina announced her arrival to the dock master who assigned her a vacant bay. Once she docked and secured the ship, she left the transport area and sought out the dispatcher.

The transportation section made up eighty-percent of the station. Once Marina left that area and entered the main corridor, Kat's security team surrounded her. They wore casual clothing and an odd variety of head garb. Attached to their hips were pulse pistols and swords.

Marina drew her daggers and prepared to take them on. When the men mocked her, she considered slitting a throat or two just to end their laughter. Nothing irritated her more than chauvinist pigs who put her down.

"Who are you?" asked a tall, turban-wearing man named Ansl.

"It doesn't matter who I am," replied Marina. "I'm here to pick up a parcel from Kat."

The men chuckled again among themselves. Marina crouched and prepared to make an example of them but Ansl instructed her to stow the daggers and come peacefully. She reluctantly obeyed and followed him through a large hall. The remainder of the security team stayed behind and resumed their patrol of the premises.

The hall was crowded with vendors of contraband and illicit drugs as well as several of the traffickers who transported slaves, products and wares to the vendors. Marina felt their eyes on her as she followed Ansl. She knew there was nothing good about her presence there. Being female, outnumbered, and disliked could guarantee only one thing – death.

A young female's voice caught her attention. "Please, help me," she pleaded. "Don't leave me here."

Marina noticed the girl and felt bad for her. She was young and barely clad. Her wrists were tied to a pole and a noose around her neck. A man near her, apparently her owner, became annoyed with her pleas and tightened the noose until she nearly fainted. He smiled at Marina and displayed the few teeth he still had. "You like her? I sell her to you cheap."

Marina stood face to face with the man in an attempt to intimidate him.

"Make me an offer I can't refuse," he said with a cynical smile.

Marina could only imagine how horrible it was for the young girl to be treated like a whore, beaten and even worse, raped. Marina was a virgin at thirty and had no intention of changing that. *"But what if I was this poor girl?"* she thought and became belligerent.

"How about your life?" Marina countered brazenly and reached for her daggers. Ansl grabbed her wrist and stared her down.

The man yanked on the noose and nearly snapped the girl's neck. "Perhaps I'll kill her just because you speak out of line, woman."

Ansl stepped in and explained that Marina is Kat's courier and knew little of their etiquette on Magnus. The man eyed her suspiciously and released his hold on his slave.

Marina continued to stare him down until Ansl pulled her away and shoved her toward a dim corridor. When they were out of sight of the marketers, Marina twisted his arm behind his back and placed a second dagger to his neck. Ansl was amazed at her skill and grew amiable. "So you are the infamous Marina. It's an honor."

"What about him?" she asked and pointed to the slave owner. "I'm supposed to just walk away?"

"You must not interfere or you will die," he warned. "These people pay good money to use Magnus as a safe haven for their businesses."

Marina bit her lip. It was just another scumbag establishment she had to cater to. Reluctantly, she released her hold on his arm.

"You are as tough as I've heard from around the sector. No one does to me what you just did."

"I can show you more if you like," she replied sarcastically.

"That won't be necessary."

Ansl led her to an elevator at the end of the corridor. "Go to the seventeenth floor and follow the red carpet," he instructed. "Kat is waiting for you."

Marina peeked over her shoulder as she entered the elevator but Ansl had returned to the hall.

When she reached Kat's floor, music from a harp put her in a sedate mood. Something wasn't right but it was too late to turn back. Marina gripped her daggers tightly but she felt her defenses waning as if she were in a trance. She tried to fight it but it crept over her like a warm blanket.

The red carpet led her down the corridor to thick blue drapes. The walls were decorated with Indian décor and the ceiling was painted with mythical dragons. Marina recognized the interior art from an Indian palace she visited on Earth while making a delivery many years ago. She wondered if Kat had been there before.

Marina peered through the drapes. Two muscular guards stood on either side of the entrance with scimitars and pulse pistols. A young woman played the harp from across the room. The music was soothing and had a peaceful, hypnotic influence on Marina. A beautiful, dark-skinned female, stretched naked across a plush couch.

Marina grew impatient as she waited to be acknowledged. "Kat, I presume."

Kat had long, silky hair colored platinum that lay across her shoulders and over her breasts. She smoked sweet-smelling incense from a pipe and when she opened her eyes, she stared at Marina as if she saw through her soul. Gracefully she motioned with two fingers for Marina to approach.

"I am Kat. I've waited a long time for this moment, Marina. Dix is very protective of you."

Marina kept eye contact and showed no emotion with Kat. "You have something for me? My time is precious."

"I certainly do." Kat stood up and circled Marina, eying her carefully.

Marina was uneasy being ogled by the woman. "Look, I don't have time for games. Can we get this over with?"

Kat was amused and ordered her men to leave them. They promptly obeyed, exiting the room.

Kat gazed at her seductively and pointed to the balcony. As Marina followed her, she felt as though she floated on air.

"Is this some kind of witchcraft?" she wondered.

The aroma of fresh brewed tea from a small teapot on the table filled the air. Next to the pot were two cups.

"Sit with me," Kat requested.

Marina took the seat near the railing to ensure her back was protected. She glanced down at the hall many stories below. "Quite a view you have from here, Kat."

"It serves its purpose," she replied and poured tea for the two of them. Marina waited for Kat to drink first before she sipped from her cup.

Marina grew more impatient and nervously tapped the table with her finger.

Kat reached out and took her hand. She turned it over and studied Marina's palm. "You have an interesting destiny ahead of you," remarked Kat. "I think you and I can be of great help to each other."

"Sorry to burst your bubble, Ms. Kat, but I work alone."

"You have the data chip, I understand."

Marina responded defensively, "I don't have the damn chip!"

Kat smiled and sipped from her tea. "Do you know who I am?" she asked curiously. "I mean who I *really* am?"

Marina folded her hands and stared into Kat's eyes in an intimidating fashion. "Yeah, a customer who is wasting my time."

Now Kat became annoyed. "I know many things about you, including your deepest secrets. You'd be surprised what I can do for you."

Marina smirked at her. "You know nothing about me and I prefer to keep it that way."

Kat gazed into Marina's eyes and drew her into a hypnotic spell. Again, Marina felt as though she floated. Kat took her by the hand and led her inside to the couch. They embraced in a passionate kiss that left her reeling. Kat backed away from her and vanished.

The room blurred until Marina heard her mother's voice and then felt her embrace. "We love you so much, Marina," she told her. For once, Marina realized that it felt good to be loved. She savored the feeling.

With no will to fight, Marina wondered if it was an illusion or if she was being manipulated by Kat for her own pleasure. For what seemed like hours, she felt the joy of human touch but didn't know why. Nothing made sense to her. She felt so many emotions, both new and strange. At one point, she felt a rush of pleasure and joy that left her whirling out of control. Then she awoke in Kat's bed wearing only her panties. She felt...different.

The music from the harp still played but there was no sign of the player or the instrument. Kat lay next to her and again kissed her passionately. It was then that Marina realized Kat's lips were glazed with a powerful drug, one which had made Kat's seduction of her all too simple and still had her under its influence. She felt Kat's body against hers as she became her unwilling pleasure toy. With each kiss, she was overcome by the hypnotic drug and the swirling emotions.

When the chemically-induced passion wore off, Marina regained her composure. She sat alone on the edge of the bed feeling violated. Kat returned from the balcony and sat with her.

Marina's anger took over and she attempted to grab Kat by the throat but she felt controlled and could do her no harm. "I don't appreciate being drugged and raped, Kat. This wasn't part of the deal."

Kat brushed her hand gently across Marina's cheek. "I only gave you what you need to survive. You need to be loved, to feel love."

"Not by you!"

Kat was not affected by Marina's anger and responded calmly, "Think of it as ....therapy. You are blind to the obvious, Marina, and that will get you killed." She playfully fingered Marina's dreadlocks and revealed, "You have so much hate inside you, so much darkness in your soul. It will consume you unless you let it go."

"Can you skip the psychobabble and get the package? I'm on a tight schedule," she complained, then stood and dressed.

Kat took Marina's chin in her hand and kissed her. Again, because of the drug, she had no will to oppose Kat. This time, the substance on Kat's lips created a hallucinogenic image. Marina wondered if she used a different drug to change the effect. She was confused that it didn't affect Kat in the same way. She fell into another hypnotic trance.

In this vision, Marina saw her mother march through a snow storm. Next, she saw her father lying on a table, near death. The hallucination ended and Marina was more confused than ever.

"Your parents suffered greatly but their love for each other never waned." Kat's voice was softly compassionate.

Marina felt her parents' pain from the illusion as if it was real. "I don't believe any of this! My parents abandoned me a long time ago."

"Your parents loved you. You will find that many others love and care for you as well," she replied and kissed Marina again with unbridled passion. Marina's head spun and she lost herself between reality and fantasy once more. She had no will to fight.

Who was this woman that could manipulate her against her will? Again Marina awoke alone on Kat's bed. She looked about but there was no sign of her.

"Holy shit!" she exclaimed nervously. She vowed that if she ever saw Kat again, it would be on her terms and Kat would pay for what she did to her.

On the edge of the bed next to her was a small box with instructions on it. It was of grave importance that the box be delivered to Dix on Glomus-5. Marina tucked it inside her bodice and stood in front of a mirror. Content that her dreadlock wig and clothes were in place she turned to leave.

From the corner of her eye, she noticed something glimmer on a small corner table. When she investigated, she discovered a small tray with several transparent strips, some with Kat's lip prints on them. It was then that she realized Kat protected her lips with the ultra-thin transparent tape. By brushing the drug of choice across the plastic, she could disable her prey without arousing any suspicion. Feeling her temper rise, she left Kat's suite and hurried to the elevator.

When she stepped off the elevator, she found Ansl waiting for her. "I trust all was to your satisfaction," he remarked. Ansl clearly suspected something happened but knew better than to inquire.

"How long have I been here?" Marina asked.

"Four days."

Marina froze and thought about what happened to her over those four torturous days.

Ansl saw the fear in her eyes. He felt sympathy for her and explained, "Kat can be a great ally. Accept her friendship or you will suffer much misery."

"Screw this!" she shouted and stepped cautiously away from him. She rushed back to her ship.

Once on board, tears streamed down her cheeks and she felt as though she would have a nervous breakdown. She considered that it could be the remnants of the opiate Kat used on her or maybe the combination of her adrenalin injection with the opiate. Then, it occurred to her that she felt vulnerable because she felt love. That was a weakness she could not afford in her line of work.

When she regained her composure, she found several items on her ship disturbed and the case of adrenalin syringes was empty on her bed.

"Those bastards robbed my ship!" she cried out. Frantically she removed her dreadlock wig and felt inside for the hidden data chip. When she found it, still pinned to the weaving, she breathed a sigh of relief.

Marina sat at the controls and started the ship's engines. To her surprise, the engine alarms were clear. The transmitter beeped and she acknowledged it. Kat's smiling face appeared on the monitor.

"You have a lot of nerve, Kat!" she exclaimed angrily. "You had no right to search my ship."

"Your ship has been repaired and I removed the poison that pollutes your body," answered Kat. "I hoped that you would share your thoughts with me and let me help you through your dark times."

Marina suspected this was about the data chip. "Why do you want the damn chip so badly? You can't use it."

Kat was amused by Marina's suspicions. "Need it? I only want to know who possesses it."

"And why is that?" questioned Marina.

"If there is to be war, I need to prepare my forces," she explained in a more somber tone. "There is a new balance of power, a delicate balance if you must know, since your parents' disappearance. We cannot afford to let that balance tilt in favor of the wrong people."

"There will be no war," declared Marina. "And we are finished."

"I don't think so, Marina. One day you will realize what I've given you."

"What did you do to me?" Marina shouted angrily.

"You need to know love if you are to achieve your destiny and I will help you learn."

"Screw you and your love!" Marina blurted tearfully. "I don't need anyone."

The pupils in Kat's eyes turned white and she uttered a spell. Marina felt a strange sensation take hold of her and she panicked. She suddenly felt vulnerable and knew Kat was able to affect her at will. "You don't know who you're screwing with, Kat! I will get you for this," she warned and ended the transmission.

Kat stood on her balcony and looked down on the crowded hall. She laughed sadistically and folded her arms. "We will do this the hard way, Marina. You will need to feel your parents' pain to know and understand their love. That is your salvation." She left the balcony and returned to her room.

Marina heard Kat's words and feared she was losing her mind. The transmitter was off and yet she still heard her quite clearly. She received clearance from the dock master and eagerly set the ship's auto-pilot system for Glomus-5. Once clear of the station, she went to the shower stall in the rear of the ship and scrubbed herself, thinking she could remove her shame. She cried, knowing that Kat had taken her innocence from her.

"Thirty years old and I'm worried about my innocence," she babbled. "I am so screwed up!" No matter how many times she washed, she still felt dirty. Finally, she was too exhausted to continue and left the shower. She collapsed on her bed and slept.

***

Glomus-5 was a huge space station equipped with a repair shop; parts depot; and a shipping department. The station was designed for short term stops, minor repairs and taking on supplies with docks for up to fifty ships.

Marina's ship glided into a small bay on the top tier of the space station. She shut down the ship's engines and breathed a sigh of relief.

"Marina, are you alright?" a voice crackled from her transmitter.

Marina was exhausted and reluctantly answered, "Yeah, Dix. I'll be there in a bit."

"I was worried about you," he responded. "I heard you had quite a crowd after you in Stanton. Are you sure you're okay?"

"Yeah, just marvelous," she uttered as she fitted her dreadlock wig over her natural hair.

Dix ignored her sarcasm. "What happened with Kat?"

"I got the package. Don't worry." She turned off the transmitter and laid her head on the console. "Two bad jobs in a row," she thought. "Something's wrong with this picture."

The image of her and Kat together in bed haunted her. Marina had never been with anyone before and this experience left her an emotional mess. She couldn't even be sure that it really happened. Why Kat insisted on showing her physical love was beyond her. If she ever met her again, she would deal with her in the way she was accustomed – with force and violence. Now that she knew about the protective strips Kat used, she would be prepared next time.

Marina stood and opened a cabinet on the wall behind her seat. Inside were three bottles of antiseptics and two bottles of whiskey. She opened the cap on a nearly empty bottle of whiskey and finished its contents.

"Alright, let's get this over with," she convinced herself as she dropped the empty bottle in a trash crate and left the ship.

Marina walked down a long corridor inside the station to the elevator, pressed the 'down' button, and waited impatiently. She stared at her reflection on the steel door and became despondent. Her cheek and eye were blackened, accented by the cuts on her chin and neck. "I look like one messed up bitch," she muttered dejectedly.

The doors squealed and slid open. Marina was annoyed by the sound and wondered if everything in the universe had degraded into disrepair just like her. She stepped inside the elevator and pressed the '3' button. When the doors closed, she pondered further about whether her assignments were becoming more perilous or if she was getting sloppy. "Get soft and you get dead" was always her motto.

When she stepped off the elevator, the smell of stale cigar smoke nauseated her. There were four ragged sofas in the waiting room, two on each side. Ahead of her was a red door with a small, mesh-covered window. A closed-circuit monitor in the top left corner focused on her as she moved.

Marina stood with her hands on her hips. "It's me, Dix. Open up."

When the lock buzzed, Marina opened the door and stepped through. Ahead of her was a thick glass window with a steel cage in front of it. A slot was cut across the bottom of the glass and cage for an access point. Beside it was a heavy, steel door leading into Dix's office.

Behind the glass sat Dix, a dark-skinned, bald man of about forty-eight years of age. He wore a dirty T-shirt, equally dirty work pants, and a sweat band.

"I preferred your old office to this," she complained. "I feel like I'm in a roach-infested motel."

Dix chuckled at her remark and responded, "It's part of my cover. I was afraid I'd lost my number one courier."

Marina placed two boxes on the counter: one from Balthus and one from Kat. "Seems a lot of people were expecting me at Balthus' place," she commented arrogantly. "You wouldn't know anything about it, would you?"

Dix lowered his eyes and appeared saddened by her insinuation. "Marina, I'm hurt that you would even think that. I do know that I need to be more selective about my clients. I understand Balthus was mixed up in militia business and I don't like being dragged into other people's wars."

"The militia's officers were very inquisitive as to my background."

"You didn't tell them anything about my operation, did you?" Dix asked nervously.

"No, they weren't interested in you, just me. It seems I fit the bill of a rebel leader they were hunting."

Dix was entertained by the thought. "They obviously don't know you very well. You look like hell."

"No worse than usual," she answered. "And what the hell is with that bitch Kat?"

Dix grew extremely nervous. "What happened with Kat? You didn't attack her, did you?"

"Not this time. Seems to me that she thought we were on a date."

"Please tell me you didn't piss her off. That could be really bad for both of us."

"I wouldn't sweat it. She got what she wanted."

"You should be very careful with her. I've heard she's a witch with great powers."

"So am I. Want to try me?"

Dix declined to comment further about Kat. He opened the velvet box and was surprised by the number of diamonds inside it. "Balthus is going to want some of this back."

Marina smirked at him. "Balthus was taken away by the Space Fleet's soldiers. They really wanted their chip back."

Dix looked panicked and asked, "What happened to the chip?"

"Two of Balthus' civilian clients showed up to collect. They were quite agreeable with the situation."

"So the militia didn't get the chip either?"

"No. The clients vanished before the soldiers *and* the militia arrived."

Dix was stunned by her turn of events. "I'm so sorry for involving you in this," he said somberly. "It wasn't supposed to be this way."

"Things worked out," Marina remarked cynically. "Balthus is behind bars. The militia didn't get the chip. Kat took me for a test drive and I didn't kill her. It doesn't get any better than that."

"There is something else, Marina. You can't keep beating my clients up. It's bad for business."

"I do what I have to. Nothing more. Nothing less."

Dix reached under the counter and retrieved a small leather pouch. He slid it under the glass to her. "That's not what I heard through the network."

"Screw the network!" she screamed at him in a tantrum. "They weren't there. First, the Fleet's soldiers were waiting for me and then the militia showed up. They were considering turning me in to the Fleet for a reward because they think I'm a traitor! That's just the good stuff that happened to me."

Marina took the pouch and stowed it under her cloak. "Besides, I didn't hurt anyone who didn't deserve it."

"And the innocent girl?" inquired Dix.

"Just a harlot that learned to keep her mouth shut and her hands to herself."

"I hear she doesn't have a mouth anymore."

"It was Balthus' little tramp. Don't preach innocent to me, Dix." As she turned to the door, Dix asked her curiously, "How much longer are you going to stay in this business? You must have a lot of money saved up by now."

"You know I don't like questions." She opened the door, hesitated, and looked back at him. "If you must know, I want a faster ship. My time's valuable."

Marina noticed that Dix didn't open the second box. "You tell me what's the deal with Kat and I'll tell you what I plan to do with my future."

"Touché," replied Dix. "I guess we'll both keep our secrets for now."

"All you need is love," Marina replied sarcastically. "Just ask Kat."

Dix chuckled as Marina closed the door behind her. "If she would only listen to reason," he thought to himself, "things would go so much easier for everyone."

Marina returned to her ship and recalled her earlier conversation with Britt. She opened the cabinet behind her seat and took out the full bottle of whiskey.

After a few drinks, she opened a horizontal panel and rolled out a cot. Painfully, she removed her clothes and her dreadlock wig. As she shook her dark hair down onto her shoulders, she looked somberly in the mirror. Standing in her black lace panties, she saw a badly bruised left thigh and hip with red welts on her shoulder. With the bruises and cuts on her face, her first thought was that she was a stranger in the mirror, especially since she rarely removed the wig. After two more hits of whiskey from the bottle, she lay back and rested on the cot. "I really hate myself," she complained and fell asleep.

Chapter 3

Unwanted Company

Thirty militia soldiers marched along a winding trail in a densely wooded valley, led by a dark-haired woman in an armored helmet and a chain mail tunic. They hunted the rebels who fled from the Palace District after a short and bloody battle.

The men were rough-looking and muscular; armed with swords, axes and pulse pistols. The woman, a sultry but vicious assassin named Fiona, paused at a fork in the trail. She looked up at the trees suspiciously.

"Take half of your men down the trail and circle around. I want them cut off," she ordered the sergeant. He nodded and took fifteen of his men down a rutted trail.

Fiona motioned for the remainder of the men to spread out behind her. She stood alone in the center of the trail and drew her pulse pistol. "Surrender now and I'll be merciful!"

An arrow whizzed from the trees and struck her left hand. She dropped the pistol and clutched at the wound.

"Come out now, you cowards!" she demanded angrily as she pulled the arrow from her hand. "You're surrounded!"

A woman in a red cloak stepped out of the trees and stood twenty feet from her. Her name was Rebecca but Fiona knew her as Red because she had long, auburn hair draped over her shoulders. "The next arrow will be through your heart," she taunted, staring at Fiona with sharp, piercing eyes.

One of the soldiers raised his pistol. A young man emerged from the trees and fired an arrow from his crossbow that pierced the soldier's throat. The man groaned briefly and fell to the ground dead.

Fiona reached with her good hand for the pistol but Red calmly raised her crossbow and fired an arrow, nearly striking Fiona's other hand.

"Damn you, bitch! I'm gonna' kill you," Fiona shouted angrily.

Red lowered the crossbow and reloaded it. "This is the last time I'll ask you to leave my people alone."

"I tried to show you mercy, Red. Now, it's time for you to die."

Red lowered her crossbow and smiled. Fiona felt her blood boil as Red refused to show proper fear and respect.

"Get her now!" Fiona ordered her men but there was no sound. She looked behind her and grew concerned that her soldiers were gone. Filled with rage, she dove for the pistol.

Red instinctively targeted Fiona's hand and fired another arrow. Fiona pulled her hand back as a second arrow just missed her hand. Frustrated, she looked up but Red was gone. She leaned against a tree, perturbed by the game that Red played with her, and tried to plan her next move. "This isn't over," she screamed. "I will tear you apart, piece by piece!"

An arrow whizzed from the foliage and struck the tree an inch from her ear. She fumed while scanning the forest, but there was no sign of Red or the rebels. "Damn you!" she screamed. Her hatred for Red masked the pain she felt from her wound.

Fiona hurried down the trail and searched frantically for her soldiers. Victor would be irate with her if she lost more of his men to Red and her band of rebels. A short distance away, she found them hanging from the trees by their ankles. Beneath each man was a muddy pool of blood.

In a panic, she paced about like a rabid animal. She needed to bring Red in now, dead or alive, or she'd surely feel Victor's wrath. Fiona returned to the fork in the road and waited. Filled with anger, she bit her lip until blood trickled down her chin. Her psychotic side took over as she raced from tree to tree, looking for any trace of the rebels.

As if on cue, ten rebels emerged from hiding and stood before her. They were young men and women in their late teens or early twenties.

Fiona grew more incensed that a group of 'kids' could give her so much trouble. "Drop your weapons, cowards, or I'll kill all of you."

One young man stepped forward and warned, "Surrender now or we'll kill you."

Each of the rebels raised their crossbows and targeted her.

Fiona laughed at them. "You are no match for me, you fools!" she taunted and quickly threw a dagger from her belt at the young man before any of them could react.

The dagger struck him in the throat. He clutched at the lethal wound and fell to the ground, his life slipping away from him. The other rebels fired their crossbows at her.

Fiona dove to the ground and rolled into the trees as arrows whizzed past her. The second group of soldiers, those Fiona sent to circle back, appeared from the trees and took position behind the rebels. Flashes of pulse fire illuminated the forest as the young dissidents were quickly gunned down from behind. Smoke rose from the searing wounds in the corpses left by the energy pulses.

The sergeant and his soldiers examined the bodies of their victims. There were three wounded survivors: Two men and a woman. He ordered his men to stand them up and secure their arms. There was no sign of Red.

Fiona questioned the prisoners, "Where is Red? I want her now!"

The sergeant glanced at Fiona with a perplexed expression and pondered who Red was.

The prisoners refused to answer and stared at the ground in defiance. Each weakened as blood flowed from their lethal wounds.

"I see you need a little encouragement." Fiona drew a dagger from under her tunic and slit one man's throat from ear to ear. She wiped the blood on the lips of the second man and the woman. They gasped, nauseated by the blood from their fallen comrade.

"I'll ask once more. Who and where is the rebel leader?"

The two prisoners refused to answer. Fiona grabbed the woman's left ear and cut it off. The woman cried out in pain.

"Now answer the question!" Fiona demanded as she tossed the ear into the trees.

The man shuddered and sobbed but still refused to speak.

Fiona stuck the knife in the woman's eye and cut it out of its socket. The woman became hysterical.

The man pleaded, "Please don't hurt her anymore!"

"Then answer the damn question!" Fiona insisted as she pried the woman's mouth open and pulled on her tongue. She held the dagger against it and waited impatiently for his reply.

"We don't know who she is, I swear!" cried the prisoner. "She travels with a man named Cristos. They come and go at random. Now, please let her go."

Fiona smiled smugly at the man. "You're in no position to make requests," she reminded him and cut the woman's tongue off anyway.

"You bitch!" he blurted tearfully.

Fiona stared at the tongue briefly in amusement and discarded it into the bushes. She punched the man in the bridge of his nose. He was stunned and slumped forward. Fiona reached into his mouth and pulled his tongue out.

"Is this really necessary?" the sergeant asked with a disgusted look on his face. "They're already as good as dead."

Fiona focused on the tongue as if it was a complicated item. "You have much to learn about control," she answered and sliced it off. "Take him away but leave the woman," she ordered.

The soldiers released the woman's arms and she dropped to the ground in shock.

She noticed their distaste for her and explained, "I'm leaving a message for these rebels. They'll know that I won't stop killing until I have their leader."

The sergeant departed with his men and the male prisoner.

Fiona lay the woman down delicately in the wet clay and slit her abdomen open. She stroked the woman's cheek as if she cared and then delicately cut out her entrails. Her eyes bulged with pleasure as she spread the woman's organs across the trail. The woman quivered briefly then became still as her life passed from her.

The soldiers marched the male prisoner along the main road back toward the palace.

Fiona followed them from a distance. As she walked, she fretted how she would explain her failure to her commander. She and Victor, were involved romantically and she expected that, when he assumed the title King of Yord, she would be his Queen.

Fiona was once a maid in the palace until she was expelled from the palace for infidelities. Fiona swore that one day she'd get revenge on everyone in the kingdom.

Victor, a militia officer rising quickly through the ranks in the 1st Militia, entered the Palace District one day and found her alone near the local pub. She lived as a beggar, shoeless and dressed in tattered clothes. Victor offered her money to bed her and they retreated to an inn. When she cleaned up, she seduced him and performed lewd acts of pleasure for him that he had never known existed. He was so enamored with her that he offered her a job as his aide. She won his loyalty by killing anyone who threatened him. Though he never said it, she knew they were destined to be together forever.

Victor, now the commander of the 1st Militia, had little patience for failure and a temper to go with it. His goal was to capture the rebel leader and arrange a truce. Fiona, on the other hand, had a penchant for bloodshed. She would not rest until she captured the rebel woman she called Red and tortured her to death. Now she had the injured hand as an added incentive to find Red and inflict pain and suffering on her.

The soldiers disappeared briefly from Fiona's view. When she reached the top of the hill, the soldiers' bodies were scattered across the moss-covered ground, slain by arrows from the rebels' crossbows.

Fiona exploded with rage. She searched through the bodies and found the lone prisoner dead with an arrow through his heart. Desperately, she rushed through the dense forest and searched for any sign of Red or her rebel army. After hours of futility, she returned to the palace alone.

***

Dawn approached and the sky above the Palace District brightened. The streets were empty and quiet until the sound of soldiers' boots broke the silence. They started as a faint thumping just outside the city and grew to a loud rhythmic beat on the city streets.

Victor, tall with long, dark hair and a thick mustache, marched through the center of the town with fifty of his soldiers. He carried a broad sword and two pulse pistols, holstered on each hip.

The soldiers were an intimidating sight in their black leather uniforms, armed with one pistol and one hand weapon of their choosing. Some carried battleaxes, while others carried swords for hand-to-hand combat.

Victor and his militia migrated ten years ago from Dax-7, a neighboring planet, intent on conquering Yord and restoring it to the business metropolis it once was, thus making them its wealthy rulers. They arrived in four battleships, great craft built by aliens-for-hire in a distant sector of the galaxy.

Their former home, Dax-7, was inhabited by numerous militias that overthrew kingdoms forged by the King and Queen of Yord during the Great War. Victor had grown impatient with the warring groups and targeted Yord with the intent of claiming the entire world for himself.

Once he achieved control of Yord, his next goal would be to return to Dax-7, conquer the other militias, and absorb their resources to create a unified army. From there he would turn on the Space Fleet and the neighboring alien races until no one could stop him.

Yord was the center of all activity in the sector and the core of the alliance at one time. When the young King and Queen disappeared mysteriously, the alliance was torn apart by warring militias and greedy leaders as Yord became an insignificant planet that fell into ruin. Now it was the last remaining kingdom not controlled by the militias. Only the dwindling army of rebels prevented Victor from achieving his goals and destroying Yord's last thread of hope.

The rebels were determined to hold out in hope that, Marina, the surviving daughter of the royal family, would someday return to unite their people and restore the alliance. Marina, after her parents' disappearance, was in the care of priestesses who were protectors of a sacred crystal from the Temple of Icarus. They were rumored to have raised her in hiding from the enemies of the kingdom until one day she fled, never to be seen again.

Militia soldiers dispersed down the side streets in search of survivors of the rebel army. When they returned, they formed up in front of the palace gates behind their leader.

Victor announced a warning for those inside to open the gates and surrender. No one responded to his threat. His impatience led to anger and he ordered the gates destroyed.

His men detonated explosives and brought the rusted steel gates crashing to the ground. When the dust settled, Victor led his men into the courtyard and they raided the palace, seizing anyone found.

As Victor waited, he lit a cigar and removed his broad sword. He ran his finger along the edge of the blade with a sadistic grin.

Fifteen servant girls raced out of the palace and fled down the street. Neither Victor nor his men displayed any interest in them.

The soldiers dragged a dozen men and women down the palace steps and tossed them on the ground in front of him. They sobbed and pleaded for mercy.

The prisoners were bureaucrats and a sorry excuse for leaders. They lived in the palace and pretended to be of importance in ruling the poverty-stricken planet.

Victor approached them and motioned for silence with a wave of his hand. "Where is the Princess of Yord?" he demanded.

The prisoners glanced at each other with surprised expressions. One man answered nervously, "The Princess has not been seen in many years. We doubt that she even lives."

Victor paced in front of the man and puffed on his cigar. He blew smoke in the man's face and rested his sword on his shoulder. "If that is so, then who does the rebel army protect?"

"Sir, we do not know these rebels," he replied humbly. "They come and go as they please."

Victor lifted the sword and glanced at his reflection on the blade. "Then you do not know who their leader is?"

"No, sir."

Victor gritted his teeth and smashed the man in the face with the hilt of his sword. The man fell to the ground unconscious, his jaw dislocated and nose broken.

"Who is the rebel leader?" Victor asked sternly.

No one replied, which added to Victor's ire. He severed the injured man's head from his body and kicked it away. The other prisoners panicked and sobbed.

"You were paid to protect us," shouted an elderly woman angrily. "We have a contract with you!"

Victor paced along the line of prisoners and looked away as if disinterested. Suddenly, he paused in front of the woman and rammed the hilt of his sword into her stomach. She let out a brief moan and fell to her knees. He struck her in the face with the broad side of his blade and knocked her to the ground unconscious. Her nose was grotesquely disjointed and shattered. Victor was amused by the sight of blood streaming profusely down her cheeks and neck. "There is no contract, you fools!" he announced mockingly.

"The priestess might have the answers you seek," replied another woman. "She knows things but her health is failed and her powers are limited now."

Victor approached the woman and studied her suspiciously. "Where is this priestess?" he inquired.

The woman grew uneasy and avoided eye contact with him. "On the second floor of the palace."

Victor placed his sword at her throat. He grabbed her hair and tilted her head back, ready to slit her throat. The woman displayed no fear from his threat. "Why are you so cooperative? Do you not fear for your life?" he asked.

"No, Sir. I only hope to see Yord become what it once was, regardless of who rules it."

"As do I," he replied and looked away, recalling his dreams for dominance.

"It hasn't been the same since the king and queen vanished," she continued. "I curse those responsible for their disappearance and the fall of a great kingdom."

Victor suddenly turned and faced her with renewed interest. "You curse them, do you?"

"Yes, sir. I suspect they were victims of deranged criminals. Who else would be sick enough to kill them after all they did for us?" The woman was proud she spoke up and beamed confidently at the other prisoners.

"I see," replied Victor curiously and rubbed his temples as if he was pained by her remark. "Would you curse me?" he asked.

"No, sir," she assured him.

"I don't believe you," he replied and pierced her abdomen with his sword. As he shoved it through her torso, he whispered into her ear, "I don't like to be cursed."

The woman's eyes widened with horror as she realized it was he who killed them. She gasped and died. The other prisoners were oblivious to his remark and shuddered in fear.

Victor turned to his soldiers and waited for confirmation that this priestess actually existed. Three soldiers descended the steps and approached him.

"Sir, there is a woman upstairs," one reported. "She is gravely ill. What would you have us to do with her?"

"I will speak with her," he responded as he looked over the prisoners. "Imprison them all. Nothing to eat or drink until they have something of value to tell me," he ordered and entered the palace alone.

The soldiers dragged the prisoners to the rear of the palace and locked them in the empty wine cellar. Their pleas for mercy fell on deaf ears.

Victor ascended the stairs to the second floor and eyed the long decrepit hallway in disdain. Burning torches lined the right side of the hall. Their flames flickered, sending eerie shadows across the dirty ceramic tile floor. Ornate lights lined the left wall. They no longer worked without power to the palace and looked ghastly with floor-length cobwebs draped over them.

Victor sneered and thought to himself, "How could these scum let such a beautiful palace fall into ruin like this? Perhaps I'll have them restore it as punishment."

Two soldiers appeared at the end of the hall and stood at attention. Victor ignored them and peeked inside the dimly lit room.

The windows were covered with black, moth-eaten curtains. Dirty panes of glass filtered the incoming daylight. In the center of the room was an oval crystal, opaque white in color, on a small round table covered with a tattered white cloth. The cloth bore an emblem with the royal crest above two crossed sabers. It draped to the floor and was discolored by soot. The only significant light in the room came from three candles in a trident-shaped candelabrum on another table.

A very old priestess lay on a stone table in the center of the room. She wore a plush, burgundy robe and her head was propped up with a small pillow. Her pupils were white, indicative of her blindness. She breathed faintly and seemed oblivious to Victor's presence.

Victor noticed the crystal nearby and his heart raced. "Could this be the mythical crystal of Icarus?" he thought to himself.

The crystal was rumored to foretell near future events but could only be interpreted by the Priestesses or Seers of the Temple of Icarus. Allegedly, there were few, if any, left with the ability to read the crystal.

As Victor approached the priestess, he grew more excited by the prospect of using the crystal to defeat the rebels. He stood by the woman and pondered the good fortune he believed was unfolding before him.

"What do you want from me?" the priestess asked.

He was startled by her sudden response. "Is this the sacred crystal of Icarus?" he inquired as he studied the crystal. It flickered briefly adding to the thrill of the moment. "Please, you must tell me!" he urged her anxiously.

The dying priestess summoned her strength and replied, "Yes, it is. It has been in my care for many years."

"Can you read the future from this crystal?"

"Perhaps," she whispered.

"Then tell me of my future here on Yord," he demanded and held the crystal close to her.

The frail woman wheezed and struggled to speak. Victor knelt next to her and listened intently. A pained expression crossed her face as she strained. The crystal glowed dimly for several seconds and then even that faint light faded. "The image is vague," she replied. "A woman you know well will kill you."

Victor was appalled by her words. He stood and stepped back from the table.

"You are right to fear her," she continued.

"Is she the rebel leader?"

The priestess trembled and coughed. Victor waited anxiously but she didn't respond.

"Is there another who can read the crystal?" he asked frantically. He feared that she would pass and leave him in futility with nothing but a worthless crystal.

The woman gestured with one finger for Victor to come closer. He knelt by her and listened carefully.

"There is only one. Her name is... Marina," the woman whispered weakly. "She is not a Priestess of the sacred Temple of Icarus."

Victor was stunned as he recalled a heinous act from his childhood. Marina was the Princess and, to his surprise, a Seer as well. He asked eagerly, "Where can I find this Marina?" he pleaded. "Please, tell me." He again knelt closer to her and leaned his ear toward her mouth.

"With criminals," she replied faintly. She coughed and turned her head sideways.

"Is she the rebel leader?" Victor inquired again anxiously.

The priestess lost consciousness and did not reply. A stream of spittle seeped from her mouth and pooled on the pillow.

Victor paced the floor and considered the value of keeping her alive. He left the room frustrated and returned to the palace entrance.

Fiona approached the palace, looking grim. Victor stood at the top of the steps outside the palace and noticed her demeanor. Eagerly he scanned the courtyard for the garrison of soldiers who accompanied her but there was no sign of them.

Fiona ascended the steps and stood before him, her hand bloodied. "We killed another dozen," she informed him. "They're down to women and children."

Victor frowned and asked, "Where is my garrison?"

"Casualties, my love, as expected. This *is* their turf."

Victor failed to suppress his anger and slapped her to the ground. "Get your hand fixed and see me later."

"Of course," replied Fiona smugly as she stood up. She entered the palace and sought out a rest room to tend to her hand.

Victor summoned Lech, a bald, clean-shaven man in his fifties, and one of his four captains. He ordered him to secure the perimeter outside the palace. The loss of thirty soldiers left him feeling somewhat vulnerable to a small rebel force that was inflicting a steady flow of losses on his army.

A transport ship arrived and landed outside the palace walls. A dozen soldiers exited, followed by three of Victor's captains; Britt, Crow and Meloche, the last missing most of his fingers.

Victor approached them and inquired anxiously, "Did you recover the chip?"

Britt stepped forward and answered humbly, "The Fleet's agents escaped with it before we arrived."

"Not acceptable!" shouted Victor angrily and punched Britt in the jaw. Victor turned and grabbed Crow, pressing a dagger against his throat.

"I needed that data chip to defeat the other militias!" he exclaimed bitterly. When he regained his composure, he released his hold on Crow. "And what of the courier? Do we know who she is?"

Britt got to his feet and rubbed his chin gingerly. He placed his hands on his hips and shook his head 'no.' "The courier was just a merc with no real training," he answered.

"And you did what with her?" Victor asked arrogantly.

"Slit her throat," he lied. "We couldn't take a chance that she was one of them."

"Very well," Victor replied. He noticed that Meloche had bandaged hands. "What, pray tell, happened to you?"

Meloche was embarrassed and looked shamefully at the ground.

"He chased the merc and nearly fell off a fire escape," answered Britt. "The frame gave way and severed his fingers. We rescued him before he fell."

"Your clumsiness was well rewarded," remarked Victor with no sympathy whatsoever. He walked away from them. "Meet me in one hour for a briefing," he shouted back.

Meloche held his hands up and grumbled, "I owe that bitch for this."

"I warned you not to mess with her," Britt scolded him as he recalled their encounter with Marina. "Fingers – I like that for a nickname," he said with a sly grin.

"Screw you, Britt!"

The three men laughed at the now re-named Fingers.

"Do you think she's the one?" Crow asked.

"Which one – the Princess or the rebel leader?" complained Britt. "You tell me."

Crow glanced at the other captains. They shrugged their shoulders at him, also unsure of whom the courier really was. If he was going to keep their allegiance, he needed to know Marina's true identity soon.

***

Victor sat inside the priestess' room and wondered if she could provide him with the names and location of the rebels?

Fiona hurried down the hall, dressed in an open back, tight-fitting gown with a plunging neckline. Her sharp facial features were accented by dark eye shadow and bright red lipstick. The wound on her hand was wrapped in a blood-stained bandage. She noticed the two soldiers at the doorway and assumed Victor must be inside.

"Sir, Fiona approaches," announced one of the soldiers at the door to Victor.

"Very well," he replied and stood. "Send her in."

The soldiers stepped aside and allowed her access. Fiona looked quite seductive as she sauntered toward Victor. She placed her arms around him and nibbled at his neck. "The palace is yours, my love. Now, it's just a matter of time before we crush the rebels."

Victor was unimpressed with her words. He ran his finger along the deep-V neckline of the dress and commented, "It seems you know your way around the palace quite well, including the closets."

Fiona was pleased by the attention and answered, "I spent my time here as a child and then as one of the maids, if you recall."

"I thought you might be of better stock than that of a lowly maid," he teased playfully.

Fiona placed her arms around his neck and whispered, "I have a room prepared for us. Let me show my love what stock I have to offer him. He will not be disappointed."

Victor removed her hands from his neck. He placed his hands on her hips and stared into her eyes. "We won't have any more losses like this, Fiona. I expected you to finish off the rebels, not..."

"And I will," interrupted Fiona. "We are so close to victory. Give me twelve of your best soldiers and we'll finish this by tonight."

"No, this is just another trap waiting to be sprung on my men."

Fiona touched Victor's cheek affectionately and pleaded, "Just twelve, I beg of you."

Victor swatted her hand away and focused his attention on the crystal. Fiona nestled against him from behind and ran her hands up and down his chest. "Have I ever let you down, Victor?"

"Sometimes I wonder. How many of my men have you lost in your quest to vanquish the rebels?"

"We knew this wouldn't be easy."

"Perhaps you aren't up to the task," he suggested disappointedly.

Fiona grew concerned by his attitude toward her. She always manipulated him through seduction in the past but today proved more difficult.

When she attempted to kiss him, Victor broke contact with her and pointed to the priestess. "She claims there is another who can read the crystal."

Fiona sneered at the priestess with an air of arrogance. "That wretched creature?" she complained. "So what will we do, hide inside these walls while the rebels regroup and recruit?"

Victor grabbed Fiona's shoulders and turned her toward him. "She tells me a woman I know will attempt to kill me. I need to know who it will be; the rebel leader, the princess, or perhaps even you, Fiona."

"All lies!" she exclaimed angrily and stomped across the room. "There is no truth to these priestesses or their stupid crystal!"

"And you know this for sure," he replied condescendingly.

Fiona placed her hands on his cheeks and pleaded, "Forget the priestess! We are so close to victory."

Victor became incensed. "Is that what you call it – victory?" he challenged. "We lose twenty soldiers for every rebel we kill! We will use the priestess to find the Seer of the crystal."

"But she is nearly dead!"

"Unfortunately so," replied Victor with a somber expression. "With a Seer and the crystal we could not only defeat the rebels but control the other militias as well. Until then, we only risk additional loses."

"Forgive me, my love. Would it make you happy if I extracted the information from her?" offered Fiona.

"Perhaps you could redeem yourself and restore your favor with me."

Fiona gazed at him coyly and nudged him toward the doorway. "Give me a few moments with her," she requested. "I know how to handle this woman."

Victor retreated to the entrance and watched curiously.

Fiona whispered into the old woman's ear, "I need your help, Charisse."

The priestess' eyes opened and displayed white pupils. "Who is there?" she asked faintly.

"A friend in need of your help."

"I can no longer help myself."

Fiona noticed that Victor stared impatiently at her. She realized that she needed to get her information quickly. "There is one thing you can do to save your people from further suffering," she whispered. "You need to tell me who the last Seer is."

Charisse grinned sadistically at her but didn't respond.

"The kingdom is in trouble!" pleaded Fiona. "I have to know who the Seer is and if she is the rebel leader!"

"If you are a friend, then you already know who she is."

Fiona was befuddled. "I have been away a long time. I need to know."

Charisse broke into a wicked laughter. "So, Fiona, after all these years, you've returned. I didn't think you'd dare after what you did."

"Alright, crone, tell me now or I'll kill you!"

"Marina isn't the rebel leader you fool, but the daughter of our long lost king and queen. She is the only one who can read the crystal and she will soon lay claim to her throne."

Fiona became enraged and appeared psychotic. "I'll make sure that it will never happen, dear Charisse," she remarked angrily. "I always hated you and the others.

Charisse responded with surprising spirit, "Because you were evil. You're a whore, a filthy abomination!"

Fiona looked back at Victor. He looked disappointedly at her and folded his arms, oblivious to the conversation. She took the candelabrum from the table and removed the three candles, one at a time.

"It is she who will never take the throne," declared Fiona. "Your secret dies with you today." She raised the candelabrum and rammed it into Charisse's eyes. She leaned on it and ground it into her face. Charisse shuddered and moaned briefly.

Fiona whispered into Charisse's ear, "I will be queen and no one else." When Charisse ceased breathing, she released her hold on the candelabrum and confidently approached Victor. "I told you I'd get you the information," she announced proudly.

Victor backed away from the door and followed her down the hall. Fiona turned into one of the bedrooms.

When Victor entered, she closed the door and kissed him passionately. She pulled him to the bed and sat down. On a table next to the bed was a bottle of wine and two glasses. Fiona clearly had her evening well-planned.

"What did she tell you?" Victor asked anxiously.

Fiona slid her dress off her shoulders and revealed her supple breasts. She took Victor's hands and rubbed them delicately. "The rebel leader is named Marina. The Seer is a priestess on Dax-7."

"That's it? That's all you got from her?" Victor shouted at her in frustration. He suspected that she knew more than she revealed and that she deliberately misled him. He already decided that he would keep Marina's identity to himself and let Fiona hang herself.

"That's enough for me, Victor. Tomorrow, I will find the rebel and kill her."

Victor hesitated and looked away. Fiona grew frustrated and stepped in front of him. "Is this how a mighty warrior treats his woman? I'm disappointed, Victor."

Victor slapped her face and floored her. He pounced on top of her and held her wrists. "Is that what you want?"

Fiona became excited. "Oh, yes. You know I like it like this," she crooned.

Victor lapped at her breasts ravenously. She wrapped her arms around his head and savored the attention.

A knock at the door interrupted them. Victor grew irritated. "Who is it?"

"It's Lech. Something's come up, sir."

Victor stood up and straightened his clothes. "Come in," he grumbled.

Fiona was stunned as she lay bare-breasted on the floor. More so, she was shocked by Victor's disrespect for her. Lech entered the room and immediately got an eyeful of Fiona's bosom.

"This had better be important," warned Victor.

"Three survivors of Fiona's garrison have returned. They have a message from the rebels for you."

"Very well. Let's go."

Victor and Lech left the room. Fiona became red-faced and threw the wine glasses at the wall. "You'll never be man enough for me, you coward." she uttered defiantly as she glared at the doorway. She hurled the wine bottle at the wall. The bottle exploded and red wine streamed down the walls. "For once, someone can clean up after me," she declared vengefully. In a fit of rage, she flipped every piece of furniture she could.

When the room was in shambles, she stormed about like a crazed woman. Eventually, she regained her composure. Rushing to the end of the hall, she looked down at the courtyard from the window.

Three naked men knelt at the base of the palace steps. All had scores of wounds on their bodies. Several townspeople gathered to see what happened but the soldiers dispersed them as fast as they assembled.

Victor and Lech descended the stairs and approached the men. "What message do you have for me?" Victor asked.

One of the men struggled to speak and answered hoarsely, "Red will kill you and many others for what Fiona has done to her people."

Victor became frantic and paced. "Who is this Red?" he asked impatiently.

"She is more dangerous than Fiona, sir," answered another.

"And this rebel thing is all about Fiona?"

"Yes, sir," answered the first. "Fiona didn't offer your terms for peace four months ago. She slaughtered them and hunted the others.

Fiona was shocked by their revelation. When Victor looked up, she quickly left the window.

"Take them away!" ordered Victor. "Treat them and report any additional details of their ordeal."

Victor was irate as he realized for a second time that Fiona betrayed him.

***

The four captains played cards in a small chamber off the main parlor. A dozen empty ale bottles littered the table. Fingers needed two hands to hold his cards and cussed every time he had to draw a card. The other three felt little sympathy for him and laughed each time he fumbled his cards.

Victor entered and slammed the door behind him. The captains quickly stood at attention.

"What do you require of us, sir?" asked Crow.

"The Seer of the crystal is a woman named Marina. She hides among criminals. Find her!"

The captains grew interested at the mention of Marina's name.

"Are you sure she's the one we want?" inquired Lech.

"Yes, I'm sure! And not a word of this to Fiona," Victor emphasized.

The men nodded in concurrence and hurried out of the room.

"How are we going to find her?" Crow asked Britt.

"We'll go to the prison on Kappa-Rigo and speak with Balthus. He knew how to find her once before."

"Perhaps we'll schedule a pickup," suggested Lech. "Then she can come to us."

"That may be the only way we'll find her. If she wasn't so elusive, she'd have been caught a long time ago."

Hopeful that they could obtain information from Balthus at the prison, they exited the palace and descended the steps.

Victor stared into space and thought, "We can play your little game, Fiona, but you will lose." He stormed out of the room into the main parlor. He knew she lied about Marina being the rebel and the Seer being on Dax-7. She also lied about offering a peace treaty to the rebels. It was disappointing that, after all they'd been through together, she betrayed him.

"Perhaps it was better this happened now rather than later when she became my queen," he thought. Suddenly he realized it was all about the throne. "That greedy whore!" he shouted angrily.

Fiona stood at the top of the stairs and looked down at him nervously. "What is wrong, Victor?"

"Take twelve men and find Red, now!"

Fiona was shocked that Victor knew the name she gave the rebel leader. Even more so, he knew it wasn't Marina who led the rebels. She hurried back to her room and changed.

Chapter 4

Bait

Marina lay motionless on her cot, immersed in another maddening dream. As a young girl, she stood on the balcony of the palace and looked down at her parents. They were dressed in their battle attire and both looked up at her with smiles.

"Please don't leave!" Marina cried. Her parents waved to her and left the palace. Each time they went away on a mission, it seemed like an eternity to the four-year old.

A young Charisse escorted her back to her room as she cried. "They'll be back soon," she assured Marina.

The transmitter beeped loudly and stirred Marina from her rest. She jumped up in a panic with tears in her eyes. "Who the hell is calling me at this hour?"

Marina sat at the ship's controls and pressed a switch on the transmitter. "What?" she yelled abruptly.

"Well, good morning to you, too," Dix' voice crackled from the speaker.

"I just got to sleep. What's up?" she asked.

"I figured after three days, you'd be ready for another job."

"Three days?"

"Are you sure you're alright, Marina?"

"Of course," she said, embarrassed by her condition. "I just lost track of time."

"What did Kat do to you?" he asked uneasily.

"Nothing you need to be concerned about."

Dix considered pressing her for more information but then thought better of it. "I have a job if you're up for it."

"What's the pay?"

"The usual. It should be much easier than the last one. I figured you could use a break."

"Just tell me when and where," Marina answered eagerly.

"I'll get back to you as soon as I validate the client."

"Thanks, Dix." Marina flipped off the switch and sighed. "That damn witch is in my head!" she blurted as she rubbed her eyes and reached behind the seat for the whiskey bottle. Marina fretted and stared at the bottle and complained, "And what am I supposed to do about it?" Three more gulps and she was asleep again with the bottle resting on her lap.

***

Britt and Lech entered the prison on Kappa-Rigo. An older soldier with scraggily hair and missing teeth greeted them at the entrance to Cell Block 17.

"What business do you have here?" he questioned the captains. "We don't usually get militia visitors, only prisoners and Fleet sentries."

Britt held out three gold coins. The soldier eyed them greedily and replied, "Whatever you need, sir."

Britt dropped the coins in his hand and requested, "We need to see the slob that was brought in a few days ago. Balthus is his name."

The soldier was surprised by the request but unlocked the door anyway. "Cell 27A, third corridor on the right. Oh, and don't get too close. He's a spitter."

Britt and Lech glanced at each other briefly. Lech drew his pistol and displayed it. "We'll fix that problem for him."

The soldier laughed and stepped aside. Britt and Lech marched dutifully down the long hall. Prisoners on either side shouted obscenities and grabbed at them.

One prisoner taunted Britt, "I ate your mother. She was good."

Britt drew his pistol and instinctively grabbed the man by the throat. He shoved the pistol in his mouth. The prisoner's eyes grew wide with fear. He tried to retreat from Britt but couldn't.

"My mother had the Blood Plague," explained Britt. "You should die as pleasant a death." He released his hold on the prisoner and continued down the corridor.

The prisoner fell to his knees and clutched at his throat. "You can't touch me!" he yelled. "That's against the rules!"

Britt paused and returned. The prisoner backed away from the bars nervously. Britt drew his pistol again and shot out both the prisoner's kneecaps. The prisoner fell to the floor clutching his knees in pain.

"Whose rules?" he asked cynically. "Anything else you want to say?"

"No, sir," whimpered the prisoner.

"I thought so."

Lech smiled at Britt in approval. The two men resumed their walk down the corridor. "I see you haven't lost your touch," kidded Lech.

"I hate these scumbags. That's what ruined the kingdoms - tolerance for felons."

They reached cell 27A and peered inside. Balthus lay on the floor with his back against a broken bed. He moaned tearfully.

"Hey, Balthus, we came to see you, old pal," Britt announced playfully.

Balthus looked up and grew angry. "You did this to me!" he shouted as he struggled helplessly to get to his feet.

"Come on, Balthus. You had to know everyone was on to you, including the Fleet."

"You should be after the bitch!" he complained. "She breaks into my home, violates my privacy and somehow I'm the one in prison!" Balthus rolled onto his belly and crawled to his feet.

"I have a deal for you," Britt informed him. "You look lonely in there."

"I have nothing to say to you." He hacked up phlegm and prepared to spit.

Britt drew his pistol and aimed at Balthus' face. "If you spit at me, I'll make sure you never do it again."

Balthus reconsidered his intentions and swallowed the glob. "What do you want from me?"

"Information," answered Lech.

"I won't be cheap, you know."

Lech glanced at Britt and chuckled.

"I told you I had a deal for you," replied Britt. "How would you like to see your old friends Sonia and Jerrold?"

Balthus' eyes lit up with joy. "You would do that for me?" he asked anxiously.

"I sure would. I need to know how you found the courier."

Balthus went into a rage. "That bitch! If I ever get my hands on her again, I'll..."

"Easy big fellow," advised Lech. "Let's discuss the details."

"Yes, we don't want you to have a heart attack and die on us," joked Britt.

Lech turned away and spoke into a transmitter on his wrist.

"I don't trust you," he stated defiantly.

Lech returned and faced Balthus, "Your friends are on their way."

Britt continued the interrogation. "Now, I need to know how you found the courier."

Balthus considered the request. "This must really be important if you're doing this for me."

"It is. My commander wants this woman, dead or alive."

"Oh, he does, does he?" said Balthus with a note of pleasure in his voice. "Can you make her suffer before you finish with her?"

"We can do anything you like if we capture her," Lech assured him.

The sound of footsteps echoed down the hall, interrupting their conversation.

"Here they come now," Lech announced.

Two soldiers escorted Jerrold and Sonia, both handcuffed, towards them. On her chest, Sonia wore a plastic bag half-full of clear liquid connected with a tube to her neck. She had no lower jaw and her face was grotesquely burnt. Jerrold had a plastic neck brace to immobilize his damaged throat. Both were frightened.

Many of the prisoners shouted and jeered at the two of them. They were especially enamored with Sonia and what her deformity could do for them.

The soldiers paused with Balthus' subjects in front of the cell.

"Alright, Balthus, time to talk," Britt ordered.

"Oh, my kitten," groaned Balthus. "Look what she did to you."

"Balthus – the information," warned Britt.

Balthus looked up at him with glaring eyes. "Glomus-5, level three. See a man named Dix. I asked for someone eye-pleasing. That's how I met that she-devil."

Britt nodded to Lech, who turned away and whispered into his transmitter.

Britt instructed the soldiers, "Move them inside the cell."

"Stand back," the soldier ordered Balthus.

"You mean they get to stay with me?" he asked excitedly.

"Assuming your information is correct. I have two of my men on Glomus-5. We're staying around until we get confirmation. If you're lying, you know what we'll do to them."

Balthus was ecstatic and retreated to the rear of the cell.

"I promise you, it's the truth! Thank you so much!"

The soldier unlocked the cell door and stepped aside. The second soldier unlocked the cuffs on Sonia and Jerrold. He shoved the two of them into the cell and locked the door.

Balthus anxiously waddled to his friends and hugged them.

"Put up a privacy sash," Britt instructed the soldiers. "I don't think the prisoners want to see what's going to happen in there."

The soldiers frowned in disgust and complied.

***

Fingers marched down the long ramp at the docking station on Glomus-5. Remembering his last encounter with Marina, he studied each of the docked vessels, hoping to find hers.

Crow rushed toward him from the other direction. "Let's go! We have a location," he shouted.

Fingers joined him and they turned down one of the corridors leading away from the dock. They reached an elevator and rode it down to the third level.

A dagger ejected from a special sheath on Fingers wrist to overcome his handicap. He displayed it proudly, but Crow chastised him, "Put that away, you fool."

Fingers reluctantly retracted his dagger. The two captains stepped off the elevator into the crude waiting room, pausing in front of the closed-circuit camera.

Dix's voice sounded from a speaker, "Can I help you, gentlemen?"

"We need to ask you a few questions," replied Lech.

"About?"

"About open the door before we turn you in to the Fleet for treason," warned Crow.

"One moment," Dix replied shakily.

"That was real subtle," quipped Fingers.

"Sometimes you have to change on the fly."

A buzzer sounded and the door unlocked. The two captains entered the next room and approached the window. The door slammed shut behind them and the buzzing ceased.

Dix was edgy at the sight of the soldiers and proclaimed, "I haven't done anything illegal, you know."

"Then you won't mind letting us inspect your office," replied Fingers.

Dix broke into a sweat as he considered the alternative if he defied them. "Can you tell me what this is about?"

"Open the door," instructed Crow, "and we'll gladly explain what we need from you."

When Dix left the caged window, the steel door clanked and slowly opened. His face appeared from behind the door. "Come in, gentlemen," he invited them with an unwelcome tone.

Crow and Fingers stepped inside. There wasn't much to the office other than a table with four computers and monitors, an old-fashioned radio transmitter, four folding chairs, a safe under the counter, and a brown cabinet.

Crow and Fingers sat in the chairs and stared at Dix. He wiped the sweat from his forehead and brow as he waited for them to explain the real purpose of their visit.

"How about something to drink?" requested Fingers. "We're a bit thirsty from the trip."

Dix opened the cabinet and brought out a bottle of bourbon. He set the bottle on the table with a thud.

"That's not very polite," Crow remarked.

Dix ignored him and set two glasses on the table next to the bottle. Crow and Fingers glanced at the bottle and then at Dix expectantly.

"You're not guests. I didn't invite you," Dix replied sarcastically. "Pour your own damn drink."

Fingers reached for the bottle with only two fingers on his hand. Crow grabbed his wrist. "I'll get it. You might drop the bottle."

"You know, Crow, one of these days..."

Crow poured a glass of bourbon and handed it to Fingers. He poured one glass for himself as well. The two held the glasses up for a mock toast.

"To our new friend, whatever his name is," Crow heckled. The two men tapped their glasses and drank.

"My name is Dix, if you don't mind."

"Well, Mr. Dix, since we're on speaking terms now, we're looking for Marina," explained Fingers. "I certainly hope you can accommodate us with her location."

Dix fidgeted for a moment and then answered, "I don't recall a courier named Marina."

Crow finished the drink and slammed the glass on the table. He stood up and grabbed Dix by the throat. "We can do this the easy way," he warned and took out a long, sharp knife. "Or we can do this the messy way. Get my drift?"

Dix was frightened and nodded obediently. Crow released his hold on him and burst into laughter. He stowed the knife and remarked pleasantly, "Now that's more like it." He slapped Dix on the back and poured himself another drink.

"Recently, she was hired to deliver a data chip to a known felon," Fingers explained. "This chip had certain weapons technology on it that creates a threat to our brotherhood of militiamen."

"I had no idea," said Dix apologetically. "I only arrange delivery of items. I don't inspect them."

"Of course you don't," Crow responded calmly. "How do we get in touch with her?"

Dix hesitated and looked away.

Crow reached down and removed his pistol and a knife, calmly setting them on the table.

"She had no idea what she was carrying," Dix replied nervously.

"Of course not. That's why she swapped it out with a bogus chip," Crow responded cynically. "How long has she been with you?"

"Almost twenty years. She came here as an orphan and needed a job."

"Twenty years, huh?" remarked Fingers. "That meant she came here when she was what... ten?"

"I'd say so."

"Get her in here, now!" demanded Crow.

"What will you do with her?" inquired Dix nervously. "I know she wouldn't take that chip."

Crow lifted the pulse pistol and rubbed it affectionately. He smiled at Dix and started to point it at him.

"Okay, I'll contact her!" Dix turned on the transmitter, set a frequency, and then entered a code into the computer next to it. He turned around and folded his arms.

"Now what?" asked Crow impatiently.

"She'll contact me when she's ready."

"I'll wait down the corridor," volunteered Fingers. "When she comes in, I'll make sure she doesn't get out."

Dix chuckled at him.

"What's so funny, Mr. Dickhead?" asked Fingers arrogantly.

"Why do you think she handles my toughest clients?" he chided. "She knows how to play rough."

"He's right," replied Crow. "We'll arrange a pickup on Yord. "There we'll have the advantage over her."

"Fine," grumbled Fingers. "But I owe that bitch for what she did to me."

"Not unless I say so," warned Crow. He scribbled on a piece of paper and handed it to Dix. "Give her this name and address to pick up a parcel," he instructed. "Screw this up and I'll make sure they find you in a lot of little pieces."

Crow stood and took another swig of bourbon from the bottle. "I'll contact Britt and make the arrangements."

Fingers nodded and poured another glass of bourbon using his thumb and forefinger to grip the bottle. "Have a seat, Dixie. We're going to be good friends by the time this is over."

Dix reluctantly sat down. Fingers filled Crow's glass and shoved it in front of Dix. "Drink up, friend."

Dix trembled as he feared what would happen to Marina because of his weakness.

***

Marina slept soundly on the cot inside her ship. The near empty whiskey bottle lay on the floor nearby. The transmitter beeped repeatedly until she awoke with an annoying headache. She rubbed her eyes and face. "Alright, I'm coming!" she groaned and programmed the transmitter to contact Dix.

Dix voice immediately answered. "Marina, I'm so glad you're there."

Marina dropped into the pilots' seat. "Yeah, I'm here. What's up?"

"I have a hot one for you. How soon can you get here?"

Marina thought that was strange of him to ask. They never discussed details like that to avoid being tracked.

"Don't know. I'm kind of out of reach," she answered. "Got to clean up a little mess first." She felt her hair underneath the wig and cringed at the matted texture from sweat.

"I understand. Get here when you can," he requested.

"Will do," Marina replied and turned off the transmitter. She took a vial of painkillers from the cabinet and popped two. Unable to swallow them dry, she picked up the bottle and chased the pills down with what remained of the whiskey.

"There's got to be a better way to earn a living than this," she muttered. Her image in the mirror frightened her: bruises on her face and one eye; cuts on her arms. Her hair was disheveled when she removed the wig and hadn't been washed in days. She opened the syringe case but it was empty. A tear streamed down her cheek as she recalled that Kat took away her 'poison.' This was the day she always feared. Now she would have to go cold turkey without the adrenalin injections.

Marina undressed while the water in the shower heated up. When she stepped into the stall, the hot pouring water over her body provided the best feeling she had had in some time. As the pain subsided, she felt better, even though it was just a temporary reprieve.

***

Dix slept in the chair while Fingers waited patiently. The silence was interrupted by a loud beep followed by Marina's voice. "Let me in, Dix."

Dix jumped up in his seat. Fingers motioned for him to handle it. He saw Marina's face on the monitor and pressed a button under the desk. Marina shoved the door open and approached the window in the dispatcher's office.

Fingers stood beside the window, positioned away from her view, his blade from his wrist sheath aimed at Dix.

Marina wore her standard mission gear: black leather pants and bodice, covered by a dark brown, hooded cloak; her dreadlock wig with flash grenade balls, two leather belts strapped on her thighs, each with two knives; and a pulse pistol holstered on either hip.

Dix was glad to see her. He always thought she looked sexy in her work attire but knew better than to comment about her appearance. Despite Finger's presence, he believed she'd handle things however necessary.

"I see you came dressed for work," he quipped.

"This job better pay well. I had plans tonight."

Dix wiped sweat from his brow and countered, "Come on, Marina, you never have plans."

"Seriously, you know I don't like rush jobs. There's always a catch."

"That's true. I need you to go to the Palace District on Yord and see a man named Bolton at the East Side Apothecary." He slid a small bag of coins and the piece of paper with the address through the cutout under the window.

Marina suspected something wasn't right but played along. She dumped the coins on the counter and looked up at him. "A little light for a rush job," she commented. "Don't you think?"

Dix reached under the counter and placed another bag on the counter. He slid it under the window to her.

"It's an extra hundred but only because I like you," he explained dryly, forcing a smile. "I'm providing a vessel for you as well. It leaves in an hour from dock five."

Marina dumped the coins from the bag and counted them, one at a time. She placed them all inside one bag and stared at Dix. "What's wrong with my own ship?" she asked curiously.

"After the debacle with Balthus in Stanton, your ship was compromised."

"You know, Dix, we've done business for a long time and, if I didn't know better, I'd swear this was a setup," Marina remarked suspiciously. "How about I come back there and we discuss this? I'm sure there's more to this than meets the eye."

Dix looked embarrassed. "You have to trust me, Marina." He shifted his eyes to his right and back to her. Marina realized that it was a trap and nodded in understanding. She stowed the bag in a leather pouch on her belt. "Something tells me you've got other issues to deal with. See you soon."

"Thanks, Marina. Be careful."

Marina left the room. She considered that Dix was never very generous with payment which was a definite giveaway. He always expected her to provide her own transportation as well. The shift in his eyes indicated that someone else was back there. Marina considered these observations as she rode the elevator up to the sixth floor where Dock 5 was located so she expected company when she got off.

Dix breathed a sigh of relief. He turned to Fingers and rebuked him, "You got what you wanted, now leave me alone!"

Fingers gently stroked the blade from his wrist sheath along Dix's neckline. "Don't do anything stupid or I'll be back." Fingers warned and left the dispatcher's office.

"Keep playing with that knife and you'll lose a few more fingers," chided Dix as he slammed the door shut.

Fingers snarled and punched the window. Dix backed away nervously, surprised that he heard his quip.

***

When the elevator door slid open, Marina tumbled out acrobatically and leaped to her feet. Two of Finger's men lunged at the place she should have been but grabbed only air. She gripped both by the back of their necks, pulled them to their feet and rammed their heads together. The injured men moaned and dropped to their knees. Marina shoved them into the elevator and pressed 'three.'

"That should impress Dix's guest," she joked and continued down the corridor to the docking station.

When the elevator doors opened on the third level, Fingers saw the two soldiers sprawled on the ground. He kicked each of them in the ribs and shouted, "Get up you fools!"

The men struggled to get to their feet.

"You couldn't take out one woman, could you?" he chided as the elevator doors closed behind him.

"She was ready for us, sir," whimpered one soldier. "We never had a chance."

Fingers punched the soldier in the face and knocked him out. The other soldier stared in horror at his partner.

"What's your excuse?" asked Fingers.

"None, sir. It won't happen again."

Finger's blade ejected and he held it to the man's throat. "For your sake, I certainly hope not."

The soldier nodded in understanding and said nothing more.

***

Inside the cargo freighter, Marina sat on a bench with her back against the hull. It was rare for her to travel on a ship other than hers. She studied the crew's actions for a short while and then relented that there was nothing else to do but wait. The steady hum of the engines had a calming effect on her and she drifted off into another dream.

In it, she reached out into a thick fog but felt nothing. "Hello," she shouted but received no response. Suddenly a hand touched her shoulder from behind. Marina spun around defensively but no one was there. "Alright, enough games!" she yelled and crouched down defensively.

A woman's voice spoke softly to her, "You have a destiny to fulfill."

Marina searched madly for the source of the voice but it was all around her.

"You must fulfill your destiny," another voice repeated.

Marina grew frustrated and responded sarcastically, "I don't have a destiny and I don't want one."

"You are a part of us and you must finish what we started. It is who you are."

"Screw you and your destiny crap!" she shouted and fled aimlessly through the fog.

Marina awoke abruptly, sweating and gasping for air. She took out a flask of whiskey from under her cloak and guzzled the contents. When the flask was empty, she stared at the floor, frozen in fear. "What the hell is happening to me?" she thought to herself. "It's gotta' be that witch!"

Marina feared that Kat's recurring intrusions into her mind could jeopardize her mission. She tossed the empty flask across the cargo bay. It was only a few days since she last used an adrenalin injection but she needed something to get her edge back in a bad way. All she wanted was to do her job and be left alone. "

"*Why did Kat have to interfere with my life?*" she pondered. "*What does she want with me?*"

Two days later, the ship landed at the docking facility on the planet Yord. The complex had replaced the old orbital station and was nothing more than a large warehouse with four loading docks, two forklifts and a few freight transportation vehicles.

The hatch opened and Marina stood in the doorway. She surveyed the dimly lit dock cautiously. Several of the lights flickered or were broken. Torches placed randomly around the loading docks provided extra lighting.

Three crewmen on board the ship interrupted her and unloaded several crates onto the dock with a pallet jack.

Marina took four steps away from the hatch and paused. A dockworker rolled a steel drum past her and stood it up in a dark corner. He returned and grinned at her, displaying several missing teeth.

She ignored him and considered which way to go. The man grabbed her ass and whispered something to her while pointing behind three large crates. Women never went to the docks alone. Only prostitutes and drug dealers and even they were rare. An easy target, the man assumed she was for sale.

Marina agreed and followed him. She glanced around before stepping behind the crates. No one noticed her.

The man shoved her against the crate and clutched at her breasts, under the cloak and leather bodice. Marina instinctively shoved her palm into his nose and broke it. Before he could react, she grabbed both his wrists and snapped them. The man gasped in horror and stared at her in disbelief.

"Might as well consummate our relationship," she joked and snapped his shin with a swift kick to the outside portion of bone. "Nice meeting you," she taunted and walked away.

The man lay behind the crates, helplessly crying in agony. "You bitch!" he screamed tearfully.

Marina chuckled to herself and thought, "That's right."

Further down the dock, two workers discussed a bill of laden for another ship. Marina walked between them and pushed each out of her way. She was in a lousy mood and a fight might be just what she needed to get out of her funk. It had to be discrete though, no soldiers or mercs.

"Excuse me, Ma'am!" shouted one of the men annoyingly. Marina gave him the middle finger and continued on her way. She was disappointed that no one challenged her.

The streets in the Palace District grew foggy as cool night air settled over the town. Marina paused and looked back. She sensed someone was following her and ducked inside the doorway of an abandoned shop.

The rebel leader called Red stood in the intersection and strained to see through the thickening fog. She wore her red, hooded cloak with the hood up.

Marina watched her from the doorway but as quickly as Red appeared, she vanished in the fog. Marina continued to the next block and paused underneath a swinging sign in front of an abandoned pub. The squeaking sound echoed down the street like a church bell but she listened warily for something else.

The sound of boots grew louder as three militia soldiers approached her from behind. Marina knew they were there and chose not to run. She was confident that she could handle them.

The soldiers stood behind her and waited for her to react. Marina's disinterest in them was peculiar.

"Victor requests your presence at once," one soldier informed her.

Marina turned and challenged, "Over my dead body."

"Not today," replied another. "Your skanky ass is worth too much alive."

The soldiers laughed at her.

Marina remarked sarcastically while subtly drawing a dagger from under her cloak, "I'm sensitive about my ass and …," Before the soldiers could react, she slit the nearest soldier's throat. "… and I don't appreciate remarks about it," she finished and fled around the corner.

The soldiers attempted to help their comrade but the wound was lethal. They chased after Marina.

Four empty trashcans were lined along the alley behind the pub. Marina knocked the first two over and flattened against the wall. She fretted as she realized she broke one of her rules about killing Fleet and militia soldiers. Now, things would get personal.

As the first soldier burst into view and leaped over the cans, Marina chopped at him and collapsed his throat. He fell to the ground and gasped frantically for air.

The second soldier leaped over the trashcan and delivered a punch to her forehead. She dropped her dagger, staggered backward three steps, and then fell to the ground, barely conscious.

The soldier stood over her proudly and proclaimed, "You don't look so tough from up here, you tramp."

Marina tried to get to her knees but he kicked her in the ribs repeatedly. She fell back down and clutched her side in pain.

Red approached the soldier from behind with a plank in her hands. "Hey, asshole," she called arrogantly.

The soldier stopped smiling and turned around. Red struck him in the side of the head with the plank and knocked him out. "You don't look so tough either," she taunted and inflicted the same treatment on him that he'd been giving to Marina.

Marina struggled to her knees and cautiously placed her hand on her dagger. Red helped her to her feet and escorted her down the street.

"Who are you?" asked Marina weakly.

"Not now," Red replied. "We have to get off the street before they find us."

Red helped her up a fire escape in a nearby alley, which led to a small one bedroom apartment above a vacant block of stores. She helped Marina down on the couch and laid her flat.

A single candle barely lit the small room. Marina held one hand over her forehead and another still under her cloak on her dagger.

Red removed her robe. Underneath she wore plain jeans and a sweatshirt with a transmitter on her wrist. She retrieved a can of freeze-spray from a cabinet in the kitchen.

When she returned, Marina drew her dagger and leapt onto her. They tumbled backwards and wrestled until Marina pressed the knife to Red's throat. The can of freeze-spray rolled across the floor.

"Who are you?" Marina demanded.

"My name's Rebecca," Red replied. "I'm here to help you."

"Why?" asked Marina, pressing the knife harder until a red line formed on Rebecca's neck.

"You don't remember me, do you?" Rebecca countered sarcastically.

"No, and I don't care," Marina answered bitterly and got off of her. "Stay out of my way if you know what's good for you."

"Would you rather be a prisoner at the palace right now?" Rebecca stood up cautiously and gave her a minute to answer. When none came, she continued, "I didn't think so."

Marina warily stowed the knife under her cloak. "You'd better have a damn good reason for sticking your nose in my business."

Rebecca studied her expression and realized Marina really didn't remember her. "We met about ten years ago in Stanton," Rebecca informed her. "My sister and I were attacked by a gang of mercenaries."

Marina thought back and tried to recall the incident. Nothing came to mind.

"My sister, Sara, was killed but you rescued me."

"So what?" Marina asked as she downplayed the possibility.

"I was tipped off by a friend on Glomus-5 that you were coming to Yord," Rebecca explained and sat at the table. "That's the first time in a long time that someone took me down in a scuffle like that. I'm impressed."

"So what is it about my presence that concerns you?" inquired Marina indignantly.

"Yord's a dangerous place under militia control," Rebecca revealed and gestured for Marina to join her at the table. "Now that the Palace District has fallen, the militia commander will attempt to establish legal authority over everyone."

Marina sat directly across from her and asked again, "So, what does this have to do with me?"

"Ten years ago, you came here and saved my life. Something about you made me believe that you were the true heir to the throne of Yord."

Marina grew impatient and stood. "You have me confused for someone else," she replied irritably and walked toward the open window. "I'm just a courier."

"Same line you used back then," Rebecca ridiculed. "And still just a courier after all these years."

"Kiss my ass!" shouted Marina. When she stepped part way out the window, Rebecca called to her, "Wait!" She rushed to Marina and grabbed her arm. Marina simultaneously grabbed her long red hair and stepped back inside the apartment. She dragged Rebecca back into a chair by the table and, in one motion, bent her arm behind her back.

Rebecca threw an elbow at Marina and struck her in the jaw. Marina planted Rebecca's cheek against the table; then held the point of her dagger against the rebel's jugular.

"Touché, Marina. That's twice. Next time will be my turn," she warned.

"There won't be a next time," answered Marina. "I don't want to see you again." She released her hold on Rebecca and went to the window.

Rebecca rushed at her and grabbed her by the neck. As Marina turned around, Rebecca swept her legs out from under her with a swift move from her left leg. Marina fell to the ground and smacked the back of her head on the floor. She lay dazed and motionless for a moment. "Not bad for a peasant," Marina uttered.

"I wonder where I learned that from," Rebecca taunted.

"So you copied a move of mine," snapped Marina. "Big deal."

"Please, Marina, let me help you!" she urged and helped Marina to her feet.

"You really don't remember when you saved my life from those mercs?" Rebecca asked disappointedly. "How about the woman and boy who were burned to death in the book shop? I believe they were family to your friend Dix."

The years of violence, adrenalin injections and loneliness made memories difficult to retain, which was part of the point. Marina didn't like her memories. She wondered why she would have saved this particular woman but then realized she had business to tend to.

"Stay out of my way. I'm not who you think I am," she repeated sternly and exited through the window.

Rebecca grew more frustrated and pressed a button on her transmitter. A man's voice responded, "How did it go?"

"I wonder if we've got the right person, Cristos."

"Was there a problem?" he asked.

"That's an understatement. She fights like a mercenary and won't listen to anything I say."

"Where is she now?

"She went out the fire escape," Rebecca replied as she picked up the ice chips off the floor.

"Maybe if I talk to her," he suggested.

"I don't think she'd care," she remarked and rubbed an ice chip on the small cut on her neck from Marina's blade. "I really thought this would work out, Cristos. I screwed up."

"No, you didn't," he answered sympathetically. "We weren't aware how damaged she really is."

There was a moment of silence between them. Finally, Cristos responded, "I'll take care of it."

Rebecca sadly turned off the transmitter and sat dejectedly on the couch.

***

Marina hid behind a dumpster and leaned against the brick wall. Her head ached and her inability to remember bothered her for the first time. "What the hell is wrong with me?" she uttered and slumped down to sit on the broken concrete ground. "What else am I forgetting?"

As she thought back ten years ago, trying to remember how she might have met Rebecca, she recalled the horrors inflicted on a small town by mercenaries. Then she remembered the mercs who assaulted two women.

Marina wondered if she really did make Rebecca who she was. She sensed someone nearby but saw no one. On the roof above her, Cristos, dark-skinned, dressed in plain clothes and a raincoat, looked down at her like a cat ready to pounce. He was the same age as Rebecca at twenty-nine with a baby face, a dark goatee and mustache.

As Marina looked up, Cristos dropped from the fire escape and chopped her in the back of the head. With Marina unconscious on the ground, he handcuffed her wrists and carried her back to the apartment.

Rebecca heard scuffling noises outside the window and drew her pistol. She relaxed when Cristos dragged Marina's body inside and shoved her onto the sofa.

Rebecca felt sympathy for her and asked Cristos, "Was that necessary?"

"According to you it was."

"What do you expect from her?" Rebecca chastised him. "She's a rebel, just like her parents before they established the alliance."

Rebecca sprayed the back of Marina's head and her swollen forehead with the freeze-spray.

Marina came to but was groggy from the blow. Rebecca covered Marina's eyes and sprayed her cheekbone. "This should help ease the pain."

Cristos went to the kitchen and poured himself a glass of vodka from a half-empty bottle. Rebecca joined him, looking dejected. After chugging the contents, he hugged Rebecca. "So what do we do with her now?" he asked.

"I don't how to make her understand what's at stake."

Marina staggered to her feet and challenged the two of them, even with her hands secured behind her back.

Cristos drew two pulse pistols from under his coat and aimed them at Marina's head. "Don't make me use these," he warned.

Marina was anything but intimidated. She felt a rage explode within her and pressed her forehead against the barrels of the pistols. "Go ahead and shoot!" she dared. "You'll be doing me a favor."

Rebecca noticed the needle track on her neck. She glanced at Cristos and commented disappointedly, "Adrenalin. I should have known."

"That's none of your business!" snapped Marina.

"You gave me a shot of that when my sister died. It made me the monster I am today."

"You were weak," Marina chastised her. "I helped you overcome that moment."

"And now I kill with no remorse! I became you," Rebecca countered. "Doesn't that bother you?"

Cristos looked disgustedly at Marina and commented, "She's nothing like her parents. She's pathetic."

"Let's get something straight," Marina shouted with a crazed look in her eyes, "I have no parents and as far as I'm concerned, I never did. Now let me the hell out of here before I hurt you."

Cristos wasn't impressed with her bravado and glared at her, eyes unflinching.

Rebecca never tolerated this kind of backtalk from anyone. She pushed Cristos' guns away from Marina and went face-to-face with her. "Don't ever let me hear you disrespect your parents again. You don't know what they sacrificed for you."

"And how would you know?" Marina asked mockingly.

"Because my parents were lost with them. You weren't the only one left behind."

"Then you live with that thought!" Marina shouted and pressed her forehead against Rebecca's. "I certainly won't."

Rebecca wouldn't back down from Marina. She pressed back against Marina's forehead. "Here's how it goes," she explained. "You have two choices. Pick one and then you can do as you please."

"No one tells me what to do," Marina warned in a low, threatening tone.

The two instinctively went nose to nose again, neither one budging.

Cristos pulled the women apart and raised his hand to slap Marina for her insolence.

Rebecca grabbed his arm as she stared down Marina. She shoved Marina backward onto the sofa.

Marina jumped back on her feet and got back in Rebecca's face. "You want to go at it now?" she challenged. "I'll kill you both!"

"Shut your mouth and listen to us," Rebecca ordered. "You need to hear this." She glanced at Cristos for his explanation.

"Victor will assume the throne of Yord very soon unless you lay claim to it," he informed her.

Marina rolled her eyes and became impatient. "I'm not interested in ruling this slum planet. In fact, I can't wait to get the hell away from here."

Rebecca added, "It's about more than ruling the planet. Do you remember the Priestess Charisse?"

Marina was surprised that she did recall her name. Charisse raised her and taught her to be her own person. She taught her to be fearless, arrogant and to demand respect from others. "Rule or be ruled," Marina recalled her words to her, over and over again.

Rebecca noticed the sadness in Marina's eyes. "You should remember," she continued. "Charisse spent many hours with you at the palace when you were a child."

Marina looked somberly at the ground. "My parents abandoned me. I walked away from that life and I'll never go back."

"At least you admit who you really are," Cristos responded. He hoped they were finally getting through to her.

"It doesn't matter who you think I am," she answered somberly. "I'll never go back to that life."

"How could you think that?" asked Rebecca with a shocked expression on her face.

"How could I not?" cried Marina. "I was left to be raised by strangers in a temple!"

Cristos sat next to her and unlocked the cuffs. He and Rebecca sat down at the table and pondered what to do or say that might change her mind.

Marina gingerly rubbed her wrists. Tears streamed down her cheeks. "You have no idea how lonely I was. I cried myself to sleep every night. Now I couldn't care less about them or anyone else for that matter."

"It could have been far worse, you know," remarked Cristos.

"You are so right. I could have stayed! I could have been the good little girl - the princess of a kingdom that cared nothing about my family." She buried her face in her hands and sobbed.

"You're nothing like the exaggerated stories I've heard. You're just a junkie with anger issues," Cristos complained.

"Screw you!" shouted Marina. She went to the window and looked down. The fog hid the street from her view.

Rebecca approached her and spoke somberly. "Charisse's body was found in a dumpster last week. Both her eyes were gouged out."

Marina was stunned by the news and turned her attention back to Rebecca for further explanation.

"Victor and his assassin girlfriend know about your identity," she continued. "Charisse was killed by them, Marina, because of you."

"And how would you know?" she countered bitterly.

"You aren't the only one who carries a burden."

Marina wiped tears from her cheeks and asked, "Why did you interfere in my fight?"

"Because your people need you to lead them," Rebecca announced firmly. "I've been doing it for you the last ten years and now it's your turn. They wait and hope for your return every day. I can only prepare them for that day when you lay claim to the throne."

"Why would you do this for me?" Marina asked curiously.

"You showed me what I needed to do. You taught me to fight fearlessly but without emotion like you. I learned and I've been fighting that way ever since."

"Well, goodie for you," she replied sarcastically. Marina knew she could never become part of the life her parents lived. She was a loner and would stay that way.

Cristos sensed her inner conflict. "If you don't wish to reclaim what is rightfully yours, then you must leave here immediately and never return. Those are your choices."

Marina stood in front of him and folded her arms. She stared into his eyes without blinking and inquired arrogantly, "And why is that?"

"If Victor captures you, he will force you to interpret what the crystal knows," he revealed. "That would imperil anyone who opposes him."

Marina returned to the table. She leaned on it with both hands. How could she make them understand how she felt? "Look, I was hired to pick up a package in town," she explained. "Once that's done, I'm outta' here."

"It's a trap to lure you back here, Marina," Cristos warned her. "Use your head!"

"Traps don't scare me."

"Marina, you are the last surviving Seer of the sacred crystal," pleaded Rebecca. "Don't you get it?"

Marina slammed the table with her fist. "What's so special about this damn crystal?"

"It shows near future events," answered Cristos.

"What future?" shouted Marina. "Look at this world. What future could it possibly have?"

"That crystal brought your parents together," Rebecca informed her.

"That crystal helped them build the empire that once symbolized peace and unity," added Cristos.

"With the war over and your parents gone, it crumbled from greed and corruption," Rebecca continued somberly.

Marina looked away from them. "And where are they now, Rebecca or is it Red?"

"It's Rebecca and I wish to God we knew."

"Once upon a time, I did too. Now I couldn't care less. I'm outta' here." Marina hesitated at the window. She glanced back at them scornfully and then exited.

Rebecca and Cristos were frustrated by her response.

"This isn't gonna' be easy," Cristos grumbled disappointedly. "The fool will be captured."

"And we can't let that happen, no matter what. Let's go."

They exited by way of the stairwell to the street below.

***

Marina crept through the fog and glanced behind her often. She knew that Rebecca and Cristos would not give up on her.

After three blocks, she found a burnt out store with no door. Fatigue affected her senses so she ducked inside to rest. Nestled under the charred counter, she slept.

In another dream, Kat appeared and reminded her, "I told you there are many who love and care for you. Don't turn your back on them." Marina felt Kat's power overwhelm her again. Kat brushed her hair from over her eyes and held her close to her. Marina pushed her away.

"No one loves me!" she cried. "No one would care if I died today."

"We all care. You have a destiny that we are all part of," Kat reminded her again. She kissed Marina and sent her into a whirl. Marina felt as though she was falling and became dizzy.

A short while later, she awoke and looked up from under the counter. A young man and woman stared down at her. She drew her dagger and leaped up. The figures vanished. "What the hell is wrong with me?" she muttered to herself. "I'm losing my mind!"

Voices outside the shop caught her attention. It was the soldiers. She waited nervously until the voices faded. "I hate this shit-hole," she groaned in disgust and left the shop. "Never again, I swear."

Further down the street, Marina paused in front of a shop. The sign above read 'Bolton's Apothecary.' She looked suspiciously back and forth before she entered. The street was empty.

Cristos' warning still rung in her ears: It's a trap to lure you back here. "Why is everyone so concerned with resurrecting a princess long gone?" she thought. "Why would they think I could be Red, a leader of rebels?"

Marina wondered as she warily stepped through the doorway. "*Was Rebecca really Red the rebel leader?*" She recalled how Rebecca took her down in the apartment. No one had ever done that and walked away. "*Did she really learn that from me?*" she questioned herself as she tried to recall their experience ten years ago. Then it came to her. Whether it was another of Kat's games or her memory actually returning to her, she wasn't sure, but now she suddenly remembered that day so vividly.

Ten years ago…

One rainy day in the forest, five mercenaries beat two women relentlessly.

Marina stepped out of the trees toward them. "That's enough!" she shouted. The men ceased their attack and turned to her. She dropped her cloak to the ground, drawing two daggers.

"You want some of this, do ya," taunted one man as he unbuckled his pants.

"I wouldn't brag about that if I were you?" mocked Marina.

The angry mercenary rushed at her but she swept his legs out from under him and slit his throat as he fell towards the ground.

"Who's next?" she asked. Her eyes were filled with rage as she anxiously waited for the next attacker.

The next two lunged for her simultaneously. Marina instinctively drove both her daggers upward into their abdomens. They fell to the ground on top of her, clutching desperately at their wounds.

As she staggered to her feet, the fourth man tackled her to the ground and the fifth landed on top of them. When they rolled over, Marina got to her knees and gained the advantage. She head-butted one man and drove her dagger into the throat of the other before either could stand. The dazed man staggered to his feet off balance and shouted, "I'll kill you, bitch!"

Marina attempted to deliver a karate-kick to the man's jaw but she slipped in the mud and fell on her back. Both her daggers landed a short distance away. The remaining merc drew his pulse pistol and aimed at her head.

"You're a sorry excuse," she taunted. "You're afraid to fight a woman?"

The man felt a rush of bravado and stowed his pistol in the holster. He dove on top of her but she drew her remaining two daggers and pierced both sides of his neck, inflicting lethal wounds. The man grasped at his neck as blood spurted from both incisions. He fell to his knees and asked in a raspy, weakened voice, "Who the hell are you?"

Marina stared coldly into his eyes and replied, "I am the courier." She laid him out for his final rest with a solid kick to the side of his head. After wiping off the daggers, she sheathed them in her thigh belts, and then donned her wet cloak.

"Help me," pleaded Rebecca.

Marina knelt down beside her and asked, "Can you walk?" Rebecca tried to stand but struggled to maintain her balance. Marina helped her to her feet and leaned her against the tree for support. She checked Rebecca's sister for any sign of life but she was already dead. "I'm sorry," she told her, "there's nothing we can do." Rebecca fell to her knees and cried.

"Who are you?" asked Marina.

"My name is Rebecca. That was my sister, Sara" she answered, teary eyed and pointing at the dead woman.

Marina recalled the grief that Rebecca suffered and how she callously gave her a shot of adrenalin to 'numb' the pain she felt for her sister. She forced the memory away and regained her composure at the door.

The shop was dingy with dirty shelves and missing floor tiles. The ceiling was water-stained and the air had a musty odor to it. Various drugs and hygiene supplies, mostly black market items, were scattered sloppily on the shelves. Empty boxes were stacked on the counter next to a bell, a newspaper, and a cup of coffee. Steam rose from the coffee.

Behind the counter was an open doorway, cluttered with brown boxes, some empty and some partially-filled with goods.

Marina approached the counter and tapped the bell twice. The shop had all the makings of a trap. It was just a matter of how it would spring on her. The owner had been coerced by either mercenaries or Fleet soldiers because of his possession of illegal goods. Whoever he was, he wasn't walking away when this was over. They never do. She placed her hands down by her side and touched her daggers for assurance.

A grizzled old man in his seventies emerged from the back room. He stared at her with intimidating eyes. Marina thought, *"How naïve you are, old man. They're gonna' kill you when we're done here."*

"What do you want?" he asked in a raspy voice.

"You Bolton?" she inquired.

"Who's askin'?"

"Doesn't matter. I'm here to pick up a package."

Bolton grunted and returned to the back room.

Marina scanned the shop uneasily. Then Britt emerged from the back room with a pulse pistol aimed at her. "How nice of you to join us again," he commented in a pleasant tone. "It's been a while, Marina."

"I figured this was a set up," she responded cynically. "Shit stinks a long way around here."

"Keep flapping that smart mouth of yours and I'll knock a few of those teeth out for you. We have to talk now."

"I don't think so," she remarked defiantly and slapped the cup of coffee over.

As Britt jumped back, Marina drew one of her daggers and flung it at him. The knife struck Britt's left bicep and he dropped his pistol.

"You bitch!" he shouted and clutched at the wound.

"That's right! That's all I am so stop chasing me!" Marina shouted sternly and rushed out the door.

Britt removed the dagger from his bloody arm and uttered, "Playtime's over."

Lech and Fingers waited outside on either side of the shop's door. Marina burst out the doorway, confident that she was free. Both captains punched her in the forehead at the same time and knocked her out instantly. Marina dropped like a rock to the ground.

"Damn, that felt good," remarked Fingers as he shook off the pain in his injured hand.

Lech placed a sack over her head and Fingers tossed her unconscious body over his shoulder. They carried her off to the palace. One soldier remained outside the shop.

The buzz of a single pulse fired from inside echoed in the quiet night. The soldier peeked inside the shop uneasily. Bolton lay dead on the floor with a burning hole in his forehead.

Britt emerged with his pistol in one hand and held his wounded arm gingerly with the other.

"You killed him, sir?" asked the soldier curiously.

"Yeah, I hate rats," grumbled Britt. He looked both ways on the street and followed the others.

The soldier shrugged his shoulders, confused by Britt's logic, and obediently followed him.

Chapter 5

Revelations

Lech guarded the entrance to Charisse's room in the palace. Inside the meditation room, Marina lay unconscious on the stone table just as Charisse once did. Her eyes were blackened and one cheek was badly swollen. Velcro straps bound her wrists and ankles.

Britt stood next to her with his arm bandaged and studied her face. He wondered if she really could be the princess, the rebel leader or both, and then what he needed to do about it either way.

The crystal on the table atop the tattered table cloth with the royal emblem flickered briefly and caught his attention.

Marina opened her eyes and noticed it, too. The crystal grew brighter for an instant as if acknowledging her awareness of it.

Lech observed the brief illumination of the crystal from the doorway and was curious. Britt looked back at him and nodded. Their suspicions were correct. She was indeed the Princess of Yord and the Seer of the crystal. Lech disappeared from the doorway to report the news to the other captains.

Marina raised her head and peered at the blood-stained candelabrum which was set back on the table behind the crystal. The crystal now glowed steadily.

Her mind was filled with a vivid image of Charisse's death. She saw Charisse telling Fiona, "Marina isn't the rebel leader, you fool, but the daughter of our long lost king and queen. She is the only one who can read the crystal and she will one day take the throne."

"It is she who will never take the throne," whispered Fiona. "Your secret dies with you today."

Marina was shocked that Charisse would reveal her secret to an assassin. Perhaps this was her way of making Marina's fate take shape. Marina saw the gristly finale as Fiona gouged Charisse to death with the candelabrum. Mercifully, the image ended there.

Marina gasped. She looked at the candelabrum with horror. Charisse's dried blood still marred the silver instrument.

Britt leaned against the head of the table, looking down on Marina. "Who are you really? I need to know now," he questioned her desperately, "before it's too late."

Marina's head pounded and her vision was blurred. She tried to sit up but couldn't.

Britt untied the Velcro straps that bound her hands and feet. She shifted her legs off the table and sat upright. He folded his arms and warned her impatiently, "For your own good, you'd better tell me now."

"I'm just a courier! Why can't you get that through your thick skull?"

He leaned closer and whispered, "Well, Victor thinks you're a lot more than that. I think he's right."

"Well, goodie for you," she retorted sarcastically.

"Look, you can trust me or you can deal with him."

Marina blurted out in frustration, "And I don't give a crap!"

"He'll soon be your king so you'd better care," Britt advised. "And I don't think he plans on letting you leave your favorite planet either." He took a handkerchief from under his leather tunic and gently wiped the dirt and dried blood from Marina's cheek.

"He's not part of the royal family," Marina reminded him. "No one will accept him as king."

"Who's going to stop him?" countered Britt. "The rebels have been chased from the city. Their numbers dwindle a little more each day. There are few residents left."

"But what if there was an heir to the throne?" Marina queried. "The other kingdoms might support him or her."

Britt chuckled cynically. "My men and I can't stop him alone so long as he has the support of Fiona and her mercenaries. We need something to justify our actions to the other militias."

"And others will support you?"

"They will. Our fear is that Victor will either imprison or marry Marina, the true princess, and legitimately control Yord. After that, he'll use his power to conquer the Space Fleet and the militias. He'll no doubt continue to wage war with the alien races until he either conquers or destroys everyone."

"Or the bastard will die trying!" she exclaimed. Marina felt a renewed fire inside her. She tried to hide it but controlling her emotions was never a strong suit of hers.

Britt was amused by her reaction but before he could say another word, Victor and Fiona entered the room.

Victor gestured with a wave of his hand for Britt to leave. Britt trained his eyes on Marina as he walked away from her.

Victor paced around the table and ogled Marina. He found her attractive and considered the possibilities of an alliance rather than imprisonment.

"It's good to see you're awake," he commented. "I hope you enjoyed your little nap."

"No thanks to your goons," she responded.

"I'm sure you'll find me quite accommodating under the circumstances."

"Gee, I feel so much better," she replied sarcastically.

Fiona grew uneasy. This wasn't how she expected Victor to treat a rebel leader who had decimated more than half of his militia.

Victor gently touched the swelling on Marina's cheek and forehead. "Fiona, summon Lech," he ordered. Fiona nodded and left the room.

Victor circled the stone table again and admired Marina from all angles. "It's hard to believe a woman of your beauty is the mighty leader of my enemies," he remarked.

"And who told you that crock of crap," she quipped. "As I told your goons, I don't play well with others. I'm strictly a loner."

"So you don't go by the name of Red?"

"Of course not, you idiot! You sent your thugs to Glomus-5 to trap me. How could I be a rebel leader here on this cesspool of a planet if I'm working somewhere else?"

Victor recalled what Charisse told him about her. He glanced at the doorway suspiciously.

Fiona and Lech entered the room. Lech approached Victor and stood at attention. "Yes, sir," he barked.

Victor placed his hands behind his back and stared at him with sharp piercing eyes. "Lech, didn't I tell you not to harm Marina?"

Lech became uneasy and responded, "Yes, sir, but it was necessary to subdue her. She is quite a worthy adversary."

Victor frowned at him disappointedly. "That was an order, not a suggestion!"

Lech cowered and looked nervously at the floor. "I'm sorry. It won't happen again," he uttered humbly.

"I'm sure it won't," Victor agreed.

Fiona drew a dagger and handed it to him. "I think you should do the honors," she suggested.

Victor refused the dagger. "Your penchant for death and suffering has done more damage to my cause than the rebels themselves."

Fiona was stunned by his accusation. She folded her arms and paced the floor, unsure of what to say or how to react.

Victor punched Lech in the gut. He fell to his knees and gasped for air.

Fiona was irate over his loyalty to his captains and reached a decision. It was time she asserted herself as a dominant figure in their relationship and took control. She brazenly stepped in front of Lech and slit his throat.

Lech gazed pleadingly at Victor as he desperately clutched at his torn throat. He fell to the floor and blood pooled around his neck from the lethal wound.

Victor was appalled by her actions.

Britt watched from the hall in horror. He felt his hatred for Fiona mount. He wanted to rush in and rip her to shreds but he knew better than to act irrationally with Victor.

"You had no right to kill him!" Victor shouted at her.

"It's time that you soil your hands with the blood of those who defy you," she declared. "You must earn the respect of your men as well as your enemies or they will see you as weak."

Victor bristled at her behavior in front of the others and slapped her across the face. "We'll discuss your insolence later."

Marina noticed that Fiona relished the pain inflicted by the slap. She stood and reached to her thighs for her daggers but the sheaths were empty. Panic set in as she felt trapped.

Victor noticed her unease and placed his hands on her arms to calm her. "You have nothing to fear if you pledge your allegiance to me, Marina. We could end the bloodshed right here, right now."

Fiona was shocked by his offer. She clenched her fists and fought to control her urge to lash out at both of them. Victor relished the envy he instilled in Fiona and felt it necessary to repay her for her disloyalty.

"I'm sure that's not all you want," Marina commented, amused by her own brazenness.

Fiona sneered at the two of them in disgust. "Let me silence this traitor once and for all," she requested as she bristled with rage.

"Silence! You've done enough," responded Victor as he turned his attention back to Marina. "I like that in a woman - direct and to the point." He placed his hands on the sides of Marina's head and gently touched her cheeks with his thumbs.

Fiona became red-faced with anger and jealousy. Marina noticed and decided to push her over the edge. "So, Victor, what do you hope to gain from a relationship with me besides a hot piece of ass?"

Victor considered that perhaps he was getting somewhere with her. *"Fiona may have outlived her usefulness, especially if Marina can help contact the rebels,"* he thought. *"A treaty with them would cement my reign."*

"Don't know what to say?" Marina ribbed.

"I want you to reveal who my true enemies are through the crystal," Victor requested with a coy grin. "Can you do that for me?"

Fiona was agitated and wondered where he was going with this. She fretted that he may already know Marina wasn't the rebel leader. "Victor," she blurted, "I told you the rebel and the Seer are two separate people!"

"Silence, Fiona!" he ordered. "Don't interrupt me again or you will be punished!" He picked up the crystal and held it in front of Marina. "Can you do it?" he asked anxiously.

"Well, that's a relief," quipped Marina with a fake sigh. "I was afraid you'd want me to marry you so you could become the legitimate king of this shit hole.

Seeing his opportunity to expose Fiona's traitorous acts, Victor set the crystal down and glanced distrustfully at Fiona. "What does she mean, Fiona? Pray tell, will you."

Fiona nearly exploded with rage. "She lies! I'll rip her lying tongue from her mouth!" Fiona stepped toward Marina with her dagger, poised for attack.

Victor blocked Fiona and grabbed her wrists. "I think it's time I was done with you, my treasonous lover."

"But, Victor," she cried, "this woman's a fraud!"

Britt was stunned by the turn of events. He debated whether to intercede or let things play out. He chose the latter for now.

Marina smiled cynically at Fiona and attempted to intimidate her further. "It sounds like someone's been keeping secrets from you, Victor."

Fiona lost control and shoved Victor out of the way. "I'll show you a secret, you bitch!" she shouted and lunged at Marina.

Marina grabbed her arm and wrestled the dagger from her hand. Fiona slapped Marina who, in turned, slapped her back so much harder that her lips bled. She wiped the blood off with her finger and gritted her teeth in anger.

Victor stood up and attempted to stop the two women from fighting each other.

"You're not dealing with Red now and you're certainly not dealing with a blind old woman," Marina taunted.

"So you know of Red, do you?" queried Fiona as she took a fighting stance. She again poised to attack with her knife. Victor backed off and listened intently. Now the truth was unfolding. He was sure that Marina was only the Princess and Seer. The rebel leader was still at large.

"I've already kicked Red's ass twice," boasted Marina. "I'd be happy to take care of yours as well."

Fiona screamed like a banshee and charged at Marina.

Victor's eyes bulged in anger. He grabbed Fiona by the waist and threw her to the ground.

"You don't know what you're doing, Victor," pleaded Fiona. "She needs to die."

Victor stood and shouted at Fiona. "Why didn't you tell me she was the Princess of Yord?"

Britt panicked when he heard this. He had to do something quick.

"She lies, Victor!" shouted Fiona tearfully. "There is no princess!"

"We shall soon see," he declared.

Marina seized the moment. "The only thing you'll see is..." She raised her fist to strike Victor.

Victor blocked the punch and slapped Marina against the stone table. She covered her jaw with her hand and pretended to be repentant.

Fiona got up off the floor and felt some degree of satisfaction. "Well done," she praised Victor.

"Shut the hell up, Fiona!" he screamed. "Get out of here, now!"

Victor focused on Marina with rage in his eyes. Fiona stood her ground and refused to leave.

Marina pretended to be frightened. "I'm so sorry. I will show you the proper respect, Victor."

"That's more like it. So you are the heir to the throne of Yord," he remarked. "Anything else I should know about?"

"Yes. I'm just... I'm just... a bitch from hell!" she screamed and kicked Victor between the legs. As he doubled over, she punched him in the face.

Fiona grabbed at Marina and was left with two of the silver balls in her hand. She was perplexed by their purpose. "What trickery is this?"

"Just for you - a real set of balls!" Marina mocked. She dove and flatted against the ground, face down.

The balls exploded in a bright flash. Fiona fell to the floor and writhed in agony. The right side of her face was severely burnt. Her clothes were charred. Victor was stunned by the flash as he dove behind the table.

Marina snatched the tattered cloth and wrapped it around the crystal. She rushed into the hall with it.

At the far end of the hall, five soldiers approached. At the near end, only Britt stood between her and the second floor window.

"Halt!" shouted Britt.

Marina laughed and mocked him, "You haven't learned, have you!" She charged at him and rammed her shoulder into his gut. The two of them fell out the second floor window and crashed through a wooden cart loaded with ceramic jars onto the cement. The jars shattered across the cement.

Marina landed on top of Britt with the crystal still wrapped in the table cloth. She moaned and clutched her right shoulder.

Britt gasped for air as Marina rolled off of him. She picked up a shard of the ceramic material and placed it under her cloak.

Victor rushed to the window and looked down at them.

Marina stepped up on the broken cart and climbed on top of the palace wall. She was dazed and in pain. Her right arm hung awkwardly by her side.

Britt tried to sit up but was in excruciating pain as well. He reached out for her and pleaded, "Wait!"

Marina paused and looked back. There was something about Britt that she couldn't figure out. Was he an ally, an enemy or a mercenary? "Why?" she asked hesitantly.

Britt grimaced in pain and couldn't speak.

Marina glanced up at Victor with a smile and then disappeared over the wall.

Victor screamed at his soldiers, "Get her or else!"

The soldiers raced down the hall to the stairs.

Victor stared at Fiona, filled with rage. "You stupid bitch!" he shouted and punched her repeatedly until she was nearly unconscious. Content that he made his point, he stormed out of the room.

Moments later, Fiona got to her knees and sobbed. "I killed for you, Victor," she cried desperately. "I earned the right to be your queen."

"You earned nothing, Fiona," Victor's voice faded as he marched angrily down the hall.

Fiona was shocked. She felt her damaged face and shrieked as her world just fell apart over another woman – Marina. As she tried to walk, she stumbled and fell to the ground unconscious.

Victor met Britt on the palace steps. He clutched his ribs and tried to ignore the pain.

"You couldn't hold onto a simple woman," complained Victor.

"A two story fall will do that, sir," responded Britt in frustration. "I'll find her immediately."

"I thought you killed the courier."

Britt hesitated as he remembered their report to Victor. "We did. She wasn't the one outside Balthus' warehouse," he lied. "I'll have her back shortly. "

"I hope so," replied Victor. "We are so close to victory and I won't tolerate failure."

Britt turned to leave but Victor placed his hand on Britt's shoulder. He gripped it tightly. "Do you know who this woman is?" inquired Victor.

"No, sir."

"Do you suspect who she is?" he asked suspiciously.

"Perhaps," answered Britt. "If she is the Princess, she's a better fighter than the rebel leader. If she fought the rebel leader, then there is no alliance between them."

"Then you are sure they are two separate people?"

"I am, sir."

"Then they are both here on Yord now," concluded Victor.

"I believe that to be true, sir. I don't understand the relationship between the two, though."

"Then she was likely the Princess and the Seer of the crystal," replied Victor.

"I intend to find out," Britt promised. His breathing was labored as he walked away in pain. He was relieved that he convinced Victor he was still loyal to him.

Victor marched down the hall intent on killing Fiona. He called for her but there was no response. As he returned to the stairs, two soldiers approached.

"Sir, the rebels have struck again," one soldier announced anxiously.

"What happened?" inquired Victor angrily.

"They ambushed the garrison behind the palace, sir," answered the second soldier.

"Casualties?"

"Ten, sir. They escaped with the prisoners."

"Summon everyone to the palace immediately," ordered Victor. "Lock it down for the night." The two soldiers hurried away.

Victor stormed down the stairs and crossed the main chamber to the dining area.

Fiona sat in the garden where two of her medical techs tended to her wounds. One of the men spread salve over the damaged tissue of her right cheek and neck. The second tech placed gauze over the wounds. A third exited the palace and handed her a small detonator.

"The device has been planted as you directed," he informed her.

Fiona noticed that Victor appeared at the glass doors and watched them. She nodded in affirmation to the tech and carefully hid the detonator in her boot.

Victor, now accompanied by five of his men, seethed as he watched Fiona and her mercenaries. He pushed the doors open and stared Fiona down.

"Yes, my lord?" responded Fiona innocently.

"Ten more of my men have been killed. You've cost me almost half of my forces from your petty war with Red."

Fiona motioned for the techs to leave. When they were alone, Fiona stood and placed her arms around Victor's shoulders. He pushed her away.

"It's my face, isn't it?" asked Fiona dejectedly. She covered her bandaged face with her hands and became teary-eyed.

"You have failed me, Fiona," said Victor stoically. "Now, when I needed you most, you turned on me."

Fiona was determined to make one last try at saving their relationship. She stood before Victor and promised, "I will find the rebel, and when I do..."

"She is not the rebel, you fool!" shouted Victor. "She is the Princess Marina and she has the ability to read the crystal. I had them both in my grasp and now, thanks to you, they're both gone."

"But what about us, Victor? We can work through this!" she pleaded.

"There is no *us*, Fiona," he replied. "There never was." Victor punched her in the side of the head and floored her.

Fiona lay dazed on the ground and was stunned by his ongoing disregard for her. "I've done everything for you!" she screamed.

"Take her away," he ordered his men and struck her in the head with the butt of his pistol. She lay dazed on the ground with a bloody wound on her forehead. He stormed out of the garden. His men grabbed her by the arms and nearly dragged her through the palace.

"Don't do this to me!" Fiona pleaded. She became red with rage and continued her rant, "You bastard! I'll get you for this!"

The men took her downstairs to a store room where they locked her inside. Fiona eyed the hinges on the door and knew she had only to pull the pins to escape. "*Vengeance is mine,*" she thought to herself.

As soon as the men left the area outside the store room, Fiona removed the hinge pins and removed the door. She defiantly returned to the second floor in hopes of confronting Victor once more.

Chapter 6

Allies and Enemies

Victor met with Crow and Fingers at the main entrance to the palace. As they spoke, one soldier hurried out of the palace and reported that Fiona escaped. Another hurried out and informed them that she was upstairs in the meditation room. Victor seemed unconcerned and continued his conversation with the captains.

"Keep an eye on Britt," ordered Victor. "He's up to something."

"Do you think he's helping the rebels, sir?" inquired Crow.

"No, but I don't think he's telling me everything he knows either."

"I'm sure there's a good reason, sir," replied Fingers. "I believe he can be trusted."

"None the less, I want to know what he's up to. Make sure Lech has a decent burial."

"Yes, sir," answered Crow. "In the meantime, we've sealed off the Palace District. There's no way the courier can escape."

"I hope so. Leave me now," instructed Victor. "I have another pressing issue to deal with."

"Fiona?"

"Of course."

The two captains looked pleased. They turned and departed the palace.

Victor summoned six soldiers and sent them upstairs in the palace to kill Fiona. He warned them of her skills as an assassin and to make sure she was dead no matter what. Victor left the main entrance and disappeared down one of the many hallways.

The soldiers warily approached the room at the end of the hall with their pulse pistols drawn.

Fiona peered out the window at the dilapidated town. She contemplated how to make Victor pay for turning on her. Also on her mind were Marina and Red. The two would have to die a horrible death.

Fiona approached the doorway to the hall. As she peeked out, one of the soldiers ordered, "Come out with your hands up, Fiona!"

"Come get me if you dare!" she challenged them and stood behind the door with her back flat against the wall.

The six soldiers barged into the room and fanned out. Before they could react, she grabbed the last soldier and slit his throat from behind. The soldiers fired immediately at her but she used the soldier's corpse as a shield. She took the man's pulse pistol and backed into the hall. She stopped dragging the corpse randomly and fired back at the doorway. The soldiers were kept at bay briefly.

There was no one else on the second floor, so Fiona retreated down the hall toward the stairs, still using the soldier's corpse as a shield. She targeted the doorway with her pistol trained for headshots.

When the hall grew quiet, three of the soldiers rushed from the room toward her while two hung back in the doorway. Fiona easily cut her assailants down with pinpoint accuracy. The three men lay crumpled over each other with smoking holes in their heads. The remaining two fired continuously at Fiona but struck the corpse repeatedly. Smoldering holes from the bursts of hot energy filled the hall with the stench of burning flesh.

Fiona kept her pistol ready and at each pause in gunfire from the soldiers, she selectively fired until she wounded them both. While they lay on the floor, writhing in pain, she dropped the corpse and fired a red burst of energy from her pistol into each one's head, killing them instantly.

Fiona listened carefully for reinforcements but the hall was silent. From the top of the stairs, she heard Victor's voice. He paced about like a rabid animal at the palace entrance and screamed out orders to anyone who came near. She snickered and retreated to the room at the end of the hall.

***

Marina, still gasping for air, made her way into an alley with the crystal wrapped and tucked under her cloak. She clutched at her dislocated right shoulder and winced with each step.

The alley led behind a row of shops. Most were abandoned and dilapidated. Three of the occupied shops had barred windows and steel doors. Trash dumpsters were located at each end of the alley.

Two mercenaries, carrying transmitters on their belts, stepped out from behind one of the dumpsters and blocked Marina's path. One approached her with his pistol drawn, pushed back her hood and briefly studied her face. "That's her," he announced assuredly. "Don't move or you're dead."

Marina remained cool and kept eye contact with him. "You want something?" she asked impatiently.

"I think you'll be coming with us," he replied. "Fiona has a bone to pick with you."

Marina looked down at the ground dejectedly. She slid her good hand under her cloak and retrieved the shard of ceramic material. "You don't understand," she explained innocently with a saddened look. Before the man could respond, her hand swung from under her cloak and slit his throat. The second man aimed his pistol at her but she quickly kicked at his wrist and knocked the pistol away. The pain in her injured shoulder was too much and she dropped the wrapped crystal to the ground.

The man clutched his injured wrist in pain and cursed her. When Marina spat in his face, he punched her in the mouth. She was stunned from the hit, blood streaming from her mouth, but she still buried the shard under his ribs. They stared at each other with hatred in their eyes. Marina pushed the ceramic shard deeper into his abdomen but he gripped her throat and choked her. The two were relentless and refused to yield. Finally the man's strength waned and he lost his grip on her.

Marina was fading from consciousness. She shoved him away and stumbled backwards. Her cloak was stained with his blood. The man fell to his knees and retrieved his pistol. He attempted to fire at her but his life drained from him. He fell face first into the broken concrete pavement with the shard embedded deeply inside him.

Marina searched for other mercenaries but saw none. She breathed with difficulty and tried to maintain her balance. After three steps, she collapsed on the ground unconscious.

The rear door of the nearest shop clanked as someone unlatched it from inside. It creaked and opened slowly. An old woman, Dora, stepped out and poured water from a bowl into a storm drain in the middle of the alley. As she poured, she noticed Marina lying a short distance away. She feared that the soldiers would soon come and hurried back inside the shop to summon her husband, Clem. The two returned and went to Marina's aide.

Clem noticed the blood stains on her cloak, her bloody mouth and that her hand was marred with deep gashes. He opened her cloak and urgently checked her vital signs. The sight of Marina's leather rattled him as he fretted who she was and how much trouble she could bring them. If she was an assassin, his family was at risk. If she was a mercenary, others would come for her.

Dora saw the royal emblem on the cloth and stared wide-eyed at the symbol. "Clem!" she cried out, while unwrapping the crystal.

Clem saw the crystal and panicked. "This is bad, Dora. This is real bad." He lifted Marina into a sitting position. "We have to get her inside fast!"

"Is she alright?" Dora asked as she wrapped the cloth around the crystal again.

"I don't know."

The two of them lifted Marina to her feet and ushered her toward the door. Dora, carrying the crystal under one arm, felt Marina's disjointed shoulder and released her hold on her. Clem continued into the shop with her. Dora looked both ways in the alley but saw no one. She locked the door behind them.

Dora and Clem operated a used clothing shop with Kara, their twelve-year old grand-daughter. Kara's parents were killed by Victor and his soldiers a year earlier during one of their raids. Since that time, Kara lived with them.

Dora set the crystal on a small table in the corner. She lowered the shades on the lone window and darkened the room. Clem cleaned Marina's hand with an antiseptic and wrapped it neatly with a bandage.

Kara entered the rear room and was stunned by Marina's presence.

"Get a cot, Kara," ordered Clem. "Hurry!"

Kara opened a closet and removed a rickety old cot. She set it up against the wall by the table and stood back. Dora left the room.

Clem set Marina down gingerly on the cot. He delicately removed her blood-stained cloak and set it aside. Marina's leather attire still concerned him. He didn't want to interfere with the warring factions and preferred to stay neutral but the sight of the crystal meant a new movement could be underway for their freedom.

Dora returned with a candle and set it on a coffee table in the middle of the room. "Who is she, Clem?" she inquired anxiously.

"I suspect someone of importance."

Kara unwrapped the tablecloth from around the crystal and gazed at it in awe. "Grandmother, is this...?"

Dora glanced back at the crystal nervously. "Hush, child," she said sternly.

"But..."

Dora went to Kara and placed her hands on Kara's shoulders. "It's not our business to pry," she explained. "This young lady is injured and needs our help."

Kara backed away from the table but couldn't take her eyes away from the crystal.

Clem felt Marina's shoulder and determined that it was separated.

An hour later, Marina finally awoke and instinctively reached for her daggers, before remembering that they were taken by Britt's men earlier.

Clem sensed her concern and assured her, "You are safe with us. We mean you no harm."

"Who are you people?" Marina asked and grimaced in pain.

"We are simple folk just trying to survive," replied Dora humbly. "We'll help you any way we can."

Marina saw the crystal and was relieved. "Thank you," she replied weakly, almost in a whisper.

Kara noticed that the crystal flickered whenever Marina spoke. She grew more curious.

"Dora, mind the store. No one must know of her presence here," Clem instructed. Dora passed through thick curtains to the front of the shop.

Clem knelt down by Marina. "Your shoulder is dislocated," he explained. "It has to be set."

"I'm fine," Marina responded and held her arm securely against her side. She tried to get up but couldn't. Her throat was bruised from the recent assault and she had difficulty swallowing.

"You don't look fine," he argued. "Let me help you."

Marina relented and allowed him to manipulate both her arms by her side. The right shoulder was grossly misaligned. He probed it with his fingers and frowned. "Turn around, Kara," he ordered. "This is extremely painful for her."

Kara reluctantly obeyed.

"On 'three,'" he said to Marina. She nodded and expected Clem to yank her arm and shoulder into place on 'one.'

Clem lifted Marina's arm gently and placed his foot against her side. "One, two…" Clem yanked on the arm. Marina's shoulder cracked and popped back into place. She cried out briefly and then sighed with relief.

Kara watched Marina with great concern. She was sure that Marina was the Princess with the mythical crystal she heard so many people talk about. Everyone believed that the crystal was the way to their freedom and that only the Princess had the power to wield it.

Marina rubbed her shoulder gingerly. "Thanks so much. It feels better already."

Clem smiled at her. "It will be tender for a few days but you'll be okay. Your hand should be stitched. Those gashes are pretty deep."

"It'll be fine, thanks."

"No, it won't. We'll fix you up."

Kara poured a glass of water and offered it to Marina. "Please have some water," she offered kindly. "You must be parched."

Marina graciously accepted the glass and drank from it. "Thank you both for your concern," she said appreciatively and suddenly realized that she displayed kindness to someone. "*Is this something that Kat instilled in me or is it because I'm in a weakened state?*" she wondered.

"It's no problem," answered Clem. He noticed her distracted look as she seemed to have much on her mind. "*Could she really be the Princess finally returning to claim her throne*? He wondered.

Kara stood in front of Marina and gazed into her eyes. Marina smiled at her and touched her cheek affectionately.

"Are you the Princess?" Kara asked.

Clem was shocked by his grand-daughter's brazenness. "Kara!"

Marina was amused by the young girl's boldness. "Why would you ask that?" she responded. "I certainly don't look like a princess."

"The crystal flickers whenever you look at it," Kara revealed. "It responds to you."

"I'm sure it's just a coincidence. I'm not a princess but you can call me Marina."

"That's a pretty name," said Kara.

Clem couldn't believe his ears. He knew the daughter of their king and queen was named Marina and here she was with the crystal and a cloth with the royal emblem.

Marina was impressed by her observation and hadn't been aware of it. The warmth of new friends made her feel ...better. She stood up awkwardly but Clem nudged her back down on the cot.

"You must rest for a bit," he instructed her. "You've been through a lot."

He retrieved a first aid kit and sat next to Marina. She watched as he threaded a needle with cat-gut.

"I haven't seen that in a long time," she kidded and forced a smile.

"We don't have the luxury of lasers here on Yord anymore. That technology was either stolen or sold off a long time ago."

Clem stitched the gashes in her hand methodically. Marina cringed from the pain. How she missed her adrenalin injections. This would be a difficult spell for her to beat her dependency on the drug. Few have ever succeeded in overcoming the addiction. Now, she'd have to manage it out of necessity.

Marina was impressed with Clem's work and was relieved when he covered the wounds with bandages.

Kara brought the crystal to Marina and it glowed steadily. "You are a very special person," Kara remarked. "That's why you have it."

"I don't know about that," she replied humbly. "I took it from a man named Victor who had no right to it."

"You don't know the story of the crystal, do you?"

"No, Kara, I don't," she lied.

"Do you have a right to it?"

"Kara, shush!" exclaimed an embarrassed Clem.

Marina placed her hand on Clem's arm. "It's okay" she assured him. "I don't mind."

Marina put her arm around Kara's waist and nestled her head against her. "You see, Kara, this man got into my business and now he has to pay. That's why I took it from him. Why are you so interested in my story?"

Kara became saddened. "Victor killed my parents. I hope you make him suffer a lot."

Clem took Kara by the arm and pulled her away. "That's enough, young lady."

Marina felt bad for her and related to them how she lost her parents at a young age. She pulled the crystal to her bosom and cradled it in her arms. It glowed more brightly.

Kara and Clem watched in awe.

Marina suddenly had a premonition. A vision appeared. In it, Fiona and three mercenaries searched the shops on the street. The vision faded as rapidly as it appeared. Marina looked panicked. "I have to leave here now. You'll be killed if they find me here with you."

Male voices in the front of the store startled them. Marina stood and staggered to the back door. "I must go now."

"No," replied Clem. "I have a better idea." He bent over and raised a small section of the wooden floor. "Down here, quickly!"

Marina set the crystal down on the floor and descended a wooden ladder into a small basement. Clem passed the crystal and her cloak to her. Before he placed the floor boards back in place, Kara noticed the cloth with the royal emblem on it, still on the corner table. "Wait!" she exclaimed.

"There's no time, Kara!"

Kara grabbed the tablecloth and scurried down the ladder.

"That's my girl," Clem said proudly as he placed the wooden floor back in place. He slid the cot over the loose flooring and laid down on it.

The basement was small and shallow enough that Marina had to duck her head to avoid the floor joists above. She sat on a small wooden crate across from the ladder. The crystal glowed faintly as if it called to her. "*What does it want from me?*" she kept thinking.

Kara took a pack of matches from a small shoe box and lit a candle. She gazed at Marina with innocent eyes. "You knew those men were coming," she whispered. "The crystal told you so."

"No, I just figured that they'd come looking for me."

"I know you really are the Princess."

"I'm no one important," insisted Marina.

"We need you, Princess," pleaded Kara. "You are the only one who can save us."

"If I were the Princess, why would your people need me to save them?" she inquired curiously.

Kara was stumped that Marina would ask such a foolish question. "Because you represent hope that we can have a better future," she said condescendingly. "The elders say that your mother and father were the glue that brought our people together, especially with the other races."

"I'm sorry, Kara. I can't be that person."

Kara grew frustrated with Marina and became teary-eyed. "You're right. You can't be the Princess because you're a coward."

Marina was struck by her words. No one ever dared to call her a coward before. She wondered if Kara was right. Was she running from her future or even her past? Maybe she was afraid to face her destiny.

Marina reached out and held Kara's hand. "Maybe one day, I can be that person, just not today."

"Are you afraid?"

"I... I don't know what I am."

"I'm afraid of the soldiers," Kara said shamefully. She nestled her head against Marina and wrapped her arms around her. Marina was touched by the young girl's affection for her.

"It's okay to be afraid," Marina remarked. Kara smiled at her.

***

Two of Fiona's mercenaries, both large men, searched the aisles of used clothing. They were dressed in brown, denim pants and long-sleeved shirts. Each had a shaved head and a thick mustache, and each armed with a pulse pistol and a dagger.

Dora approached the men and asked politely, "Can I help you, gentlemen?"

The nearest man, Josh, approached her with an intimidating stare. "We're looking for someone - a woman."

"No one's been here all day, sir. I don't have to tell you that business has been bad and customers are scarce."

The second man, Artur, stooped under racks and searched for any sign of Marina.

"I think we'll look for ourselves," Josh announced.

Artur grew frustrated and approached her. "If we find out you're helping her, we'll kill you," he warned.

Dora cringed as she sensed their determination. "I told you, there's no one here. You are more than welcome to search the shop."

The two men noticed the curtain to the rear room. They glanced at each other and hurried toward it.

In the back room, Clem lay still on the cot and acted sickly. He breathed irregularly and moaned in a low voice.

The two mercenaries burst through the curtain with their pulse pistols drawn. They ignored Clem and searched the room for any sign that Marina had been there.

Clem realized the first-aid kit was on the table and was terrified. "Please don't hurt us, good sirs," he begged.

"Shut your yap," ordered Josh.

Artur placed his hands on his hips in disgust. "There are only so many places she can hide."

Josh grumbled, "If she was smart, she hopped a flight out of here."

Artur started toward the curtain. "Let's get out of here," he said dejectedly. "Fiona's gonna' be hot if we don't find her soon."

The two mercenaries left the room. Dora trembled near the entrance to the shop as they stormed past her. She pretended to go about her usual business for several minutes.

Josh appeared outside the shop once more and glanced in at her. Contented that she was telling the truth, he finally left.

Dora breathed a sigh of relief. She approached the front door and watched them depart. She returned to the back of the shop and informed her husband, "They're gone, Clem."

Clem sighed and sat up. "That's a relief," he said. "They were persistent." He slid the cot to the wall and lifted the floor boards. "It's all clear," he announced to Marina and Kara.

Kara looked sadly at her candle and blew it out. She followed Marina up the ladder.

Marina emerged from the basement with the wrapped crystal and cloak under her arm. She looked exhausted as she sat on the cot. Clem and Dora studied her with concerned expressions. Clem took the bloody cloak from her and promised to dispose of it.

Kara restored the planks on the floor and turned her attention to the adults.

"Thank you, Kara," said Clem sheepishly. "You saved our lives by hiding that cloth."

Kara stared at Marina disappointedly. Marina bent over and whispered, "I will take care of Victor and his assassin witch first. Then I'll return and we'll talk about the Princess."

Kara grew optimistic and responded cheerfully, "Promise?"

"I promise," assured Marina. Kara seemed pleased and hurried out of the room.

"I must go now," Marina informed them. "I have some issues to deal with."

Clem unlatched the rear door and stepped aside. "We'll pray for you," he said with sadness in his eyes.

Dora hugged her and stepped back. She gazed at her proudly as if she were her own daughter. "You'll find your destiny," she said with a tear in her eye. "Be safe."

Marina was stunned by her words, the same damning words she kept hearing from everyone – find your destiny. "Thank you for everything," she responded, unsure if she should hug Dora back or just walk away.

Affection wasn't her strong point. Kat's image burned in her brain again and her words: There are many who love and care for you. Marina shuddered as she wondered how so many people knew about her once secret life.

Kara returned and handed Marina a backpack and a brown cloak. "You'll need these to avoid the soldiers' attention. Please come back safely."

"I promise," she assured her and stroked her hair gently.

Kara's eyes welled with tears and she left the room again.

Marina put the crystal inside the backpack. She gazed at Dora and Clem enviously and forced a smile. At least they had some semblance of a family.

Her mind raced backwards to a time when she was two-years old. She sat on her mother's lap. Her mother caressed her long hair. Her father entered the room and sat next to them. He hugged her and set her on his lap. It was such a happy time. Marina trembled for a moment and regained her composure.

"Are you alright?" asked Dora worriedly.

"I'm fine. It was just... It was nothing," Marina answered and donned the cloak.

Clem opened the door and Marina stepped out. She looked back once more with a smile and walked away. "That's strange," she thought. "They cared for me and I liked it."

Clem glanced out the door in both directions. There was no one outside. He quickly closed the door and latched it.

Kara sat on the stairs with tears in her eyes. Dora gestured with her hand for Kara to come down. Kara approached and asked, "Is she really the Princess, grandmum?"

Dora glanced at Clem uneasily.

"Yes, she is, Kara," he replied, "but she may not be ready yet."

"Will she stand up for us soon?"

Now Clem glanced at Dora for an answer.

Dora reluctantly answered, "Only Marina knows the answer to that."

***

Marina approached the end of the alley. She heard commotion as the mercenaries found their dead peers. Instinctively, she tucked her dreadlocks back under her hood.

One of the men, Cletus, spotted her and summoned her. Marina approached cautiously. To run would attract more attention than she was prepared to handle right now. She hid her bandaged hand under her cloak.

"Who are you, woman?" he asked.

"I am Shayla, just a vagrant in search of food. Can you spare me any morsels?" she asked humbly.

The men glanced at each other in disgust.

"I'll do anything for you," she offered and reached her good hand toward Cletus in mock affection.

The other men laughed at him. One taunted, "You finally found yourself a woman, Cletus!"

The mercenary was embarrassed and pushed her away. "Beat it before I cut you to pieces," he grumbled and shoved her to the ground.

Their laughter angered her more than the abusive treatment. "We'll meet again, Cletus, I promise."

"Not in my dreams," he scoffed at her. The men continued to mock her over her appearance.

Marina stood and left them. She peeked back periodically but no one followed her. Once she limped onto the main street, she scanned both sides for mercenaries but saw none.

On her left, she noticed a cloaked woman that resembled Red. For a moment, Marina was glad to see her and welcomed an ally. As she drew nearer, she realized it was an old woman. Disappointed, she thought, *"Perhaps it's better that I work alone."*

The sky darkened as night approached. Marina looked about for a place to rest for the night. She considered going to the transportation hub and slipping onto a ship but Victor would expect her to try just that. No ship would leave the hub without a thorough inspection.

"This planet sucks!" she complained aloud and continued down the street.

***

Victor entered the palace through the front entrance. Crow and Fingers descended the stairs toward him.

"Sir, Fiona has escaped," Crow informed him. "The men you sent after her were slaughtered."

Victor grew red-faced and clenched his fists in anger. "There are going to be two more casualties if you don't find her soon!" he shouted. "I want her head now!"

"Yes, sir," Crow answered nervously. He and Fingers both left the palace.

Veins bulged in Victor's temples and he was rabid with rage. He glanced toward an antechamber to the garden. Next to the glass doors he noticed a wooden cabinet with its door slightly ajar. Inside the cabinet were several bottles of wine.

"That gold-digging traitor is driving me to drink!" he complained and approached the cabinet.

Outside the glass doors to the garden, Fiona hid in the bushes. Two soldiers entered the garden from the rear of the palace. She slid further into the bushes to avoid detection but stepped on a branch with her boot.

She scanned the garden and searched for an escape route. In front of the west wall was a bronze statue that spouted water. It was three feet high and the wall was eight feet high. It wouldn't be easy but she was confident she could get over it, even with her bandaged hand.

Victor heard the branch snap outside as he placed his hand on the cabinet door. Sensing something amiss, he left the cabinet and stepped through the glass doors to the garden. He immediately spotted Fiona in the bushes. She retrieved the detonator from her boot and held it up for him to see.

"You traitorous whore!" he shouted, unaware of what she held.

"Die, you bastard!" Fiona replied angrily and pressed the button on the detonator.

Before Victor could react, the cabinet exploded. He was thrown across the cinderblock patio and knocked senseless. Blood seeped from several cuts on his forehead and left cheek.

Three soldiers tried to reach them from the hall but the door was locked and the handle rigged to fall off.

Fiona climbed on the statue and pulled herself to the top of the wall just as the statue broke under her weight. She glanced back at him. "We could have had it all," she shouted angrily. "You weren't man enough for me."

"You won't get away from me, Fiona!" he replied. "I will see you to the end."

The soldiers broke through the door and rushed through the antechamber to the garden.

"I'll see you in hell," Fiona swore and disappeared over the wall.

Victor pointed to her. "Kill her now!" he ordered as he reeled from the blast.

Victor got up gingerly and hobbled to the garden doors. He glanced back at the wall and punched the glass door, shattering it. Blood seeped from cuts on his fist but he was oblivious to it. There was one bottle of wine on the floor that wasn't broken. He snatched it up and stormed out of the room.

***

Marina awoke in an alley behind a trash dumpster. She was hungry and miserable. If only she had her ship with her, she could leave this dismal place, never to return again. Tears streamed down her cheeks as she realized how much she hated what her life had become.

The sky brightened and the fog dissipated. Marina left the alley and walked cautiously along the street. She stopped in front of a weapons shop and considered going in. Without her daggers, she was defenseless.

A few men and women walked by, glancing at her suspiciously. She wondered what it was about her that stood out to the locals. The cloak and hood should have hidden anything she wore that would reveal her identity. *"Perhaps it was the look of mistrust in my eyes,"* she thought. *"But shouldn't everyone have that same look here?"*

Marina peeked through the window inside the shop at a variety of knives and swords. In a reflection off the window, Marina spotted Britt.

He stood in the middle of the street nearby with Crow and Fingers. They were in a heated discussion.

Crow poked a finger in Britt's chest and warned, "We're running out of time. The other militias know Victor plans to take them out with the new weapons once they're built."

Fingers added, "We still don't know who has the data chip either. Without it, there will be a war."

"I'm well aware of that," replied Britt miserably. "What do you expect from me?"

"Find that damn Princess so we can mobilize before it's too late."

"Are you sure we have the support of the other groups?" Fingers asked uneasily.

"I'm sure," answered Britt. "If the Princess steps up, it's all legal and we'll have lots of help. If not, no one wants to be branded a traitor."

"Then do something quick," advised Fingers. "The other militias are already making plans to take us all down unless we prove we weren't part of this."

Britt spotted Marina by the weapons shop. "Don't go far," he instructed them. "I see someone who might help." Britt entered another shop.

Crow and Fingers wondered what he was up to. They noticed two mercs and a cloaked female watching from a distance.

"Could be Fiona," suggested Crow.

"Let's get that filthy slut!" exclaimed Fingers. "I want to kill at least one of these bitches today."

They rushed toward the three figures with pistols drawn.

Their targets fled down an alley and disappeared. Crow and Fingers grew frustrated as they searched behind dumpsters and crates.

Before Marina could leave the front of the shop, Britt appeared behind her. She spun around and tensed for a fight.

Britt took a step back and held his hands out in a peaceful gesture. "Relax, Marina," he said calmly. "I thought you might want these back." Britt unlatched a package wrapped in brown cloth from his belt and tossed it to her.

Marina eyed him suspiciously. She opened the sack and peeked inside at her daggers. "I suppose a 'thank you' is in order."

"That's up to you," he replied modestly.

Marina stepped toward him, almost nose to nose. "What's your deal?" she inquired, sounding bitter. "I tried but I can't figure you out."

Britt chuckled and walked away.

Marina was more confused than ever. She stowed the daggers under her cloak in the sheaths. When she realized that Britt wasn't going to wait for her, she hustled after him.

Britt was surprised but pleased when she appeared alongside of him.

Marina grabbed him by the arm and spun him toward her. "Cut the shit!" she warned angrily. "What do you want from me?"

"I don't want anything from you," he answered and walked on.

Marina walked with him. "I'm not going away until we put this behind us, Brett."

Britt paused and smiled at her. "It's Britt. All I want to know is this: Are you the daughter of our king and queen - yes or no?"

Marina grew more frustrated with him. "What's it to you?" she asked sarcastically.

"It's really quite simple. If you are, then my allegiance is to you," he explained. "If you aren't then I must return to Victor."

"And why should I believe you?"

The two walked along the street. Several people watched them curiously. They were a strange pair – a militia officer and a peasant woman.

"My father served the king and queen before their disappearance. I was raised and trained to do the same."

"And what if I'm not the Princess?" she queried. "Would you turn me in?"

"Not this time," he answered sincerely. "I'd give you a chance to escape for good. I'm obligated to serve Victor unless the circumstances change."

Marina was amused by his response. "I suppose you want the crystal, too. Am I right?"

Britt halted and stared into her eyes. "I don't want anything to do with it but I sure don't want Victor to have it, either."

"So we do have something in common."

They turned the corner and approached the transportation hub. Hovercraft-style trucks passed back and forth through the entrance to the hub.

Britt glanced back and noticed six Fleet soldiers behind a parked taxi. "Keep walking," he urged her anxiously. "We have company."

They walked quickly toward the docks.

"Are you shipping me out, Brett?" she asked curiously.

"It's Britt! You can't stay here, you know."

She felt satisfied, knowing that she got on his nerves.

They stepped between stacks of crates and slid toward the rear of the loading area out of sight. Britt tucked Marina behind him in a corner. He watched warily for the soldiers.

Marina noted that his concern seemed genuine. "Suppose I am the Princess. What do you plan to do about it?"

"Protect you until I can get you away from Victor's jurisdiction."

"I may just pay Victor a visit and take him out myself," Marina suggested arrogantly. "That would put an end to this crap." She attempted to push her way past Britt.

Britt blocked her path. "Not so fast, young lady. You have other pressing issues besides Victor and one of them is Fiona."

Marina enjoyed the attention of a man for a change and was amused. "And why should I be concerned with her?" she asked playfully.

"Because she's an assassin and a very dangerous one," he explained. "After the rebels were crushed and Victor took the throne, she expected to be his queen and you just ruined her meal ticket."

"So she wants revenge on me."

Britt glared at her and complained, "You don't get it, do you?" He grew frustrated and led her back toward the street.

"There's another issue that involves you as well," he informed her.

"And what could that be?" she asked.

"The leader of the rebel alliance – a woman called Red."

"And what does that have to do with me?" she asked curiously.

"Victor isn't sure if the Princess and Red are one and the same or two different pains in his ass."

"What do you know about this woman called Red?" inquired Marina.

"She's a real bad ass like you. She also would have good reason to steal the chip and give it to the militias on Dax-7 to turn them against Victor. Kind of a peace offering between the groups."

"You give me too much credit, Brett."

"It's Britt, damn it!" he sniped at her and became more annoyed. "Besides, you weren't intimidated at all by Fiona. That's Red's trademark – don't kill her, just humiliate her."

"Fiona didn't seem that tough to me," commented Marina. "Neither did Red for that matter."

"You really fought Red before?" he asked curiously.

"I did and I kicked her ass – twice actually, although she did beat me once," she admitted sheepishly.

Britt grabbed her by her arms and pressed her against the crates. "How well do you know her? We could use her help."

Marina pushed Britt's hands off of her and replied, "Red and I don't see eye to eye on things. I don't expect she'll get involved in my business again."

Britt grinned at her. "If Red has an interest in you, there's a reason…Princess. She won't go away."

Marina blushed but advised him, "Don't call me that if you know what's good for you."

"Why are you so ashamed of your title?" he asked.

Marina grew angry and shoved Britt against the crates. She pointed a finger in his face and warned, "I am not the Princess and if you say it again, I'll kick your ass!"

Britt grew angry as well. He grabbed Marina and shoved her against the crates. "If you're not the Princess, I'd be more than happy teach you a lesson," he threatened. "In fact, I think I'll put you over my knee and spank that arrogant little ass of yours!"

Marina promptly kneed him in the groin and he doubled over in pain. "Don't make promises you can't keep," she mocked.

Britt groaned and mumbled, "You …are …such …a…"

Marina smiled at him and finished, "I know - a bitch. I hear that all the time." Marina helped him upright and escorted him into the street.

"That wasn't necessary," he uttered, still hurting.

"As you can tell, I don't play well with others. Still think I'm princess material?"

Britt stopped and leaned against a light post. "Why'd you do that?"

"I saw you with your two pals. Where are they and what are you up to?"

"I told you already," he answered painfully.

Marina placed her blade against his throat. "Let's try again. You want my trust then tell me the truth."

"That data chip you delivered. It has valuable technology on it for new weapons," he explained. "I have to prove that Victor is the only one behind this treason against the other militias and that we don't have it."

"With my help," added Marina.

"Yeah, with your help," he answered. "My men make up a small portion of the militia. They won't revolt against Victor for fear of being charged by the other groups for treason. It's a code thing with us."

"So you need the Princess to make all of this legal."

"It's more like we want to follow the true ruler of Yord. That makes the revolt legal, in addition to returning to a period of prosperity."

"What about Red? It seems like she's doing pretty well for herself."

"She's not royalty. She's branded an outlaw and no one in the militias will support her, especially when she's killed so many of them."

"And you think I can pretend to be the respectable Princess who will emerge from her evil past and lead everyone to the Promised Land, right?"

"I'm not judging you on the way you conduct yourself," he admitted. "I'm not asking for any explanations for your actions past or present. All I want to know is whether or not you'll assume the throne. I don't care when but I need a promise."

Marina felt embarrassed and considered that she had been a bit hard on him. "I think you already know the answer to that," she replied honestly for the first time. "For what it's worth, I'm sorry about the knee ..."

"And my second question?" he interrupted.

"I think we have ..."

Britt held his hand up for her to stop when he heard boots striking the street. They were masked by the sound of a forklift. He pushed Marina into the doorway of a dark abandoned shop.

A forklift turned the adjacent corner with a large crate on its forks. As it passed them by, Britt noticed seven Fleet soldiers marching past the crates.

"What is it?" whispered Marina.

"A Fleet patrol. We need to get away from the hub for a few hours until they move out," he advised. Britt nudged her toward the next alley and they disappeared into the darkness.

"Why are they here?'" she asked curiously.

"Looking for you, smart-ass," he chided. "They think you have the data chip." He grabbed her arm and hustled her into a back alley. They remained hidden as he watched for any sign of the soldiers.

Marina cringed in pain from her injured shoulder. As Britt turned to her, she shoved him against the wall and placed the blade of her dagger against his throat. She grimaced as she struggled to apply pressure to the dagger with her injured hand.

Before Britt could grasp her hand, she reached with her free hand for his neck just above the shoulder and gripped it tightly.

"What the hell is wrong with you?" asked Britt in frustration.

"Tell me why should I trust you?"

"Because I trust you. I won't risk revealing who you are to my men yet, either because it's too risky."

"You really do care about me," Marina remarked almost sympathetically. "I'm impressed."

Britt glanced behind her and blinked twice. Marina understood that someone approached them and Britt didn't acknowledge them.

Marina pulled the blade slightly away from his neck and placed it in her good hand. She gripped the tip of the blade and waited for his cue. Britt nodded for her to attack.

Marina turned and threw the dagger into a cloaked mercenary's eye. He fell to his knees and was stunned by the impact of the knife. Marina then directed a kick into the hilt of the dagger and drove it deeper into his brain. The man's eye stared at her with a shocked expression for a moment and then he fell to the ground dead.

"Nice shot," Britt complimented her.

"I was aiming for his forehead," Marina answered cynically. "I missed."

Two more mercenaries dropped down from the fire escape above. They were Josh and Artur.

"A homeless person, huh?" remarked Josh. "You won't escape us this time."

Marina drew a second dagger as Josh drew a Taser and fired at her. She dropped the dagger, staggered backwards and fell to the ground next to a heap of broken crates.

"Marina!" cried Britt. In a fit of rage, he rushed at the two men and threw early punches. The men still drove him against the wall near Marina and floored him with a series of blows.

Marina struggled to get to her feet but couldn't move. Her body quivered from the Taser and she had little control of her neural functions.

Britt glanced at her as blood streamed from several cuts on his face. The men continued to punch his face and kick his ribs.

Marina regained enough control to draw a second dagger. She crawled close to Artur's legs and wrapped an arm tightly around his knee, while cutting his calf with her free hand. The man screamed in pain and fell to the ground. He clutched desperately at the severed tendon that disabled his leg. Marina cringed and fought back tears from the pain as she tried to stand and fight.

The second mercenary, Josh, turned on Marina and punched her in the head. She fell backwards next to the crates and lay dazed.

Crow and Fingers paused at the end of the alley. They saw Josh standing by Britt and rushed toward them to investigate.

Marina crawled between the broken crates out of sight, still partially paralyzed.

"Stay right there," Crow ordered Josh.

Josh drew his pulse pistol and shouted "Screw you, soldier boy!"

Before he could fire, both Crow and Fingers fired two shots each into his chest. He dropped his pistol to the ground and glanced in horror at the smoking holes and red splotches of blood.

Fingers approached him with his pistol aimed high. Despite the loss of his fingers above three knuckles, he was able to aim his pistol reasonably well. Josh fell to his knees and looked up at Fingers in fear of his lethal injuries. Fingers fired a shot into his forehead from close range. His brains sprayed out the back of his head against the wall and he slumped to the ground dead.

Fingers blew at a tiny plume of smoke from the tip of his pistol and commented, "That feels better each time."

Britt rolled his eyes in disbelief at Fingers.

Crow helped Britt to his feet and eyed him suspiciously. "I hope you have a good explanation for this," he remarked sarcastically.

Britt rubbed his swollen eye and replied, "I'm helping the Princess."

"With what – your good looks?" he joked.

Artur struggled to stand despite his wounds. Fingers fired two shots into his chest and then joined Britt and Crow.

Britt rubbed his jaw and turned away from his comrades. He realized that Marina took cover from them and thought better of involving his friends in her predicament right now.

Crow took exception to Britt's silence and inquired, "Can you trust her?"

"How can I not?" rebutted Britt.

"If we go out on a limb for her and she bails, we're screwed," complained Fingers.

"Besides," Crow taunted, "Fingers can't afford to go out on a limb with hands like his."

"Kiss my ass!" shouted Fingers. I'll get my revenge on her one day. I don't care who she is."

Britt became disgusted with Fingers and challenged, "Would you prefer the services of Victor and a war with the other militias instead?"

Neither man responded.

"I thought so."

Crow knelt down next to the dead mercenaries and rifled through their pockets.

"Where is the crystal, Britt?" Fingers asked suspiciously.

"Fiona's mercs have it. Where's Fiona now?"

Crow stood up and shoved a small wad of bills in his pocket. "Fiona made an attempt on Victor's life and escaped."

"Why didn't you tell me? That changes a lot of things!" Britt exclaimed.

"You think! The only thing I see is that he wants her as dead as we do."

Britt grew concerned and digested the new information. "I'm sure Fiona wants revenge on Marina, too. That means we have two problems." He staggered away from them toward the street.

Crow grabbed him by the shoulder and stopped him. "We're going with you."

"No," answered Britt. "It's too dangerous. I need you to thin out Fiona's merc force as much as possible. They're swarming all over the town."

"How do we do that?"

"Use the Fleet soldiers to help. The mercs are packing pistols …which are illegal, remember?"

Crow motioned with a wave of his hand for Fingers to leave. "Stay in touch," he warned Britt. "Victor and Fiona are hunting you as much as they are the bitch, I mean the Princess."

Britt shook his hand and thanked him. It bothered him that they spoke of her with such disrespect but she really made their lives much more difficult since she fled Balthus' warehouse *with* the chip.

"Oh, and another thing," mentioned Crow, "the chip that our dear princess delivered was a dummy."

"Oh, shit! That means Rock and Tulley will be on our trail as well."

"Watch your back, brother," warned Crow. He scanned the alley once more and followed Fingers.

Britt leaned against the wall in pain and clutched his ribs. He stepped toward the pile of broken crates to assist Marina.

Rebecca and Cristos descended from the rooftop on ropes. Cristos crept up behind Britt and placed the barrel of his pistol against the back of Britt's head. "Don't move or you're dead."

"What the hell!" groaned Britt. "You've got to be kidding me."

Rebecca searched through the crates and found Marina. She helped her to her feet. "Looks like you could use a little help," she commented.

"For once, I'll agree with you," answered Marina. She held onto Rebecca for support. Her legs were still wobbly and she teetered shakily. "I'll be fine in a minute," she said weakly.

"Where's your stash of adrenalin?" Rebecca asked. "I'll give you a shot."

"Don't need it anymore."

Rebecca smiled at her proudly. This was a good start in her eyes.

"Get on your knees and place your hands behind your head," Cristos ordered Britt.

"We have to get out of here or we're all dead," Britt warned.

Cristos didn't respond but pressed the barrel harder against the back of Britt's head. Britt reluctantly knelt down and placed his hands behind his head.

"We're gonna' get you out of here," Rebecca assured Marina. "It's a good thing you have friends."

Marina looked at her with a confused expression. "Friends? Since when?" she asked.

"Just keep quiet and let us handle this," Rebecca ordered and escorted her toward the street. Marina balked and looked back at Britt. Rebecca wondered why.

Cristos was anxious to shoot Britt and leave the alley. He became impatient with the women and complained to Rebecca, "Now what?"

"He goes with us," Marina interjected.

"Are you crazy?" exclaimed Cristos.

"You heard me." Marina's voice echoed her determination.

"Listen to her, Cristos," Rebecca instructed him.

Cristos glared at her with a confused expression.

Marina pushed away from Rebecca and helped Britt to his feet. They exchanged a fleeting glance then looked away from each other.

Rebecca and Cristos were both confused by her loyalty to a captain in Victor's militia.

The four of them approached the street. They paused behind a truck and watched as twenty Fleet soldiers marched past them. The soldiers spread out and searched shops, people and vehicles.

"That's strange," remarked Rebecca. "I've seen a lot of Fleet soldiers here on Yord lately."

"They must want something," replied Cristos. "Perhaps it's you they're hunting, Marina. Who did you piss off in the Fleet?"

Marina grit her teeth at Cristos and refrained from a crude response. Rebecca again took note of the change in Marina and was pleased. She was learning self-control.

Britt informed Rebecca and Cristos, "We already had this conversation. She knows it's about her."

"This is more than just her. Look at them all," said Cristos nervously.

"We should split up," Britt suggested to Marina. "The Fleet wants their data chip; the militia and Fiona's mercs want you. Neither will stop until they get what they want."

"The chip?" Marina asked innocently.

"Yeah, they know you delivered a dummy to the Fleet's agents."

Marina grinned sheepishly. "I didn't know they were the Fleet's agents."

Britt became annoyed again and chastised her, "Can't you take anything seriously?"

"So why not copy the chip and return the original?" suggested Cristos.

"That chip can only be used in a system designed specifically for the Fleet," explained Britt.

"Then why all the concern?" inquired Rebecca curiously.

"Because the inventor of the system disappeared last year. Fleet suspects that she's working for Victor."

"Does 'she' have a name?" asked Marina.

"We have no idea. Now do you see why it's so damn important to all of us?"

Rebecca and Cristos were surprised that Marina kept the real chip and realized its value to each group. "We stay together," declared Rebecca. "The two of you are sitting ducks without any backup."

"Britt's right," Marina concluded.

"But Marina!" blurted Rebecca. "You have no backup."

"You wanted to help, didn't you," she reminded Rebecca callously.

"Don't screw her over, old man," warned Cristos. "We will find you."

"Look kid..." Britt started. Despite his injuries he wouldn't back down from Cristos' threat. Marina grabbed Britt by the back of the collar and pulled him back. "Knock the shit off already," she shouted at the two of them, "... or I'll go alone."

The men continued to stare each other down.

"We'll meet you on Glomus-5," Marina informed Rebecca and Cristos.

"Negative," answered Rebecca. "We go to Orpheus-2. I have friends there who can help us."

Marina glanced at Britt. He nodded, agreeing with Rebecca's suggestion. Marina took off the backpack and handed it to Rebecca. "Take this for me. You know what to do with it."

Rebecca reluctantly took it from her. "Are you sure about this?"

"Of course, I'm sure. Do you think I give a hoot about that stinkin' crystal?"

Rebecca and Cristos looked nervously at each other and walked away. They looked back once more before disappearing around the corner.

Britt took a deep breath and gazed at Marina. She stared back and grew uncomfortable with his look. "What's wrong?"

"I take it that was Red."

"She claims her name is Rebecca. You'll have to ask her about the *Red* part."

Britt shook his head in disappointment. "Nothing is easy with you, is it, Marina?" he complained.

Marina looked away for a moment and turned back to him. "This is who I am," she stated bluntly. "Take it or leave it."

Britt folded his arms and responded. "I made it this far with you. I might as well keep going."

Marina cracked a smile. "You're tougher than I thought. Let's get out of here before I change my mind."

Chapter 7

Flight from Yord

A forklift rumbled toward them with a stack of folded tarps on the back.

"I have an idea," Britt announced. "Wait here."

Marina watched curiously, wondering what he had in mind. Oddly enough, she found herself becoming more and more interested in Britt. He was strong, intelligent and, most importantly, he cared for her despite her shortcomings. Perhaps, they could get along as friends. In her life, that was a big deal.

Britt approached the forklift and motioned for the driver to stop. He climbed up on the side to speak with the driver. "I need you to do me a favor," Britt requested. "Take a walk for fifteen minutes and when you come back, I'll need you to place a crate on one of those ships."

The man noticed the cuts and bruises on Britt's face and laughed at him. "How about I kick your ass?"

"You want to try?" challenged Britt.

"Looks like someone already did."

Britt drew his pistol and placed it against the man's head. "And now they're dead. Want to join them?"

"Okay! I get the point," the man complained and leaped off the forklift.

Britt handed him some money. "This is for the inconvenience."

The man's attitude improved considerably. "Fifteen minutes. You got it, buddy." He dropped the money in his pocket and walked away.

Britt hurried to the schedule board and found one ship departure, the *Golden Falcon*, destined for Orpheus-2. He returned to the containers next to the forklift and inspected them. One was marked "Frozen Goods" and another had an invoice with a destination marked 'Orpheus-2.'

"That'll work," Britt thought to himself. He pulled the invoice off of one crate and swapped it to the cold container. Next, he shot the lock off with his pulse pistol set at 'low' power and then fired three shots for air holes in the cover.

Marina grew suspicious of his plan and approached him nervously. "What the hell are you doing?" she asked.

Britt opened the cover on the cold container. The box was half full of frozen slabs of meat covered in ice. "Get in," he ordered.

Marina looked inside and was shocked by his request. "You're kidding me!"

"Sorry kiddo. No one will suspect that you'd stow away inside a container of frozen meat."

"I'll freeze, you idiot!" she exclaimed.

Britt took one of the tarps off the back of the forklift and laid it inside on top of the meat and ice. "Yeah, well we don't have much time."

Marina glared at him uneasily. "I trust you, Britt," she reminded him nervously. "Don't screw me over."

"Just get in before the driver returns," he urged anxiously and lifted her inside the container. "It's only until after departure."

"If not, you'll be sorry," she warned him with frightened eyes.

Britt rolled his eyes and gently pushed her down. "I'm doing the best I can. Just stay cool."

"Real funny, asshole!"

Once she laid flat on the tarp, Britt closed the cover and placed another tarp over the top to hide the missing lock and holes.

The driver returned and climbed inside the forklift. Britt instructed him, "Take this container to the *Golden Falcon*. I'll speak with the crewman out front."

"I hope you have paperwork or this crate isn't going anywhere."

"Just get it over there!" he ordered impatiently. "This is a security issue and you're impeding my efforts."

The driver drove the forklift to the container and lifted it.

Britt jogged toward the crewman standing watch at the cargo hatch of the *Golden Falcon*.

"Can I help you?" asked the crewman.

"Yeah," answered Britt. He pointed to the approaching forklift and container. "I need this container on board your ship now. I'll accompany it to Orpheus-2."

"Paperwork?" he requested.

"It's on the container," replied Britt. "Feel free to check it out."

"Sounds pretty important."

"A security issue," replied Britt.

The crewman checked the paperwork attached to the side of the container. "Seems like everything's in order."

"If anyone tries to board this ship, make sure you check their IDs very carefully," ordered Britt.

"Are you expecting trouble?"

"I'm sure of it. A woman has stolen something very valuable from a person of importance. She'll attempt to get away from here before she's caught. The box is bait to draw her out of hiding."

The crewman glanced at the paperwork once more and attached it to the container. "We'll be ready if she tries to board this ship."

"The Space Fleet is working with us on this," added Britt. "Some of their men will want to search the ship. Give them your full cooperation."

"Of course. We don't want any trouble."

The forklift stopped in front of the hatch and waited for direction.

"Go ahead," the crewman directed the forklift driver and pointed inside the cargo bay. He took out his radio and requested backup from other crewmen.

Britt noticed three Fleet soldiers approaching. He walked away from the ship and hid behind a stack of crates, waiting nervously. One of the crew operated a pallet jack and moved the crate with Marina in it toward the back.

The soldiers stopped at the *Golden Falcon*. The crewman greeted them and allowed them access to the ship.

On board the ship, two of the soldiers searched behind crates and hatches. The third climbed stairs and disappeared through the hatch. Soon after, he returned and motioned for them to exit the ship.

The crewmen arrived and briefly spoke with their peer. After he briefed them, they entered the ship and left him alone on watch. He waited anxiously at the hatch for their departure.

When the soldiers were out of sight, a cloaked woman and two burly men approached the ship.

Britt watched suspiciously but couldn't comprehend their words. He knew it had to be Fiona.

The woman handed papers to the crewman. He examined them and gave them back. The conversation quickly became heated and he refused them admittance. One of the men shoved the crewman against the hull and threatened him.

The other crewmen quickly emerged from the ship, armed with crowbars, pipe wrenches and hammers. The two men didn't want to attract any attention and backed down from the crew.

The soldiers overheard the commotion from a distance and returned quickly. The woman managed to disappear behind a truck laden with cargo before they arrived. The soldiers questioned the two men for several minutes. Finally, all of them left.

Britt returned to the ship, anxious to hear what happened. The crewman explained that they were recruiters from a spiritual group.

"They were an odd lot," he remarked. "The woman had a mask over part of her face and the men carried pistols. She did have travel papers but they weren't stamped. I did notice that she took their pistols before she left." He thanked Britt for the heads up as they boarded the ship.

Fiona and her mercenaries approached the hatch of a private ship but another crewman blocked their path and explained that the ship was about to depart.

Fiona handed him a bag of gold coins. The man hesitated and then stepped aside. Once they boarded, the hatch closed.

***

Three of the crewmen counted crates and containers in the cargo bay of the *Golden Falcon* while one of them verified that the numbers on the crate matched his sheet.

Britt was nervous as he eyed the container with Marina inside. He watched the crewmen uneasily. They reconciled the shipping manifest and finally left the area.

Britt urgently removed the tarp from the top of the container and slowly lifted the lid.

Inside the container, Marina shivered. A sliver of light penetrated the darkness and grew as the lid was raised. She reached for one of her daggers and tensed for a fight.

Aware of her defensive nature, Britt paused and leaned closer to the opening. "Put the knife away," he whispered. "It's me."

Marina breathed a sigh of relief when Britt opened the lid fully. She still clutched the dagger in her trembling hand and reached for him. He lifted her out of the container and rubbed her shivering body for warmth. Marina dropped to her knees and shook from the cold.

Britt pushed the hood from her cloak off her head and stood her up. Her dreadlocks with the silver flash grenades dropped down on her shoulders. He hugged her and rubbed her vigorously until she stopped shaking. Marina politely pushed him away and stowed her dagger.

"Are you okay?" asked Britt nervously.

Marina grabbed his chin forcefully and drew close to him. "That's a stupid friggin' question, don't you think?" She released her hold on him and studied the layout of the cargo bay and the access points. She noted the stairs in relation to the hatch and cabinets.

"Did you have a better idea?" Britt inquired.

Marina glanced back at him and replied miserably, "Yeah, but you wouldn't like it."

Britt knew better than to respond to her comment. She was right. It would be messy and he wasn't in a fighting mood with his injuries. He had a feeling that the rib injury was more serious than he previously thought but Marina was his first priority.

Marina left the cargo bay and followed a narrow corridor to the crew's empty break area. Britt followed her dutifully as he expected she would take charge now. One thing about Marina in his eyes: She was very predictable.

The break area consisted of three tables, a counter, and several appliances. Meals were typically quick and small when traveling short hops to space stations. The first and last hour of flight required the crew to be at their stations so Britt knew the break area was empty for a little while.

Britt and Marina entered and sat at the first table. He sensed that Marina was still cold and instinctively placed his arm around her shoulders. She nestled against him and gazed into his eyes.

Britt became unnerved and quickly removed his arm. "I'm sorry, your Highness," he responded apologetically. "I didn't mean…"

Marina realized that her real identity bothered him. She placed a finger to his lips and interrupted him, "I'm Marina, not Your Highness. Put your arm around me and shut up."

Britt hesitated briefly but finally gained the courage and placed his arm around her again. She welcomed his attention. Shortly after, Marina was fast asleep. Britt stayed attentive through the trip while she rested.

***

Upstairs, the passenger deck had twenty seats and all were filled with passengers. Rebecca and Cristos sat in the back row. Cristos held Rebecca's hand affectionately. He kissed her cheek and remarked, "Not to spoil the mood, but I have a bad feeling about this."

Rebecca responded despondently, "I do, too. This is different than fighting in the forest. There's no place to run."

"How do you know we'll be safe on Orpheus-2?" he inquired uneasily.

"My contact, Severin, is the Security Officer there," she explained. "She'll help us."

"Can we trust her?" he asked.

"It was Severin who tipped me off that Marina was coming to Yord."

Cristos felt more at ease and focused his attention on the passengers around them. There was no obvious sign of Marina or Britt but there were too many faces and too little time to look more thoroughly without stirring suspicions among the other passengers. "I guess Marina and her merc friend took another ship," he commented.

Rebecca noticed his unease and patted his knee for reassurance. "Don't worry. She's more than capable of handling herself."

"Do you think we can trust Marina to work with us?" Cristos asked.

Rebecca considered his question for a moment. "I think she realizes that she can't hide from this anymore. She's in too deep with us, Fiona, Victor and the militia officer she's smitten with, to turn back."

"Then her life as a recluse is pretty much over."

"And that is why I think she'll eventually accept her role as princess," Rebecca concluded confidently. "Her identity has already been compromised so no more illicit courier assignments."

Six men entered the cargo bay. When they surrounded Britt and Marina, she was surprised to see Rock and Tulley among them.

"Well, hello, gentlemen," she said with a false smile.

Rock approached her and shoved her against the crate. Britt immediately punched him in the face. Three of the men jumped on Britt and beat him down to the floor. They drew pistols and aimed at his head.

"Don't move or you're history," warned Rock as his men disarmed Britt and Marina.

Britt spit blood on the floor and remained still.

Rock squeezed Marina's jaw tightly. "I thought we had an understanding. You disappoint me, Marina."

"You wanted the chip. I gave it to you. What's so hard to understand about that?"

Rock punched her in the stomach and knocked the wind out of her. Britt attempted to stand but the three men kicked him in the ribs until he lay flat and ceased resisting.

Marina gasped for air as Rock maintained a hold on her chin. "I'm not in the mood for games," he informed her angrily.

"Who exactly do you work for?" Marina asked as she panted heavily.

"Let's just say that we promised to return the chip by a certain time to the appropriate owners."

"Bullshit!" blurted Marina.

Rock glanced at Tulley with a frown. He punched Marina again in the stomach and brought her to her knees. She gagged and nearly vomited.

"You embarrassed us with a common maintenance chip. That will hurt my reputation immeasurably," he complained to her.

"So what do you want from me?" she uttered mockingly.

"The friggin' data chip, you stupid bitch! Where is it?"

Marina chuckled despite the pain. "How do I know you aren't working for Victor?"

Tulley charged at her and grabbed her by her arm. He twisted it behind her back and lifted her in the air. Rock stepped back and watched, amused by her stubbornness.

"The Fleet and the militias are ready to go to war over that damn chip! If you have it, give it to us now."

Marina groaned in pain as her shoulder dislocated again and exploded with pain. "And what about Victor?" she cried out.

"Our only concern is that the chip is returned to the Fleet. Now, give it to us before I break your arm off!" Tulley threatened.

Marina's eyes rolled up in her head as the pain was overwhelming. She tried to speak but could not.

"Set her down," ordered Rock. "We don't want to kill her before we get what we came here for."

Tulley released his hold on her and she dropped to the floor on her injured shoulder. With her eyes still rolled back in her head, she gasped for air and shook violently.

"You'll kill her, you fools!" shouted Britt.

The men backed away and allowed him access to Marina. He lifted her into a sitting position with her weight off her shoulder. He nearly cried when he saw her shoulder grossly misaligned.

"I have to fix this fast to alleviate the pain," Britt informed them frantically. Rock glanced at Tulley and they both agreed he could proceed.

Britt knelt next to her with one knee in her side. He yanked on her arm while turning it slightly. Marina screamed as her shoulder popped back into place. Britt cradled her head against him and hugged her tightly.

One of the men offered a canteen of water. He tilted Marina's head back and slowly poured the water into her mouth. She stopped shaking and sobbed.

Britt laid her flat on the floor. One of their assailants returned to the cargo bay with a blanket from a locker upstairs. He tossed it to Britt.

Britt covered her and lifted her into a sitting position. Her breathing stabilized and her eyes returned to their normal position. He cradled her against him and gently rubbed her arm. Rock and Tulley sat on a crate with their arms folded and watched patiently.

"We will get that chip from you, one way or another," Rock guaranteed her.

Marina tried to speak but couldn't.

"Back off," ordered Britt. "If she has it, I'll get it for you."

"We'll let you two consider your options. Oh, and don't think you can escape when the ship lands either. We've got that covered."

Rock, Tulley and their henchmen left them alone in the cargo bay.

***

Orpheus-2 was a horizontal, multi-decked cylinder with vertical towers at each end, capable of handling up to one hundred ships of all sizes except for battleship-sized craft. Each tower had a series of hatches for isolation of the individual bays as ships entered and departed.

The *Golden Falcon* approached the huge space station and was guided into one of the open bays by a tractor beam operated by the Transport Master in one of the towers. Once the hatch closed and sealed behind it, the ship was secured in place against the dock by powerful magnets.

Numerous conduits and hydraulic lines automatically attached to ports on the hull for air and water replenishment.

The loud whoosh of oxygen through vents at various locations in the bay made the air breathable.

Marina was nestled in Britt's arms in the corner of the cargo bay. Rock and his crew returned and stood by them.

"Anything you want to share with me now?" Rock asked sarcastically.

Marina pushed away from Britt and stood up. Her balance was poor and she clutched the top of a crate for support. "I'll only discuss the issue of the chip with a senior officer of the Fleet. I don't trust you."

"Why do you have to be so damn difficult?" Rock complained and slammed his elbow into her jaw. "You should have stuck to the plan."

Marina bounced off the hull and fell to her knees. Britt knelt by her and held her in his arms. "Hang on, Marina. I'll call the medical team once they open the hatch."

Marina gazed into his eyes. "Thank you, Britt," she mumbled meekly like a little child.

Ten sentries armed with pulse rifles entered the bay through an air-tight door and stood on the dock. They waited patiently as the hatch finally opened.

When the crew appeared, one of the sentries inquired as to their cargo and passenger list. One crewman showed him the cargo manifest.

While they discussed the contents, the front hatch opened for the passenger deck. The sentries immediately boarded and surrounded everyone. No passenger was permitted to exit the ship while the investigation in the cargo bay was ongoing. Rebecca and Cristos were concerned about the reason for the delay. They waited anxiously for clearance to debark.

Rock showed the sentries his ID and informed them that Marina had information vital to the Fleet.

One of the sentries called for the medical team. Another ordered Rock and Tulley to follow them to the Security Center.

The medical team arrived promptly to tend to Marina. The remaining sentries shoved Britt off the ship to the dock.

Britt looked like hell. His face was bruised and his lip swollen. "What's the meaning of this?" he asked sternly as he tried to look calm. "We are here on official business."

"That is Marina, I assume," remarked one of the sentries.

"That's none of your business," Britt informed him.

"Actually, it is. It's imperative that we get both of you away from the dock."

"What's the big deal?"

"There is an unscheduled arrival coming – a private vessel. We suspect an assassin may be on board and Marina is her target."

After an injection from the medic, Marina was stable and attempted to stand. The medics pushed her down on the gurney and carried her off the ship.

Marina rolled off onto the dock and fell to her knees. Britt immediately went to her aid. The medics surrounded her but Britt stood in front of her. "If she says she's okay then leave her be."

The medics backed off but watched with concern.

Marina thanked them and assured them that she was okay now, despite her appearance.

Britt whispered to her, "I don't like this. They just left us here without knowing where the chip was."

"They're working for the Fleet, I'll bet."

"So why assault us?" he asked, looking confused.

Marina frowned at him and explained, "He mentioned something about sticking to the plan. They used me to find out who was behind the chip's theft. I was supposed to leave it and get out."

"And you kept it which made you look like a free-lancer."

"I think I also blew their chance for a finder's fee and to nail the original thief."

Britt realized the extent of her actions and understood why their assailants were so angry.

The sentries formed a protective circle around them. Britt and Marina glanced at each other nervously. Both were unsure what to expect but followed them from the bay into an isolated corridor marked 'authorized personnel only.' A short distance later, they entered an elevator.

No one spoke on the elevator ride up. When they exited on the twentieth floor, they passed through a series of hatches. Each hatch had a camera mounted above it for security purposes. After passing through the last hatch, they entered a corridor lined with steel doors. They were labeled with the letter 'R' for the zone and a number to identify the specific room. They stopped outside a door marked 'R-17.'

Marina chuckled to herself.

"What's so funny?" asked Britt curiously.

"This is the office where I used to come for my assignments ten years ago. Things got hot for my handler and he moved on to another location."

One of the sentries knocked and stepped inside the office for a brief moment. When he returned, he directed them to enter.

Marina stepped inside first, followed by Britt. 'R-17' was a simple office with a large desk surrounded by seven chairs. Three filing cabinets lined the wall behind the desk and a large flat-screen monitor was mounted on one wall. On the desk was a computer keyboard and holographic display filled with floating words and numbers.

Severin, a dark-haired woman wearing the tan uniform of a Security Officer, sat at the desk and studied the hologram. Her facial expression and sharp attention gave her a tough-as-nails but attractive appearance for a woman in her late fifties.

Marina and Britt stood in front of her desk and waited for her to acknowledge them.

"Excuse me," interrupted Britt politely.

Severin replied, "I'll be with you in a moment."

Britt observed the data in the hologram and realized they were the positions of all the ships in the quadrant.

Marina pounded the desk with her fist and winced from the pain. "You brought us in here," Marina reminded her. "Let's talk – now!"

Severin stood and studied Marina from head to toe. "You look so much like your father," she remarked and extended her hand in friendship. Marina refused it. "I was impressed by all the commotion you caused on Yord," Severin continued and both women sat down.

"I'm just a courier who got dragged into something I know nothing about," Marina stated firmly.

"Save it, Marina," Severin chided. "I know exactly who you are and what you've been doing since you ran away from the temple as a child."

Marina leaned on the desk with her hands and stared at Severin. "How would you know that?" she asked with a tone of arrogance.

Britt grew quite interested in the conversation and listened eagerly.

"Come, now, Marina. I was your invisible guardian. I knew you worked for Dix on Glomus-5 as a smuggler. It was me who sent the Fleet soldiers to Balthus' warehouse *after* you supposedly gave the chip to Balthus to make sure you were safe. You were supposed to be out of play at that point."

Marina folded her arms in front of her and was shocked that anyone could have kept tabs on her like that. She was always so careful to avoid detection. "I don't believe you," she retorted. "Someone gave you that information - Rebecca, perhaps!"

"It was my agents who came for the data chip from Balthus' warehouse, expecting him to have it."

"That's …. That's impossible," blurted Marina. "There's no way you could have known about that."

Severin was amused by Marina's defensiveness. "It was me who told Rebecca that you were going to Yord. I asked her to protect you while you were there."

Marina became visibly upset with her. "A lot of good that did!" she bellowed.

Britt coaxed her to sit down and relax.

"Do you have the chip?" Severin asked.

"What's it to you?" she asked defiantly.

"Because, I need to know that it's safe before a war of terrible proportions breaks out and a lot of innocent people die."

"Are Rock and Tulley your 'agents?'"

"They are more like secret security for the Fleet. Not military but sanctioned by the military."

"And they nearly beat the pulp out of us! Nice friends you have."

"I'm sorry about that. They have their way of handling things. Why the open hostility toward me?" questioned Severin. "You're among friends now."

"I have no friends."

"Look, Marina, I know how you feel about your parents' disappearance. We were all hurt by what happened."

Marina punched the table with her fist again and glared at Severin. "As far as I'm concerned, I have no parents. Now, drop the subject," she demanded.

Severin slid her chair back and folded her hands on her lap. She was very patient and took her time responding to Marina. "Victor is on his way with a man-o'-war and a cruiser. His accomplice, Fiona, may have arrived on another ship that is on an unscheduled stop here. Since they're both hunting you, I'd like to know if there's anything going on other than the chip between you and them."

"We can explain," interceded Britt.

Marina held her hand up, signaling for Britt to be silent. "I escaped from Victor and took some things that might upset him a little," she revealed.

"Might the crystal of Icarus be one of those items?"

"Of course," replied Marina proudly. "And I ruined his whore's good looks as well. She's a little overdone on one side."

"That whore is an assassin and a very dangerous one at that," Severin chastised. "We couldn't touch her when she was under the militia's jurisdiction but it seems all that's changed."

"Good news travels fast," quipped Marina cynically.

"So what prompted you to walk right into Victor's grasp? Is this some fantasy role that you're acting out?"

Marina jumped out of her chair and shouted, "It was my job and I'm damn good at it!"

"Why didn't you heed our warnings?"

Marina was suddenly at a loss for words.

"Just as I thought," remarked Severin. "We have a very good counselor here who'd be happy to help you with your trust issues."

"Screw you and your counselor!"

Marina looked to Britt for support. He shrugged his shoulders with a befuddled look and had no reply. She became more frustrated.

"I... I had business to tend to," she stammered, then covered her face with one hand while struggling to contain her anger.

"If I can interject," said Britt curtly, "Fiona's facial burns should help your people identify her.

"Fiona is very elusive," Severn replied. "Even with that, I'm sure she'll be difficult to find."

Two sentries entered the room with trays of food. Severin pointed to the desk. They set the trays down and left.

Severin locked the controls for the computer. "I have to meet with my officers over how we'll handle the approaching ships. There is something you might want to look at while I'm away, though."

She pressed several keys on a remote control device and the monitor came to life. The image of a sporting event appeared with a large cage surrounded by a massive crowd. Inside the cage were a young man and an alien creature.

Marina wondered what the relevance was and waited for an explanation. Severin walked to the door and paused. "See if you recognize the man," she hinted and left the office.

Marina watched the two combatants in the cage and turned pale.

"What's wrong?" asked Britt. "You look like you've seen a ghost."

Marina burst into tears. "Shut up, will you, please!" she cried.

Britt put his arm around her and comforted her. He watched the event and realized it was a death match between a human and an alien creature from Calamaar. The creature looked humanoid with reptilian traits. Its arms and legs were quite muscular. The fight was brutal and the man was severely beaten.

Britt noticed the date and time at the bottom of the video. It was from twenty-seven years ago. "That's your father, isn't it?" he surmised.

Marina said nothing as she continued to watch. When the fight ended, the man was victorious despite being badly injured. Marina could only stare in amazement at the images.

"Like father, like daughter," Britt thought to himself regarding Marina's penchant for fighting. He was amazed to see that her father was so much like her but only before he and her mother took over the role as king and queen. Once that occurred, he became a different person – a better person.

***

When passengers were finally permitted to leave the ship, Rebecca and Cristos blended in during their exit. Rebecca carried the backpack with the crystal close to her bosom.

Several bays down, another ship docked. The sentries stood by and discussed the passenger manifest on that ship and its cargo. There was nothing to indicate Fiona was onboard. The captain arrived and requested maintenance on one of the ship's systems. The sentries contacted maintenance personnel and arranged for the bogus repairs.

Fiona and her two mercenaries used the distraction to creep out of the cargo bay and cross the dock toward a maintenance container. She whispered instructions to the men and sent them toward the exit.

Three sentries stopped the men as they approached and questioned them. Fiona used the distraction to leave the dock and enter the station. She hid in a small hallway just off the main corridor and studied the passengers departing the *Golden Falcon*. There was no sign of Marina.

Rebecca and Cristos questioned one of the crewmen for directions to Severin's office. Since neither Fiona nor her men knew the faces of Rebecca and Cristos, they proceeded unrecognized.

The passengers dispersed throughout the corridor along the horizontal section of the station, or sought out elevators to other levels.

Rebecca and Cristos followed a separate corridor marked 'Authorized Personnel Only.' A sentry verified their identification and contacted Severin for instructions. With her permission, they took the elevator to the twentieth floor.

Severin returned to the room and sat at her desk. "Do you recognize the man?" she asked Marina.

"That was... my father."

"Yes, it was. His successes with the Calamaar leaders were the cornerstone to the alliance that he built."

Marina and Britt continued to watch the scrolling pictures of her parents in battle gear in front of an alien cruiser. Her mother's outfit was remarkably similar to hers. Another couple stood with them.

"That's an impressive ship," Britt remarked.

"I wonder how they got it," Marina pondered aloud.

"Your father captured it during a battle with the Calamaar forces. They boarded his ship and he boarded theirs. The catch was that his ship was too badly damaged to be of further use. The aliens from Calamaar were stranded and he escaped with the pilot, the Calamaar Prince, as his prisoner. Quite a bargaining chip."

"That was slick," responded Britt. "How did he make peace if he had to fight them?"

"He earned their respect. What he went through to do so amazed all of us here at the station."

Rebecca opened the door and peeked in the room. She was surprised to see Marina and Britt in there.

Severin looked up and saw Rebecca at the door and became excited. "You made it!"

"Severin, it's been a long time!" she said as they entered the office.

Severin pressed two keys on her keyboard, freezing the picture on the large monitor. Rebecca handed Cristos the backpack and embraced Severin as she stepped out from behind the desk.

"This is Cristos," Rebecca announced.

Cristos shook hands with Severin. "I understand you've been of great help to Rebecca," he remarked. "We are in your debt."

"Nonsense. Maybe now, we can restore the order of the alliance and you can settle down and start your family."

Rebecca smiled at Cristos contentedly and then turned to Marina. "We were afraid you wouldn't make it."

"Yes, how did you get here?" inquired Cristos.

"The same ship as you," answered Marina. "Britt kept me on ice, literally."

Cristos frowned at Britt, still displaying his distrust for him.

"We rode in the cheap seats in the cargo section."

"What happened to you two? You both look like hell."

Marina and Britt both frowned at each other. "A few of Severin's agents wanted the chip. I think they need to see your counselor for their anger issues."

Rebecca was shocked and looked to Severin for an explanation.

"They aren't part of the military structure. I have no control over how they conduct their business."

Rebecca looked back at Marina in mock surprise. "And you wouldn't give it to them, I presume."

"I didn't know if they could be trusted with something so sensitive."

"So you risked all our lives for a chip that we shouldn't have anything to do with!" Cristos complained vociferously.

"I'm serious, Rebecca, it's time for you to get out of the rebel business."

Marina was curious about Severin's remark but said nothing.

"I pray that we're close to ending Victor's rule, she replied. "Only then will I stand down."

Severin hugged her and whispered, "Your loyalty is priceless."

"Did you see any sign of Fiona during the flight?" Britt inquired of them.

"Negative," answered Cristos.

"Fiona is here already," interrupted Severin. "One of our cameras spotted her on another dock with two men. She escaped before my sentries could arrest her."

"She's going to be a problem," complained Rebecca.

"My sentries are on heightened alert with orders to shoot and kill her."

"Have you thought about how to mitigate the problem between the militias and the Fleet over the stolen data chip?" Rebecca asked.

Severin glanced at Marina for a response. Marina stood and took the backpack from Cristos. She removed her wig and retrieved the chip. The others were amazed by her appearance with her natural hair. Marina nervously placed the wig back on and pinned it in place.

Severin looked relieved and reached for it but Marina tossed it on the table with little regard for her. She handed the backpack to Cristos again.

"If Victor is defeated, the other militias will follow my orders," Britt informed Severin. "We will pledge our support to Marina if she takes the throne."

Marina elbowed Britt in the side and glared at him.

"And some of us will support her even if she doesn't," he continued, wincing in pain.

Severin inspected the code on the data chip and made a call. She acknowledged that the chip was verified and could be picked up.

Rebecca noticed the picture on the large monitor and stared in awe. The picture showed both Marina's and Rebecca's parents standing in front of the alien cruiser with ghostly images on its hull.

"Those two on the right were your parents, Rebecca," Severin explained. "Good people, they were."

Rebecca's eyes became wet with tears. "I miss them so much." Cristos placed his arm around her and consoled her.

"They were a hell of a team with Marina's parents," Severin remarked and started the images scrolling again. "This was after they found Marina's parents and brought them back together again. It took almost three years but they never gave up."

Britt turned his attention to Severin and commented, "My father told me that they were responsible for uniting human and alien races together in a way never seen before."

"That is true. Marina's father had unconventional ways, much like Marina, of dealing with situations. You saw the death match where he surprised everyone and spared the Calamaar Prince."

Britt was impressed. "I heard many men warn of the Calamaar. They are a strong and violent race."

"Very much so," answered Severin. "Marina's father used that to earn their respect."

"So why did they leave me?" Marina asked, somewhat choked up.

"They didn't," answered Severin. "Something happened with the portal system after they defeated the massive Weevil invasion force. We searched for so long but never found any trace of them."

Marina became lost in thought as she stared at the image.

"So what do we do about Victor?" Britt asked. "Is there someplace we can hide until he leaves?"

"I can't risk it," replied Severin. "I'll arrange for all of you to leave on a fast transport, the *Neutrino*."

"Thanks, Severin," Rebecca said humbly. "We're in your debt."

"I suggest that you wait until Victor's cruiser docks before leaving. That will give you your best opportunity to escape."

"Very well," Rebecca responded.

A knock on the door startled them. Rock and Tulley entered and approached the desk. Severin handed the chip to them and assured them that it was authentic. The men paused in front of Marina.

"You're a tough nut to crack," Rock complimented her. "I'm sorry it had to be that way."

"I'm sure you understand it was business," added Tulley.

"That's why I couldn't give it to you," she remarked proudly. "I'm sure you understand that as well."

"We'll arrange for you to receive a handsome bounty for your help in procuring the chip. That's the least we can do for beating you up like that."

Marina looked insulted. "Keep your money. That's not why I did it."

"Very noble, Princess," commended Rock. "Good luck to you." The men smiled at her approvingly and departed the room.

Marina was shocked that they learned her true identity. She figured their boss must have been quite upset to learn that his boys beat up a princess. *"Maybe I should have taken the money,"* she thought.

Severin stood and approached the door. She paused and looked back at Marina. "If you decide to take the throne, I can assure you the Alliance will back you,"

"The Alliance?" questioned Marina.

"Yes, or what's left of it. That includes the Space Fleet and a few alien allies."

"And the militias," added Britt. "I can guarantee that."

Marina looked down and briefly considered their words. "I don't think that will be an issue," she responded somberly. "Once Victor and Fiona are disposed of, I will be leaving the sector for a place where I can live in solitude."

Rebecca, Cristos and Severin looked disappointedly at her. Severin left the room with her head down. She sensed that Marina wouldn't budge on her opposition to taking the throne and restoring what her parents created.

Britt excused himself and followed Severin out of the office.

Marina stood in front of the large screen and stared at the images of her parents. A tear streamed down her cheek.

Rebecca handed the backpack to Cristos and whispered, "Hide this on board the *Neutrino* and, whatever you do, guard it with your life."

Cristos nodded and left the room.

Rebecca joined Marina in front of the screen and pondered aloud, "Funny how close our parents were and we never knew each other."

Marina glanced at her and asked, "How can you accept being orphaned like this and not feel pain?"

Rebecca looked down at the floor for a moment and considered her response. When she looked up, she answered, "I was adopted. My natural parents were killed when the Weevil raided our planet. I never knew them."

Marina was stunned by her revelation.

"My blood sister, Sara, died as you well know," continued Rebecca. "I think of them every day and renew my vow to avenge their deaths."

"So you and I have quite a bit in common."

"Yes, except that I direct my anger at those who took them away."

Marina felt embarrassed by Rebecca's critique of her. "Perhaps one day, I'll see it differently."

Rebecca gently poked a finger into Marina's chest. "You'd best hope you work it out before it's too late," she advised.

Marina took a seat at Severin's desk. She appeared lost in thought.

"So, what do we do now, Marina?" Rebecca asked. "We can't run for the rest of our lives."

"I don't know," she answered with a flustered expression. "I don't know anything anymore."

"Well, you'd better know. We only have one-way choices left and, whichever way we choose, there's no going back."

Britt returned and announced, "Victor's ships have entered the sector. We have to be ready to leave the station in two hours."

"We were just discussing our long term plans or lack thereof," Rebecca explained cynically.

Britt stared at Marina and patiently waited for her response.

Marina's eyes widened and she felt renewed vigor. "We know Victor will pursue us," she said with a coy smile. "We'll convince him that Fiona has me and the crystal. If we should die in a mock blast, then he'll think that both me and the crystal are gone with her."

Rebecca and Britt glanced at each other, pleased with their agreement thus far on the plan.

"Then we go after Victor," added Rebecca.

Britt stepped forward with his hands out for attention. "Let me handle Victor. I can arrange to have him captured by the other militias and charged for conspiring against them."

"No!" Marina and Rebecca replied in unison. They looked at each other with surprised expressions.

Britt was rattled by their determination.

"We have much to settle with Victor," Rebecca remarked sternly. "You can do it with us or you can leave."

"Fine," relented Britt. "We'll do it your way."

Marina pressed a button on Severin's keyboard and the images on the monitor scrolled at normal speed again.

A picture of Marina's parents with Severin and an older gentleman in a general's uniform appeared. Marina assumed this must have been General Adolpho, who gave his life to save her father during an alien attack. She noticed how the General appeared paternally protective of Severin.

Britt noticed her distracted expression. "What's wrong, Marina?"

"The picture of Severin and the General," she replied.

"The General was her uncle," answered Rebecca. "He raised her from a child and sent her into the military much like your grandfather sent your father after your grandmother died."

"How do you know so much about my family?" Marina asked defensively.

Rebecca went to the door and paused with her hand on the handle. She stared back at her condescendingly.

"Something you want to say?" shouted Marina.

"Isn't it obvious?" responded Rebecca. "Our parents were so close and they accomplished so much."

"Well, good for them," Marina countered sarcastically. "All I remember is being raised by strangers as a four-year old!"

"Marina!" Britt exclaimed in surprise of her attitude.

"Zip it, Britt. You don't have a say in this argument."

Rebecca returned to Marina and begged her. "The people of Yord need you. Can't you see that?"

Marina stared coldly into her eyes and responded, "I see Victor and Fiona out there and they need to die. That's all I care about right now."

Rebecca fumed and stormed out of the room.

Marina punched the wall in anger and flipped the chairs like a spoiled child. She dropped to the floor and cried.

Britt knelt next to her and placed his arm around her.

"She has no idea what I went through!" she cried. "It was horrible!"

"Maybe she does," suggested Britt. "How much do you really know about her?"

Marina considered his comment and said nothing more.

***

Cristos boarded the *Neutrino* with Marina's backpack. With no one in sight, he searched for a safe location to store it. He paused in front of a three-foot long panel labeled 'Data Processing Control System' and placed the backpack inside of it.

A hatch slammed in the distance and echoed through the corridors He quickly closed the panel, then glanced behind and ahead but no one was in sight. He entered the cargo bay and paused in the doorway.

A grating noise across a wall sent shivers down his spine. He turned and looked quickly behind him but no one was there. When he faced forward, Fiona stood in front of him. He was startled but quickly regained his composure.

"You must be one of the rebels who aided Red." she said pointedly.

"And you have the face of a charred steak," he taunted. "Red is none of your business anymore."

"I'll ask you once. Where is Red?"

Cristos' hatred for Fiona took over and he shoved her against the hull. She shoved him right back with a sarcastic sneer on her face. "Time to die, rebel?" she declared gleefully.

"Is it, now?" Cristos replied as he summoned his courage. He grabbed Fiona by the throat and choked her.

Fiona stared defiantly back at him with bulging eyes. Her hand slipped under her cloak and retrieved a dagger.

Cristos smiled as he gained confidence, but then she shoved the dagger into his lower abdomen and sliced upward.

Now Cristos' eyes bulged as he knew his wound was lethal. He slumped to his knees and desperately tried to contain his entrails with one hand. He clutched at Fiona's cloak and held tightly for balance with the other. Fiona bore a sinister smile as she rested his head against her stomach in mock affection.

Severin and two sentries barged into the cargo bay. The sentries aimed their pulse rifles at Fiona.

"It's over, Fiona," declared Severin. "I've waited a long time for this moment.

"Stay out of my business if you know what's good for you," Fiona warned and released her hold on Cristos. His dead body dropped to the floor.

"You murdered a man on my station," she charged. "That makes it my business."

Fiona held her hands up and feigned surrender. "I'm sure everything will work out just fine," she said mockingly. Two mercenaries took advantage of her distraction and slipped into the bay behind the sentries.

Severin fumed at her disrespect. "Kill her," she ordered the sentries.

Before they could fire, the mercenaries gunned them down from behind. Severin drew her pistol and returned fire at them. The mercenaries fell to the floor dead.

Fiona drew her pulse pistol from under her cloak and stepped toward Severin. Before Severin could turn around, Fiona fired two shots into the back of her head. Severin collapsed to the ground with a smoking crater in the back of her head, exposing a shattered skull.

Fiona rolled her over and brushed the hair from Severin's eyes. "I told you it would all work out just fine," she whispered, gazing psychotically at her corpse.

***

An hour later, Rebecca sat in Severin's office and sobbed. When Marina and Britt entered, they knew something serious had happened.

"The sentry told us there was a problem," Britt informed her but Rebecca didn't respond.

"We're supposed to be leaving," Marina complained impatiently.

"Has something happened?" Britt asked.

Rebecca looked up at them with swollen eyes and blurted, "Cristos is dead. So is Severin."

They were stunned by the news. "Fiona?" Marina asked. Rebecca nodded and wiped her eyes.

Marina was outraged. She punched the wall with her fist. "Damn it! I'm gonna' kill her now on this station!"

Britt placed his hand on Rebecca's shoulder compassionately and inquired, "The crystal?"

"I don't know. Cristos went on board the *Neutrino* to hide it. That's when she killed him."

Marina stormed to the door and grabbed the handle. "She won't leave this station alive!" she vowed and opened the door.

Britt stood over Rebecca and instructed her calmly, "We have to leave now. You understand."

Rebecca stood slowly and nestled against Britt for consolation. Marina grew red-faced and shouted, "I'm going after her now, with or without the two of you!"

Britt escorted Rebecca to the door and blocked it with his foot. "This is one time you'll listen to me," he chastised Marina. "We have to leave now. Victor will be here shortly and our presence endangers everyone on this station." He took Marina by her arm and nudged both women out of the office.

Marina glanced back once more at the image of her parents on the monitor and left the room more confused than ever.

Chapter 8

On the Run

The man-o'-war, the *Scorpion*, remained in orbit around Orpheus-2. A cruiser, the *Orion* entered one of the bays on the huge space station and docked.

Victor and twenty of his men exited the ship. "Split up!" he ordered. "Half of you will search the bays for them. The others will come with me."

Victor led his men down the corridor to the elevator. Five stood guard while the other five rode the elevator up with him.

Five Fleet sentries awaited them when they stepped off. "Stay where you are," ordered one of them.

Victor held his hand up for calm. "I'm looking for Severin," he announced. "She's expecting me."

The lead sentry informed him, "Severin was killed an hour ago in an ambush down at Dock Nine."

"Who was behind it?" Victor asked impatiently.

"We believe it was the assassin Fiona. She is here on the station."

Victor bit his lip and contemplated this new situation. "Let me and my men handle Fiona. I have a debt to settle with her."

"We'll set up a perimeter around the transportation hub. No one will go in or out without your knowledge."

Victor nodded in appreciation of their support. "She won't escape, I assure you," he promised.

"My stand-in commander wishes to speak with you. He is on the seventh floor."

"Very well. Let's make this short, shall we? I have a traitor to execute."

They returned to the elevator.

***

Britt, Marina and Rebecca walked quickly to the elevator, wary of anyone who passed. Britt kept his hand close to his pulse pistol while the girls were anxious and kept their hands on daggers under their cloaks.

"Do you have any idea where Cristos would have hidden the crystal?" Britt asked Rebecca.

She shook her head sadly. "I told him to guard it with his life. I never expected this to happen," she replied.

"Then Fiona may already have it."

Marina interrupted, "Fiona doesn't care about the crystal any more than I do. She only wants her revenge."

"Maybe the two of you should work together – two cold-hearted bitches!" sniped Rebecca.

Marina stepped in front of Rebecca and placed her hands on her shoulders. "Look, I know I'm not the most sensitive person," she admitted sympathetically, "and I'm really sorry about Cristos. I know the two of you were close."

"Should I be flattered by your fake compassion?" Rebecca responded angrily and shoved Marina away. She continued onto the elevator alone.

Marina glanced at Britt. He didn't know what to say to either woman. They stepped onto the elevator and waited with her as the doors closed.

Marina touched Rebecca's arm and repeated sadly, "I really am sorry. I can't help myself when it comes to showing no emotion."

"Maybe if you were in my shoes, you'd feel differently," Rebecca replied and sobbed.

Britt gestured with his eyes for Marina to keep trying.

"Alright, Rebecca, help me here. What shoes are you talking about that I don't know of?"

Rebecca looked at her somberly and answered, "I'm pregnant and Cristos is the father of my child."

Marina and Britt were stunned.

"Rebecca, I had no idea," Marina said compassionately.

"Would it have mattered?"

"I think so," Marina replied hesitantly, unsure how or why it would be different. "I never knew anyone who carried a child before."

"You really are out in the cold, Marina."

"I told you I was a loner!"

Rebecca touched her arm affectionately and replied, "Not anymore."

The elevator slowed just prior to stopping.

"Stay here," he whispered to the girls. "They won't shoot me."

"Britt, be careful," urged Marina with a note of concern in her voice.

Britt was surprised and patted her arm affectionately. "I'll be fine."

"What do you want us to do?" asked Rebecca.

"Get yourselves out of here. I'll find you later."

The women moved aside from the door, out of the soldiers' view. Britt stood in the middle with his hands visible.

Five of Victor's men waited at the elevator as the door opened. "Don't move!" ordered one of the soldiers.

"You know who I am," he responded. "Where's Victor?"

"You'll see Victor soon enough. Put your hands over your head."

Britt reluctantly complied and stepped out of the elevator. The doors closed behind him. He raised one arm but grabbed the soldier's gun with the other and chopped him across the side of the head. The soldier was dazed.

Britt took the man's pulse pistol and aimed it at the head of another. The other three kept their weapons trained on him.

"Back away and nobody gets hurt," he warned. "I need to see Victor."

The soldiers refused to accommodate him.

"Alright, we'll do this the hard way," he said irritably. "Back up now or he dies."

"Screw you, asshole!" shouted one of the soldiers.

Britt fired a shot into the man's head and chastised, "That's no way to respect one of Victor's captains. Anyone else have something to say?"

No one answered. Smoke and stench arose from the searing hole in the man's head. The soldiers retreated through two doorways.

Britt held onto the dazed soldier using him like a shield with the soldier's arm bent behind his back. The soldiers again aimed at Britt but his hostage prevented them from shooting.

"We're going back to the dock. Now move," he ordered, "or he dies too."

The soldiers reluctantly entered the hall and walked ahead of him, glancing repeatedly over their shoulders at him. "Stow the guns if you know what's good for you."

"Why don't you just shoot us?" asked one soldier.

"Because I'm not your enemy. Fiona and her mercs are."

The soldiers finally understood and followed his instructions.

***

Marina hugged Rebecca and stroked her hair out of her eyes. "Let's make that bitch pay for what she did to Cristos."

"Promise me when the time comes, you'll let me handle her," Rebecca requested.

"Damn, you want all the fun," teased Marina.

"I'm serious, Marina. I want to look her in the eye before she dies and see her fear."

"You got it. Now let's find a way out of here."

The elevator stopped on the fifth floor and a young Lieutenant greeted them. "Follow me," he instructed. The women cautiously obeyed. "I saw you on the security monitor and knew you needed my help."

"Who are you," Marina inquired.

"Severin's nephew, Jeffries. I'm the interim commander on the station now."

"We're sorry for your loss," Marina said somberly.

"Sometimes life sucks but it still goes on," he responded and stopped in front of double doors marked 'Station HVAC and Air Transfer.' He unlocked the doors with a key and pointed inside.

"What's in there?" asked Marina.

"Your escape route. The drawings on the wall will show you how to reach your ship."

"How?" Rebecca asked curiously.

"Through the ductwork," he replied. "Now I must go. I will meet with Victor and delay him as long as possible."

As soon as they entered the room, Jeffries locked the door behind them. "Can we trust him?" Marina asked.

"Do we have a choice?"

The women studied the large drawings on the wall for several minutes. They looked uneasily at the large vent behind them and listened to the sound of air flowing through miles of ductwork. They glanced at each other uneasily.

"Shit," complained Marina.

"Damn," replied Rebecca.

They gathered some tools from a workbench and disassembled a section of the large cover. Marina checked a flashlight for brightness and tucked it under her bodice. "You first," she instructed Rebecca.

Rebecca peered down the duct and replied, "No way! You first, your Highness."

"Great," Marina grumbled and pushed her out of the way. She straddled the lip of the duct with one leg over and looked back at Rebecca. "You are coming, aren't you?"

"I'll be right behind you. Just don't stop."

"Your scrawny ass had better be right behind me. I'm not coming back for you."

"I will, already," Rebecca promised reluctantly. "Now get going."

Marina looked down into the darkness and slid her other leg over the side. She pushed off and slid into the darkness.

The ductwork was smooth and turned at a forty-five degree angle before it leveled off. It was designed for a large volume of air flow to accommodate the immense size of the station.

Marina slid to a stop on her back in a horizontal portion of duct and scrambled to her feet. She took out the flashlight and peered ahead.

Rebecca tumbled down and nearly slid into the back of Marina's legs. "What a rush!" she blurted giddily.

Marina was amused by her reaction. She helped her to her feet and the two tip-toed quietly through the duct with only the flashlight to guide them.

"There should be an air-handler and modulator coming up," Marina whispered, aiming the light straight ahead.

"Is that a problem?" Rebecca inquired.

"I don't know."

Suddenly, Marina shrieked and fell into a vertical run of duct. Her instincts enabled her to grab the other side and hold on. The flashlight dropped to the bottom of the shaft and landed with a bang. Marina cringed, hoping no one heard them.

"Are you all right, Marina?" Rebecca yelled frantically.

"Quiet. You want them to hear us," Marina warned. She pulled herself up onto the horizontal duct, lay on her back and regained her composure.

Rebecca tested the area along the left and right side of the opening. There was a small ledge on either side. "It's not big enough," she fretted. "I can't make it."

Marina groaned and pulled herself into a sitting position. "Jump to the left or right and plant one foot on the lip, then push off. It'll be easy. Just remember to keep your head down."

Rebecca studied the width of the vertical shaft. The outline was vague with only the light through the vents to guide them now. "I don't know about this, Marina."

"Don't be such a child," Marina taunted.

Rebecca backed up a few steps and rushed toward the right side of the shaft opening. She leaped, planted her right foot on the lip and pushed off to the other side. She tumbled and fell on top of Marina.

Marina kidded, "Maybe that ass isn't so scrawny." The two women burst into laughter.

Rebecca helped her to her feet and they continued down the shaft. A short distance later, they reached a six foot drop off and lowered themselves down to another horizontal run of duct. Blocking the path ahead of them were four vertical vanes in the open position. The ductwork rumbled downstream and air flow increased around them.

"Hurry up!" urged Marina as she slid anxiously through the vanes.

Rebecca stepped through just as the vanes started to close and pinned her. "Marina, help me!"

Marina tried to pull Rebecca through but it was too late. She took her dagger and wedged it in the cam above them that drove the vanes. She stopped the vanes but couldn't reverse them.

Rebecca groaned in pain. "I... can't... move," she uttered. Her breathing grew strained as she became teary-eyed. "I ...can't ...make it. Go on ...without me," she said weakly.

"No way," replied Marina determinedly. She stepped between the middle two vanes and tried to push them open. The air flow grew in intensity. Marina took a second dagger from her thigh sheath and pried the cam while using the first as a stop. The cam budged backward slightly and she blocked it again.

Rebecca strained to get free of the vain but was still pinned. Marina pried again on the cam and budged it a little more. She immediately blocked it with the first dagger. "Come on, Rebecca. Get your ass through there," she urged.

Rebecca pushed against the vane with all her strength and moved forward a little. "I still can't get through." Her voice grew stronger as the force on her chest lessened.

The air flow increased to near gale force. Breathing was difficult and pieces of grit sandblasted their skin until it was red and raw.

Marina drove her shoulder into the vane with all her strength and pried on the cam above her. It moved a little bit more and she blocked it again.

Rebecca broke free of the vanes and tumbled forward. Marina stepped away and yanked the dagger away from the cam. The vanes slammed shut and the airflow ceased.

Both women fell to the floor, breathless. Rebecca reached over and placed her arm around Marina. "Thanks," she said appreciatively.

Marina embraced her and kissed her forehead.

"What was that for?" asked Rebecca curiously.

"You're becoming the sister I never had and a big pain in the ass at that."

"You seem to know a lot about my ass," she joked. "I never knew you noticed."

"I noticed a lot of things about you," Marina confessed. "I wish I were like you."

"But why? You're beautiful," replied Rebecca.

"I don't know how to be a woman. I can't even wear my hair like a normal woman. Instead I hide under this wig and leather outfit and... and I beat people up for a living."

Rebecca rested her head on Marina's chest. "You just proved to me that there's a woman underneath all that toughness. You're like a golden chalice that needs to be polished but you're still special."

Marina grew teary-eyed. "We'd better get moving," she suggested, fearing her emotions would get the better of her.

Rebecca kissed Marina's cheek and promised, "I'll always be here for you if you ever need someone to lean on."

"I'd like that. Now get your ass up so we can get the hell out of here," she teased.

The two women continued around a bend in the ductwork and descended again to a lower level.

"Up ahead on the left should be the vent to our bay," Marina declared confidently. "

"I hope you're right."

"Hey, I looked really hard at those drawings," Marina replied defensively. "I don't want to get lost in here either."

***

Jeffries waited in Severin's office as Victor was escorted in by two of the sentries. Jeffries stood and shook hands with Victor. After introductions, Victor offered his condolences and then requested full support from Jeffries to capture Fiona, Marina and Britt.

Jeffries agreed and instructed Victor to follow him back to the transportation hub. He assured him that the hub was secured to contain Fiona and her mercs.

"I'll be happy to see all these criminals off of my station," Jeffries remarked, "and I welcome your assistance in doing so."

"These criminals will be punished severely when we have them in custody," assured Victor.

"I understand your concern with the assassin but what of the others?" asked Jeffries. "Isn't one of them an officer of yours?"

"Yes, but I don't know if he's turned traitor or if he's onto something bigger and needs to work alone. Either way, I need him and the others to put this problem to rest."

"I understand. My men are at your disposal."

The two men approached the elevator.

***

Britt forced the soldiers into the bay near the *Neutrino's* open hatch. There were no other guards around. As he forced the remaining three soldiers to the hatch with his hostage, two mercenaries emerged from the ship and assaulted him from behind. The soldiers stood by and were entertained as the two mercenaries stomped on Britt repeatedly.

High above them, Marina and Rebecca peered down from the vent, watching the altercation.

"Damn!" fretted Marina. "Britt needs my help."

"You have a plan for this?" questioned Rebecca.

"No, but I'll think of something."

When Britt lay motionless, one of the soldiers ordered the mercenaries to put their hands over their heads. Several shots were fired from inside the ship and the soldiers traded gunfire. When the shooting ceased, the four soldiers lay dead and Fiona's mercs stood over them, gloating.

Marina pried off three of the bottom vanes on the vent with one of her daggers and peered down. Twenty feet below her was the top of the *Neutrino*. Its hatch was directly under the vent but out of her line of sight.

"Follow me," Marina instructed and slid onto the lip of the vent with her legs dangling over the ship.

"Huh?" Rebecca replied with a stunned expression.

Marina drew the second dagger from its sheath and slid out the vent. She dropped onto the top of the ship and slid down toward the hatch.

As the two mercenaries dragged Britt toward the hatch, they heard Marina hit the top of the ship. When they looked up, she descended on them, knocking them to the floor. The two men scurried to their feet and rushed at Marina. She kicked the first one in the chest and knocked him against the ship's hull. The second man punched her in the face and staggered her. Before he could strike again, she shoved the dagger into his abdomen and cut upward.

The man grabbed her by the throat and tried to choke her. Marina gripped his testicles through his pants with her free hand and squeezed. The man's eyes rolled back and his grip weakened. Marina pulled the knife back and pushed him to the ground.

The first man drew his pulse pistol and aimed at her but Rebecca slid down the side of the ship and knocked him to the deck.

"Nice timing, Rebecca," Marina commented appreciatively.

"Nice ride," she replied. "I'm starting to like this."

Marina and Rebecca examined Britt. He groaned and rolled onto his side. The women lifted him and ushered him to the hatch.

More soldiers arrived in the bay. Gunfire peppered the hatch as the women disappeared inside the ship. Marina pressed a red knob on the wall and initiated the hissing of air in pistons on either side of the hatch. Bursts of red energy pulses struck the opposite hull of the cargo bay for several seconds until the hatch finally closed.

"Can you fly this ship?" Britt asked Rebecca.

"I think so."

"Marina, escort her to the flight deck and get us out of here fast. We need to make sure the ship is secure."

"What about you? Are you okay?"

"Just fine," he said weakly. "I'll search the rear of the ship. You search the front. If Fiona or her mercs are here, we have to find them fast and kill them."

"Where are we going to?" asked Rebecca.

"Any place where they can't catch us," Britt replied sarcastically.

Marina and Rebecca climbed the stairs to the passenger deck and paused. They heard the squeal of the hand wheel on the 'flammable stores' door behind them. As Britt went to investigate, the door swung open and knocked him backwards.

Three men charged out of the room, surprised to see Britt and the women. The first man attacked Britt while the other two rushed after the women. Britt punched his attacker in the face, staggering him.

Marina dove off the stairs and tackled the two men. She leaped to her feet and kicked at the inside of one man's knee, tearing his cartilage. The man groaned and clutched at the injured knee.

The second merc grabbed Marina from behind. Rebecca applied a sleeper hold from behind around his face and neck. When he fell to his knees, Rebecca released her hold and backed away. Marina delivered a powerful kick to his jaw and flattened him. He lay motionless on the floor.

Rebecca drew her pistol and shot the injured man twice in the chest. Britt fought with the third mercenary.

Marina offered, "Want some help?"

Britt fell to the floor after a punch to the face. Blood streamed from his busted lip. "No, I got this," he uttered painfully.

Marina and Rebecca watched and were amused by his bravado.

Three more men charge down the stairs from the passenger deck. Marina and Rebecca quickly assumed a fighting stance.

Britt grew desperate when he saw the men and head-butted his adversary. He drove his elbow into the man's forehead and chopped him in the throat. The man collapsed, gasping for air.

Marina took on the first attacker and flipped him over her shoulder onto his back. As she drew one of her daggers, the merc kicked her legs out from under her and she fell on top of him. Marina lost her dagger and wrestled with her attacker. The two punched and clawed at each other as they rolled across the floor. Marina's mouth and nose bled from a series of punches to her face and her left eye swelled. In a desperate move, she spun off of the man and kicked him in the mouth.

Rebecca used a leg sweep and floored her attacker. She fled up the stairs but the man hustled to his feet and chased after her.

Britt traded punches until his assailant reeled and fell to the ground. As the wounded man raised his head, Britt delivered a powerful blow to the side of his head and injured him badly. He hurried to Marina's aid and yanked her attacker off of her. The man's face was bloody with jagged gashes from Marina's finger nails.

The two men fought while Marina staggered across the floor. She picked up a pulse pistol and targeted Britt's opponent. The two men were locked together in a tight grip.

Marina tapped the man on the shoulder. "Hey, asshole," she called. When he turned to her, she shoved the barrel of the pistol in his mouth. The man's eyes widened with fear as Britt ducked his head out of the way. Marina pulled the trigger and blew a hole out the back of his head. Brain matter and blood covered the wall behind him.

Britt dropped the dead man and vented at Marina. "What the hell was that all about?"

"He's dead. Is there a problem?"

"Yeah, that was damn close to my face!"

Marina kissed his cheek and teased, "Your face looks just fine."

Britt cussed and fell to his knees, fatigued from the fighting.

***

Rebecca hurried onto the flight deck and slammed the door shut. When she yanked down on the handle to latch the door, she felt a brief pang in her womb and placed her hand on her belly with concern. It gave her renewed strength to survive for the sake of her child. The man rammed his shoulder into the locked door repeatedly.

Rebecca frantically searched for a weapon. The loud hum from a panel at the rear of the cabin caught her attention. There were four cables plugged into it on either side. One cable was marked 'high voltage.' She yanked it from the panel but was thrown backward against the pilot's seat from the force of the arc flash. The arc flared from the jack at the end of the cable and dissipated. The panel became quiet and several of the ship's systems shut down.

When the door jamb shattered, the door flew open and the merc lunged at her. When Rebecca dodged him, he landed on the pilot's seat. She stabbed him in the back with the cable jack as he tried to stand. The man quivered for several seconds until he collapsed on the floor and died.

Rebecca breathed a sigh of relief and pulled the cable jack out of his back. She carefully wiped the blood on his clothes and pushed the jack quickly into its port to prevent another flash.

The panel lights illuminated and a low hum returned. The systems booted up, one by one. Rebecca stepped over the smoldering body and left the flight deck.

Four more of Fiona's men emerged from the ship's engine room. Marina and Britt looked dejectedly at each other.

"Here we go again," she complained and grabbed the lid off of a wooden crate. Her first attacker charged at her but she swung the lid and struck him in the temple and eye. The man crumpled to the ground dead. Yellow fluid seeped from his damaged eye.

The second assailant rammed his shoulder into her knees and leveled her. He punched her in the face but she shoved her thumb in his eye. The man screamed and covered his injured eye. Marina retrieved one of her daggers from her thigh belt and slit his throat.

The other two mercenaries beat Britt to the ground and kicked at his ribs. Marina grabbed her attacker's pistol and fired at Britt's foes, killing one and badly wounding the other. Britt slumped to the ground motionless.

Marina dropped the pistol and crawled on her knees to Britt. The wounded man was determined to finish her and staggered toward her with one of her own daggers in his possession.

Marina saw him and crawled desperately out of the cargo bay. She entered one corridor and leaned against the walls for support. The wounded man lumbered after her. Both were bloody and battered, barely coherent.

Britt lay on the floor exhausted and badly hurt. The hiss of the pistons startled him. He crawled behind one of the containers and watched anxiously.

The hatch opened and Fiona boarded. As soon as the hatch closed, she turned off the power to it. From the middle of the bay, she listened carefully. There was only the hum of the ship's systems and the increased whirring of the engines starting. Britt searched frantically for a weapon but his pistol lay near the hatch.

A metallic clanking at the hatch caught Fiona's attention. Outside, Victor's men beat on the hatch with pipe wrenches and hammers. Four of the men focused their pulse pistols on the hatch seals and fired. The seals glowed red but held firm.

Fiona stared at her dead mercenaries on the floor and bit her lip in anguish. She climbed the stairs to the passenger deck with her pulse pistol ready to fire.

Crow and Fingers arrived with pulse rifles and pushed aside their men. They focused on the seals and fired at maximum power.

Crow screamed at the men, "Fiona must not escape, no matter what! That's an order!"

***

Marina fell to her knees in front of the break room and looked back. The merc was hurting as badly as she was but he was determined to kill her. He grinned sadistically with blood dripping from his mouth and raised the dagger to strike her. She kicked desperately at his legs and knocked him to the floor. Above her was a panel labeled 'Data Processing Control System.'

The man struggled to his feet and charged at her. Marina swung the door open and rammed her shoulder into his gut. She spun him around and shoved him at the panel door where he struck his head on the door's corner. She delivered a desperation kick to his back and floored him. Blood streamed from a wide gash in his head and mouth. His breathing ceased and he lay motionless. Marina staggered to the panel door and stared down at the merc. Overcome with fatigue, her hands slipped off the panel door and she fell to the floor next to the dead merc.

Rebecca hurried down the stairs at the end of the corridor and knelt by Marina. She raised her into a sitting position. "Marina, speak to me!"

Marina opened her eyes and forced a smile.

Rebecca was relieved. "I thought you were dead!"

"I'm fine," she uttered weakly.

"Victor's men are at the hatch! We have to get away from here now!"

Rebecca helped her to her feet. Marina grabbed the panel door for support and glanced inside. Her backpack with the crystal was inside the panel. "Son of a bitch!" she declared with a smile.

Rebecca peered inside and took out the backpack. She smiled at Marina and remarked, "Cristos came through for me."

"He came through for us," Marina corrected. "Fiona's going to pay for what she did to him."

Rebecca leaned against Marina and sobbed, "He was all I had."

"I can't imagine your pain," Marina said to her compassionately. "I never had anyone like that in my life before."

"Perhaps you do and you don't even know it."

Marina smiled at her. "Maybe I have more than one person like that and never realized it."

Rebecca was pleased by her comment. She looked relieved as she returned the backpack inside the panel.

Marina looked back in the direction of the cargo bay with concern. "I'd better see if Britt is okay." She hurried down the corridor, weakened from the fight and her wounds.

When the *Neutrino's* engines reached operating temperature, the ship immediately pulled away from the dock. A loud whooshing sound filled the air as the outer bay door opened. The soldiers fled the bay and closed the hatch behind them.

Victor and Jeffries exited the elevator and heard the commotion. "What in hell is going on?" Victor shouted.

Fingers slinked toward the rear of the group and hid.

One of the men answered, "We attempted to board their ship but they escaped before we could breach the hatch."

Victor glared at Jeffries. "How could they leave the station?"

Jeffries thought for a moment and replied, "Fiona must be working with them. One of her mercs must have accessed the Transport Tower. That's the only way those bay doors open and the ship is released for flight."

Victor searched the group and spotted Crow. "Was Fiona on that ship?" he inquired.

"I believe so, sir," he replied humbly. "We will hunt her down and finish this, I assure you."

Victor fought to contain his anger and paced uneasily. "I'm disappointed in you Crow."

"I swear, I will terminate Fiona personally," he promised nervously.

Victor patted Crow on the shoulder. "I don't think you will." He drew his pulse pistol and fired a shot into Crow's forehead.

Crow fell to his knees briefly with a blank expression on his face and a smoking hole through his head. Then, as if in slow motion, his corpse fell to the floor. The soldiers were stunned and silent.

Victor stowed the pistol in his hip holster and turned to the group. "I will not tolerate any more excuses. Is that understood?"

The soldiers replied in unison, "Yes, sir!" They scrambled down the corridor to another bay, where they boarded their ship.

Jeffries spoke with two of his men and returned to Victor. "Surveillance cameras indicate that two females and a male boarded the ship just recently."

"Thank you for your assistance, Jeffries," Victor replied coldly, wondering if he was played for a fool.

"Oh, and a female wearing a cloak boarded that same ship a half hour ago with twelve men," Jeffries added. "I suspect some of the men arrived here on another ship. My men are already rounding up suspects. "

Victor scowled and left the bay.

***

On the flight deck of the *Orion*, Victor barged in behind the two pilots: One, Tibbs, a young officer, and the other, Anton, a seasoned veteran officer. "How long before we catch up to them?" he asked anxiously.

"They're headed toward the Kronus asteroid belt," replied Tibbs. "That could complicate things and slow us down."

Victor punched Tibbs in the back of the head and stunned him. His head bounced off the control console and jarred the ship briefly. "I don't want excuses!" he shouted. "Now, how long before we catch up to them?"

Anton, replied, "Six hours, sir. We'll target the most likely entry point of the asteroid belt and cut them off."

Victor glared at Tibbs and complimented Anton, "Much better. Now get us out of here before I take it out of your carcasses!" He stormed out of the cabin.

Anton shoved Tibbs. "What the hell's wrong with you?"

"I answered his question, didn't I?"

"Never express doubt or vagueness. He'll kill you and probably me, too."

"Alright, I get it," Tibbs responded, red with embarrassment.

Victor entered the passenger compartment and scanned his men from behind. There were twenty soldiers on board. When he spotted Fingers in the last row, he approached and knelt down in the aisle next to him. Fingers fidgeted and looked ahead nervously.

"Well, Fingers, you haven't exactly done yourself proud, have you?" he remarked.

The soldier next to him excused himself and left.

"No, sir. What do you require of me?"

Victor thought for a moment and inquired, "Do we know where Fiona is?"

"No, sir. We haven't seen any sign of her in some time."

Victor sighed and stood up. He brandished a dagger from his belt and ran his finger delicately across the blade. "Are you sure of that?" he asked sternly.

Fingers wouldn't look up but grew increasingly uneasy. The other soldiers were tense as well and the cabin became eerily quiet.

"I think so, sir," he stammered.

Victor's face tensed as his anger built up in him. "That's not good enough, Fingers," he responded. "You see, she was on Orpheus-2 and is likely on the *Neutrino* right now."

"But, sir," blurted Fingers as Victor rammed the dagger into the base of his neck and twisted it viciously. Finger's eyes rolled up and his head drooped limply as he died.

Victor paced slowly up the aisle, looking over his men. "For all you morons who still don't get it, Fiona must die," he announced loudly.

"Sir, yes, sir," they replied in unison.

"I want my crystal and the Princess returned to me, both unharmed," he continued. "I don't care if the rebel leader lives or dies. Any questions?"

"No sir!" they replied in unison.

"Am I clear about my expectations?"

"Yes, sir!"

"Good," he remarked calmly. "Then we'll have no more misunderstandings."

"No, sir!" they replied, again in unison.

Victor marched to the rear of the cabin and departed. The soldiers glanced uneasily at each other in eerie silence.

***

Marina returned to the cabin and winced from the odor. The burnt corpse smoldered behind them on the floor. She set the controls for 'auto-pilot' and stood, looking concerned.

Rebecca flipped several switches and the monitor displayed 'scan' mode. "Is Britt okay?" she asked.

"I didn't find him yet." She stared at the corpse for a moment and complained, "I've got to get rid of Stinky. I think I'm gonna' hurl from the smell."

"I'd appreciate that very much. It's affecting my concentration," Rebecca remarked cynically and then focused on the controls while Marina dragged the corpse out of the pilots' cabin.

Marina was anxious to find Britt and realized she might actually care for him. She teetered as she dragged the corpse down the stairs to the cargo bay. As much as she wanted to lie down and rest, rotting corpses tended to spread disease quickly on a small ship like the *Neutrino*.

Across from the hatch was the control panel for the 'refuse incinerator' with a red, a green and a yellow knob on it. Near the back wall was a large plate positioned on the floor. Marina pressed the yellow knob and hydraulic pistons raised the steel plate, revealing a large pit underneath. One by one, she disarmed both the corpses and the wounded, shoving them mercilessly into the pit.

Marina pressed the green knob and the plate slowly closed. The red knob flashed repeatedly as the incinerator activated. She searched about the cargo bay for Britt but there was no sign of him.

Dejectedly and fatigued, Marina collapsed against the wall. She failed to notice the missing vent cover above her and the wire noose that descended from the opening toward her.

Rebecca's voice called from the intercom, asking for Marina to contact her. Marina ignored her.

The incinerator grew quiet as the green knob blinked three times and went dim. Marina stared at the streaks of smeared blood near the corner of the bay by the door marked 'Flammable Stores Compartment.' She wondered if Britt was in there and if he was okay.

Fiona patiently dangled the wire noose just over Marina's head. As Marina pushed away from the wall to search for Britt, Fiona snared her by the neck and yanked. Marina barely slid her bandaged hand under the wire in front of her throat but struggled to breathe.

Fiona pulled upward with all her strength until Marina's feet left the ground. She wore a fiendish expression as she savored Marina's desperation.

Marina reached frantically for one of her daggers in her thigh belt. Her fingers danced across the belt, just shy of the daggers.

"It's time for you to die, Marina," taunted Fiona. "There's no one to help you now."

Rebecca entered the cargo bay at the top of the steps and was horrified. "Marina!" she cried out.

Fiona was distracted briefly as Marina brought her knee up and gripped one of the daggers from the sheath on her thigh. She turned and pushed away from the wall. Before Fiona could react, Marina reached up and shoved her dagger into her eye socket with what little strength she had left. Fiona let loose an ear-piercing scream.

"That should do wonders for your looks," Marina uttered, barely audible.

Fiona finally released her hold on the wire. Marina fell to the floor and goaded hoarsely, "Can't see being here, Fiona?"

"You bitch!" wailed Fiona and she retreated from the vent opening.

Rebecca drew her pulse pistol and descended the stairs. The noises from motion in the ducts faded, signaling Fiona's escape.

Marina gasped while struggling to remove the wire noose.

"Damn, Marina!" Rebecca exclaimed and helped remove the wire from around Marina's neck. "You could have been killed!"

"No shit!" Marina groaned and rolled onto her stomach. She slowly pulled herself to her knees and regained her breath. "Thanks for coming down," she said humbly. "That was the break I needed."

Rebecca helped her to her feet and hugged her. "I thought you were ignoring me down here," she said jokingly. "I came ready to rip your tail."

Marina forced a smile and rubbed her neck gingerly. "Maybe I was ignoring you," she kidded weakly.

Rebecca grinned briefly, and then turned serious. "I know where we can enter the asteroid belt."

"Will we lose Victor's ships in there?" Marina asked.

"At least for a little while. I think we can hide out in one of the larger asteroids."

Marina slumped to the floor and leaned against the wall. Rebecca was concerned about her. "Are you gonna' be okay?"

"I will be once we get that witch," she assured her. "I have to find Britt first. Stay on the flight deck and lock the door."

Rebecca left the cargo bay and fretted over Marina's condition. Despite Marina's uncanny knack for survival, Rebecca feared losing her on her watch and what the consequences of Marina's death would be for her people, who would then be forever without their one hope.

Marina crawled to the door for the 'Flammable Stores Compartment' and pulled herself to her feet. "God, I'm getting too old for this," she complained.

The handle turned, the sudden motion startling her. Before she could react, the door swung open and knocked her over.

Britt staggered through the doorway and was surprised to see her on the floor. "Are you all right?" he asked with a note of concern in his voice.

"You friggin' oaf!" she screamed. "I thought you were dead!" Tears streamed down her cheeks and she laid her arms out flat on the floor dejectedly.

"I'm sorry, Marina," he said apologetically.

"What the hell were you doing in there?" she asked angrily, while still on her back on the floor.

"The mercs rigged explosives to blow up the ship. I disabled them."

Marina stared at him and cracked a faint smile. "Maybe you're not so bad after all, Britt. I'm impressed."

Britt lay on his back next to her on the floor. Neither was anxious to leave the cargo bay. "What the hell happened to your neck?" he asked when he saw the ring of deep red welt.

"I was hanging out with Fiona."

"She got away?"

"Yeah, but I gave her something to remember me by."

Britt rolled his eyes and knew better than to ask what that meant. "Why don't we get you cleaned up?" he suggested. You're a bloody mess."

Marina touched his cheek gently and smiled. She recalled her talk with Rebecca earlier and realized how she cared for both of them.

As they staggered out of the cargo bay, Britt kept his arm around Marina's waist and supported her. When they passed through the corridor to the locker room, Marina removed her wig while watching Britt with a keen eye.

Britt secured both doors accessing the locker room and inspected the vents as well. He avoided making contact with Marina while she disrobed.

Marina was amused by his shyness as she tossed each of the belts from her thighs onto a bench. "What's wrong?" she asked coyly.

Britt went to the shower and turned on the hot water. He sat down in front of eight lockers along the wall. *"She is the Princess and I'm just a militia officer. The two just don't mix,"* he reminded himself.

"Not talking, are we?" Marina taunted as she removed her leather pants.

"It's not my place to see the Princess disrobed," he responded humbly.

"What a pity," Marina remarked and stepped into the shower stall. The stall had four shower heads in an area with eight feet on a side. Three walls were metallic and the fourth was a door of hinged Plexiglas. She savored the feeling of hot water on her aching body. The bandage on her hand fell to the floor and she flexed it delicately. Soon, the glass was fogged from the steam.

Britt considered what options were left to them. His own forces, now led by Victor, were hunting them. Fiona was on board and a threat to all of them. They were on the outskirts of the Kronus asteroid belt, a relatively unknown region of the star system. With Severin's death, he wasn't sure if they could trust the space station's forces or the Space Fleet to help them.

Frustrated over the circumstances, he searched several lockers until he found one with female attire. He held up a red bra and panties to determine if they'd fit Marina. *"Maybe a little skimpy,"* he thought but took them anyway.

Marina stepped out of the shower and toweled off. She approached Britt in the locker room. He refused to look at her. She dropped the towel to the floor and folded her arms. "Are we gonna' keep playing this game?" she questioned him angrily, while standing nude in front of him.

Britt tossed the underclothes to her and looked away. "I have an obligation to you, Marina," he stated firmly. "I'm going to honor that obligation."

Marina was amused by the bra and panties. "You like to dress me, huh? That's kinky."

"Come on, Marina," he complained. "Fiona's still loose and we're stuck in no man's land out here."

Marina broke into laughter.

Britt was confused by her reaction. "What's so funny?"

Marina stood in front of him and answered coyly, "I'll take care of Fiona. We'll find a place to hide out and then you're gonna' make love to me. That's an order from your Princess."

"And if I don't?"

"Then I'll cut your balls off for treason," Marina threatened with a stone-faced stare while putting on the panties.

Britt grew frustrated and left the locker room. Marina smiled and dressed in her black, leather attire. She enjoyed frustrating him and it took the edge off, something she sorely needed.

Britt paced in the hall as he considered his feelings for Marina. There was something about her that attracted him but she drove him crazy. He felt the need to say something about it to her but he was at a loss for words.

Marina stepped out of the locker room as she positioned her wig with the dreadlocks on her head.

"Why the wig?" inquired Britt.

"Because it's a weapon that I frequently use," answered Marina. "I'll search the cargo bay and you take the rest of the ship. If you find Fiona, send her my way."

"Why don't I just kill her and get it over with?" suggested Britt.

Marina shoved him against the hull and chided, "If you and I are going to have any kind of relationship, you'd better stop questioning me every time I say something or else..."

"I know," Britt grumbled, "you'll cut my balls off." He sighed and walked away in obvious pain.

***

Rebecca operated the controls and piloted the ship into the asteroid belt. "Can I fly the ship?" she mimicked Marina and then continued her side of the debate. "You aren't the only one with special skills and training." She maneuvered the ship between two large asteroids and landed smoothly inside a dark crater on a third.

The sound of the engines faded and only the hum of the panels was heard. Rebecca extended her seat into the reclined position and thought about a village far away where she could have lived with Cristos and her child. A tear formed in her eye as she realized her dream of a perfect family was over.

***

Victor paced back and forth behind his pilots on board the *Orion*. "Are we closing on them yet?" he inquired anxiously.

"Sir, I think we lost them," replied Tibbs.

Victor fumed and made two fists. Anton immediately interjected, "We haven't lost them, sir. The asteroids are providing interference and limiting our contact. All we have to do is project the most logical course through the belt and follow it."

Victor nodded appreciatively to Anton and ordered Tibbs to stand up.

Tibbs glanced at Anton nervously and stood. Victor exercised all his will power, restraining himself from killing the young pilot. "How long have you been a pilot on my ship?" he asked.

"Over a year, sir," Tibbs replied timidly.

"Would you like to live to see another year, you friggin' moron?" Victor threatened and threw him against the cabin wall. He pummeled Tibbs with a series of punches until his face swelled and blood covered the front of his uniform. Victor retrieved a dagger from his belt and held it against Tibb's throat until a thin line of blood formed.

"Answer the question," Victor ordered him.

Tibbs fought back his tears and trembled. "Yes, sir," he replied shakily. "I do want to live to see…"

Victor grabbed him by his blood-covered chin and warned him, "Don't piss me off again or I won't be so merciful." He released his hold on him and stormed off the flight deck.

"You haven't learned, have you?" chided Anton.

Tibbs crawled to his knees and pulled himself into his seat. "Next time you answer him," he replied feebly.

"There won't be a next time or I'll kill you myself!" exclaimed Anton. "Now, get us through this forsaken field and find them."

Chapter 9

Sweet Revenge

Marina entered the cargo bay and sat on a crate. As she sharpened one of her daggers, she wondered how much more punishment that they could sustain. The welts and cuts from Fiona's noose were still evident on her neck. Her face was badly bruised and her lower lip was swollen.

Britt, she suspected, had more serious injuries and refused to reveal how badly he was really hurt. Rebecca was exposed to minimal fighting and, because she was pregnant, it was better that way. She had a knack for showing up at just the right time in a fight, though, which made her a valuable asset.

Marina wondered where her relationship with Britt would go and where they would end up after they defeated Fiona and Victor. She had feelings for Britt but she wasn't ready to call it love. Perhaps it was only a relationship of convenience.

As if on cue, Fiona stepped into the cargo bay. She dragged her metal-tipped nails along the hull and caught Marina's attention. The screeching sound from her nails was bone-chilling.

Marina pretended to ignore her and swapped to another dagger. Fiona stepped into the middle of the bay and glared at Marina through her one good eye. The other was a puss-filled, swollen wound. Along with her burnt face, Fiona resembled more of a demon than a woman. She dropped her cloak to the ground and revealed her tight black, leather pants and black sports bra. Marina couldn't help but notice that Fiona's body was one to die for, no pun intended. Under different circumstances, they might have been friends but fate is what it is. *"There is that word again,"* she thought, *"fate."*

Rebecca entered the cargo bay at the top of the stairwell. Marina and Fiona were oblivious to her presence.

"Something you want to say?" inquired Marina in a disinterested tone.

Fiona thought for a brief moment then responded angrily, "I had it all until you showed up!"

"You only thought you did," Marina contradicted her. "How could you be so vulnerable to him?"

"We were in love and I was to be his queen. Thanks to you, I have nothing!" she screamed. "Look at me!"

Marina remarked sarcastically, "I try not to. You are quite repulsive."

"Why did you come back if you didn't want to rule?"

"I was a courier doing my job," she explained. "It was your 'Romeo' who dragged me into this."

"Then I will drag you out!" Fiona drew two daggers from her belt and stood ready to attack.

Marina stowed her whetstone. She drew a second dagger and prepared to fight.

"Wait!" shouted Rebecca. "This is my fight." She stepped down the stairs confidently with her eyes riveted to Fiona and drew one dagger.

"And you must be Red," presumed Fiona. "I've waited a long time for this moment."

"As have I."

"And now you finally show your face No hiding in the trees or behind your cloak from a distance."

"Let's get this over with. You disgust me, you ugly whore."

Marina stowed her daggers. "Have at it, ladies," she declared and sat back on the crate.

Fiona rushed at Rebecca with a dagger in each hand. Rebecca grabbed her wrist with one hand and blocked Fiona's thrust with her own dagger. The two women wrestled and slammed each other against the hull and into crates repeatedly.

When they locked tightly against each other, Fiona leaned toward Rebecca's ear and whispered, "It was so sweet killing your lover. He was so ... helpless," she taunted, "as he clutched at his entrails. While I held him, I thought of all the pain I just inflicted on you and felt so good, I didn't want to let him go."

Rebecca's face grew red. "Not nearly as much as I'll inflict on you!" she cried and head-butted Fiona. Once Fiona backed away, Rebecca grabbed her by the hair and delivered three knee kicks to her stomach.

Fiona staggered back, stunned from the blows. Rebecca charged at her and grabbed her wrists and continued to knee Fiona in the stomach repeatedly.

Fiona head-butted Rebecca and briefly stemmed her attack. She drew a second wind and charged with her daggers at Rebecca.

Rebecca kicked one dagger away and grabbed the other. She twisted violently until Fiona's wrist snapped, the bay filled with her screams of agony. She dropped the dagger and lunged with the other. Rebecca blocked it with her dagger and, in one fluid motion, slit Fiona's throat. Fiona stared at her in disbelief and clutched her throat desperately.

"That's for all of my people you tortured and killed," Rebecca declared. "And this is for Cristos." She slit open Fiona's abdomen while brushing her fingers across her cheek in mock affection.

"Would you like to do the honors, your Highness?" Rebecca asked Marina.

"Why thank you," Marina replied. "How thoughtful."

Fiona fell to her knees and looked pleadingly at Marina, blood streaming from her neck and her entrails falling from her abdomen.

Marina stood and approached her, straight-faced and calm. "You know, Fiona, I never liked your skanky ass," she taunted and delivered a powerful kick to the side of Fiona's head. A loud snap ensued and her head cocked at an awkward angle. Her eyes bore a puzzled expression and her head tumbled to the floor. Fiona's body was frozen for several seconds as blood spurted from the top of the torso in rhythm with her fading heartbeat. Blood spattered across Marina's face and chest, staining her black bodice. Under the circumstances, she didn't mind.

Rebecca glanced at Marina with a satisfied smile. They watched as the headless body fell forward and the blood slowed to a trickle, pooling on the floor.

Marina opened one of the lockers and removed a plastic box. She took Fiona's dismembered head and set it inside the box.

Rebecca grew curious and inquired, "A souvenir?"

"Let's just say it's a present for Victor."

Rebecca stared at the headless corpse with a perplexed expression. Marina noticed and asked, "Feel better now?"

"You know, I do feel better. It won't bring Cristos back, but it does feel good to see that smug bitch die like this."

"So you and I are alike," kidded Marina.

"But I'll never be you."

Marina was surprised and realized she was referring to her true identity as the princess. Rebecca did all the things Marina should have done but she can never be the princess. *"Did she ever want to be?"* pondered Marina.

Rebecca opened the incinerator pit and shoved Fiona's messy corpse into it. She started the incinerator and walked to the steps. "Coming?" she asked Marina.

Marina set the box with Fiona's head on top of the crate and activated the controls for 'auto-wash.' "Yeah, let's get out of here." She followed Rebecca up the steps and back to the flight deck.

The 'auto-wash' function sprayed a mist of cleaning agent from pores in the walls and floor. Next, the bay was saturated with steam for thirty seconds and then vacuum jets along the base of the walls sucked the moisture out of the bay into a holding tank. The cleaning agent dissipated on the walls and floor into the steam and vanished into the vacuum ports. The bay was cleaned and sanitized, leaving no chance for disease or infection.

Marina paused in the corridor and asked, "Have you seen Britt?"

Rebecca looked back and replied uneasily, "No, I haven't."

"I'll meet you up front later. I've got to find him."

Rebecca continued down the corridor to the flight deck and Marina searched the rest of the ship.

Britt lay face down in the break room. Marina rushed to him and sat him up. "Britt, talk to me!" she pleaded. He still breathed but didn't respond. She dragged him into one of the crew's quarters and set him on a cot. Frantically, she searched for a first-aid kit but found none.

An image of Kat appeared in her mind and distracted her. Marina tried to clear her head but the image would not cease. "I can help you," Kat's voice reminded her. "There are many who love and care for you." The image of Marina nestled in Kat's arms created a soothing effect on her as if she was hypnotized and she rested.

Britt came to and found Marina asleep with her head on his chest. His face was ashen and he was weak. He stroked Marina's cheek affectionately and she stirred. "Are you okay?" he asked.

"Yeah," replied Marina. "Just a little bloody."

"And Fiona?"

Marina pondered and then answered, "Rebecca fought her."

"And..."

"Fiona fought well but she fought with emotion. That was her undoing."

"And what about you? Isn't that how you fight?"

"I fight with a purpose, no emotion whatsoever."

Britt laughed at her and quipped, "You remind me of my wife."

Marina was shocked by his remark. "You're married?" she asked with a surprised expression on her face.

"Once, I was," he replied somberly. "My wife and three children were killed by terrorists."

"Did they pay?"

"I blew up a reactor on Serma-5. It killed over three hundred colonists and the terrorists."

"Did you feel vindicated?"

Britt looked down at the floor sadly and replied, "It haunts me every day of my life. It's also my motivation to make things right with you being a big part of that, just like my wife."

"Me?"

"My wife always wanted to make a difference. She started a school on the colony for orphans. Terrorists tried to recruit those kids. She and the other teachers defended the kids bravely, but their weapons were no match for their assailants."

"I'm sorry for bringing it up." She hugged him tightly and backed away to avoid further discussion of the topic.

"Why don't we get you cleaned up," he suggested.

"You need to rest," she directed him. "What happened to you?"

"I, uh... I don't know."

"Don't lie to me, Britt. Are you all right?"

Britt sat up and held his ribs gingerly. "I'll live. Let's take a walk."

Marina eyed him and wondered what was on his mind. They stopped a short distance down the corridor and Britt faced her. "Fiona and her mercs were only on board the ship for one thing."

"No shit! How'd you figure that out?"

"They planted explosives in the engine room, the Flammable Stores Compartment and the passenger deck. When I showed up with the soldiers, they were trapped inside. The fire fight was for them to try and escape."

"But how did they know that we'd use this ship?"

"Someone in Severin's group is a spy for Fiona," Britt replied sullenly. "When she realized that her mercs were discovered, she couldn't risk that the explosives would be found and we'd escape."

"I like you more and more, Captain." Marina grinned coyly and led him to the locker room. She anxiously shed her leather attire and entered the shower stall. The hot running water soon steamed up the shower stall and locker room entrance. She enjoyed the feel of hot water as her body tingled. As she rubbed soap over her body, she craved the feel of Britt against her. This time he wasn't going to get off so easy.

In the locker room, Britt stripped down and contemplated how to handle Marina. She was a princess whether or not she accepted the role. He was just a soldier in a militia, a glorified mercenary.

When the sound of running water stopped, he wrapped a towel around his waist and went into the shower area.

Marina stepped out of the stall and stood in front of him. She was shocked by the bruises on his rib cage and thighs. He moved aside and looked away modestly.

"I don't think so, Britt," she remarked and yanked the towel off of him. She took his hand and pulled him back into the shower.

Britt turned the water on again and felt a renewed sense of being. Marina held him from behind with her hands on his chest.

"This is awkward for me," he said humbly.

"Get over it," she said sternly and turned him toward her. They kissed slowly at first, then ravenously as they slid to the floor in each other's arms.

Britt reached up and turned off the water. "I can't do this, Marina? It's not right," he confessed.

Marina slapped his face and glared at him. She pressed him flat against the floor and straddled him. "I'll make a man out of you yet!"

Britt was embarrassed and tired of fighting her. "Then do what you must," he replied.

Once Marina slid onto him and became aroused, she moved in a rhythmic motion on top of him, savoring the feel of her first sexual encounter. Finally, Britt abandoned his principles and rolled on top of her and made love to her.

When they finished, Marina teased, "Was that so hard?"

Britt grinned and stood up. He helped Marina to her feet and opened the shower door. Marina grabbed his hand and commented, "There's room for improvement, you know."

Britt chuckled and pulled her out of the shower. He pressed her against one of the lockers and kissed her hungrily. Marina crooned as he kissed her neck down to her waist.

"That's more like it," Marina quipped and lay across the bench. Britt buried his head between her legs until she screamed with pleasure.

Later, Marina sat alone in the locker room and thought about how fast her life was changing. Already she was so far from the life of solitude that she lived when working for Dix as a courier. *Will I ever be able to go back to that?* she pondered. *With all that happened recently, I'll never be able to operate discretely. Too many people know who I am.*

Britt entered and interrupted her thoughts. She smiled and took his hand. "Was I your first?" he asked curiously.

Marina blushed and looked away. "Why would you ask that?" she countered uneasily.

Britt sat next to her and placed his arm around her. "I just wondered if I shouldn't have done that," he continued. "You are my Princess and one day, you'll be my Queen."

"Stop making excuses! We both wanted it and it was good."

"Just good?" he queried.

"It was fine. Are you having second thoughts?"

Britt wasn't sure how to respond and hesitated. "I'm developing feelings for you that I don't want," he finally admitted.

"Get over it!"

"But your Highness, I..." he paused, then asked nervously. "How do you feel about this?"

Marina stood up in front of him and gripped his shoulders. "I feel pretty damn good!" She was annoyed with his petty concerns about royalty and protocol. "You risked your life for me and I trust you. That's a big friggin' deal in my life. I made love to you because I wanted to. Does that answer your question?"

Britt was taken aback by her lack of sensitivity. "It's just that ... What happens now?" he asked apprehensively.

"There can be more between us or you can get the hell out now. Don't waste my time." Marina turned and walked away from him.

Britt thought about her words – 'there can be more.' He smiled and followed her out of the locker room.

Marina expressed her concern over Britt's bruises. They were deep purple in several areas of his chest and abdomen. His ashen appearance also worried her. Britt felt confident the bruises would heal in time. He did relent to resting and light duty for the duration of the trip.

Marina returned to the flight deck and met with Rebecca. "How are things?" she inquired.

"So far, so good." Rebecca noticed the concern on Marina's face. "What's wrong?"

"It's Britt. I think his injuries are more severe than they appear."

After a brief discussion about what she saw on Britt's body, Rebecca untied Marina's bodice.

Shocked and embarrassed, Marina asked, "What are you doing?"

"Just checking something. Relax."

Marina wasn't sure what to expect and grew uncomfortable as Rebecca opened her bodice. Marina had several deep bruises on her ribs and abdomen. She covered her breasts with her hands and looked away sheepishly.

"Marina, did Britt's bruises look like these?"

Marina was embarrassed but realized what Rebecca's intentions were. She looked down at her bruises and realized she was in the same predicament as Britt. "Yeah, I guess they did," she replied uneasily.

"We need to get help for the both of you! It's likely internal bleeding."

"I'm fine, really," insisted Marina.

Rebecca noted that she looked much paler than before and considered where they could possibly get medical attention.

"We can lose Victor in the asteroid belt and then return to Orpheus-2," suggested Rebecca.

"No, we'd never make it that far."

"Then where do we go?"

"Magnus," Marina reluctantly decided and tied up her bodice again.

Rebecca was stunned by her decision. "Magnus! Are you kidding?"

"Why? You know something I don't?" queried Marina.

"How about I ask you the same question?" replied Rebecca. "Magnus is not a good place to be."

"I have friends there and I'm sure they'll be happy to help us," Marina lied and cringed at the thought of returning.

Rebecca frowned but reluctantly agreed. Marina grew curious and wanted to know more about Rebecca's knowledge of the station. At first, Rebecca resisted, but Marina's persistence wore her down.

"Magnus is ruled by a woman of magic," Rebecca explained. "Many of my fighters came to Yord, thanks to her influence."

Marina was surprised by her revelation. "So they didn't volunteer to fight for you?"

'They did," answered Rebecca. "Supposedly, the woman prepared them to fight. She gave them courage and determination."

"Have you ever met this woman, Rebecca?"

"No. There was a middle man who handled the arrangements." Rebecca noticed Marina's puzzled expression. "No one's ever met this woman that I know of."

Marina became nervous and looked away. Rebecca suddenly realized that Marina had met her. She waited eagerly for an explanation.

Marina was embarrassed as she recalled her encounter with Kat. "Yeah, I met Kat. Are you happy?"

"And?" Rebecca pressed her and grew more anxious for details.

"And I have some clout with her. Just don't let her kiss you."

"That's it?" asked Rebecca. She was perplexed by Marina's response and wondered what she meant.

"Yeah, that's all you need to know."

Marina became faint and fell out of the co-pilot's seat. Rebecca lifted her and took her to the crewman's quarters where Britt lay. She set Marina down on another cot in the room and noticed that Britt's color worsened. She shook Britt repeatedly but he didn't respond. Then she shook Marina but she didn't respond either. "Damn!" she cried and rushed back to the flight deck. She weaved through the outskirts of the asteroid belt and then set a course for Magnus.

Rebecca searched and found a first aid kit with four adrenalin syringes. She cringed at the sight of them but knew what she had to do.

Britt and Marina both breathed irregularly and trembled. They sweated profusely as fever took over.

Rebecca returned and injected each with a dose of adrenalin. She watched over them for an hour but noticed no improvement. Reluctantly, she gave each of them a second injection and watched anxiously. If this didn't work, then it was a race with time to get her to Magnus. Even then, there was no way of knowing if Kat could help them.

After another hour, their breathing stabilized and the fever came down a bit but they were still unresponsive. Rebecca returned to the flight deck and piloted the ship. She set the auto-pilot system and fell asleep.

The 'auto-pilot' alarmed twice and woke Rebecca. The transmitter beeped and startled her. She was asleep for three days and they were now in range of Magnus.

Rebecca acknowledged the transmitter and a voice requested, "Identify yourself and the reason for your presence."

"I need to speak with Kat," replied Rebecca. "I have two very sick people who need help."

"This isn't a medical facility," replied the speaker.

"Tell her that Marina needs her help. She'll know what to do."

There was a moment of silence and then she was ordered to stand by. After what seemed an eternity, the speaker replied, "Shut down your engines and we'll bring you in."

"Thank you," Rebecca replied.

When the ship was docked and secured, ten armed men waited at the hatch.

Rebecca opened the hatch and allowed them aboard. She led them to the crewman's quarters and stepped aside. The men carried both Marina and Britt off the ship and down the corridor. One of them instructed her to stay for her own safety.

Rebecca reluctantly returned to the ship and sat alone in the cargo bay. Tears streamed down her cheek as she fretted for Marina and Britt's health.

A voice startled her from the corner and Kat appeared. "Welcome to Magnus, Rebecca. It's about time we met."

Rebecca was stunned. "You must be the mysterious Kat."

"I am."

Rebecca stood and shook her hand. "I owe you so much for your support of my people. We could not have lasted this long without it."

Kat touched her cheek and smiled. "You have performed your assignment well. We weren't sure if you could handle it."

"What assignment?" asked Rebecca, feeling confused by her remark.

"Your meeting with Marina ten years ago was no accident. You needed her and she needed you."

Rebecca was perplexed and listened patiently as Kat continued.

"The old alliance was a benefit to all of us. What happened to Marina's parents' was beyond criminal. They sacrificed so much."

"As did my parents," added Rebecca.

"And as you have, too. Marina will soon be ready to assume the throne and she will need all our support to restore the alliance."

"How do you know all this?"

Kat placed her hand behind Rebecca's head and kissed her firmly but passionately. Rebecca saw images racing quickly through her head of her parents, Marina's parents and many other events in the day. Rebecca saw her parents remove her and her sister Sara from the rubble at a young age from their dead mother's arms. She was more amazed to see a young boy kill their parents on a strange ship. Kat pulled away and Rebecca was jarred back to reality. "What the hell was that?" asked Rebecca, embarrassed by Kat's kiss.

"I have many powers and knowledge is one of them," Kat revealed then walked to the hatch and paused. She turned to Rebecca and assured her that everything would be fine. Rebecca's head spun and she fell to the floor. When she came to, she was alone on the ship. "Holy shit!" she said to herself. "Marina wasn't kidding about the kiss."

Kat exited the elevator and proceeded down the hall to her suite. Marina and Britt lay on cots in the center of the room, bare-chested. Kat knelt over Britt and placed her hands on his chest. With her eyes closed, she uttered a series of incantations. A dark cloud formed over Britt and two funnels reached down to his head and chest. Britt shuddered several times as Kat moved her hands in circular motions. When she finished the incantation, the cloud dissipated and Britt lay peacefully.

Kat moved over to Marina and performed the same ritual. At the end of the ritual, she placed her lips on Marina's and kissed her in her typical fashion.

Marina became alert mentally but her body was still void of motion. She knew Kat had her under her power and was helpless to say or do anything.

"You disrespected me last time we met, yet you returned to me for help."

Marina felt ashamed. "I had no choice. You were our only option."

"And I should forgive you."

"I'll do whatever you want. Just save Britt if you can. I don't care about myself."

"You'll do anything?" countered Kat.

Marina knew what that meant and agreed. She had no idea what to do about Kat's protective strips for her lips and didn't really care right now. "Why are you so attracted to me?" asked Marina. "You can have anyone you want on this station."

"You are our future. And right now, you are a scarred individual. I want to help you heal so you can achieve your destiny."

Marina was more confused and asked, "How does making love to me accomplish that?"

"You have to know what love is to share in it. If you are incapable of love, you will fail."

Kat vanished in a haze and Marina felt so much better. She realized that she was again Kat's sexual toy but now she understood the meaning. She accepted her role with Kat and released her inhibitions. As with their prior experience, she wondered if the experience was real or just an exercise in mind control. Kat was always cryptic with responses and never answered directly.

The pleasures Marina felt were beyond ecstatic and mind-numbing. She felt a strong connection develop between her and Kat, a mental connection that helped her see more clearly. The feel of someone holding and caressing her that really cared was new to her. Even her experiences with Britt were limited to self-gratification at this stage of their relationship.

When Marina awoke, Kat stood on the balcony with her back to Marina and stared down at the crowd below. She studied Kat's shapely body from behind and wondered if the two actually engaged in a physical relationship. As she approached her, she felt some tingling in her legs and an achy feeling within her womb. It was a 'good' achy that left her mentally in a good place compared to before.

Britt still lay motionless on the cot but his color returned and he appeared much better. Marina stood next to Kat and placed her arm around her waist. "I guess a 'thank you' is in order," she said humbly.

Kat turned to her and responded playfully, "For what?"

"For letting me feel the joy of love with another who cares."

"You are finally learning, Marina."

Marina felt an awkward moment but summoned the courage to kiss Kat passionately. Ironically, nothing happened this time. It was a beautiful kiss but there were no illusions or hypnotic trances. Kat was pleased with her.

"I have to ask, Kat, was our experience real or was it an illusion?"

"Love is always real, my dear."

"I should have known better than to expect a simple answer from you. Thank you again for your help."

"You are welcome any time in my house but for now, you must leave. One of Victor's man-o'-wars is approaching. They will want to search the ships in the transport bay for yours."

"Of course. And I have a date with destiny," she replied proudly. "What can I ever do to repay you for your help?"

Kat became serious and stared into her eyes. "After you defeat Victor, destroy the crystal. Promise me you'll do that."

Marina was taken aback by her request but was more than willing to accommodate her request. They kissed again. "Will there be a next time, Kat?"

"Most certainly. We have a busy future ahead of us."

Marina was pleased and hugged her. "And what about my friend over there?" she asked while pointing at Britt.

"My men will carry him back to the ship. He'll sleep for a while but he'll be fine."

Marina leaned over Britt and kissed his cheek. When she looked up, Kat vanished. She was puzzled how Kat kept doing that. Perhaps she really was a witch. Marina stepped onto the elevator and descended.

Rebecca sat on the floor and worried about her friends. It was only four hours but she needed to know if they were all right. More so, she fretted if Kat could be trusted to care for them.

Marina boarded the ship and surprised Rebecca. "You're back!" Rebecca shouted excitedly. She rushed to Marina and they hugged.

Four of Kat's men arrived with Britt and set him down on a cot in the cabin.

"We have to leave now," ordered Marina. "One of Victor's ships is approaching."

When Kat's men exited, she closed the hatch and went to the flight deck. Rebecca powered up the ship's systems while Marina initiated engine startup.

"I suppose you have a plan?"

Marina glanced at her confidently, "We're going after Victor."

"Huh!"

"Fate is on our side. We have to do this."

Marina noticed that Rebecca was strangely silent. "What's wrong?" asked Marina. "Kat got your tongue?"

Rebecca became embarrassed. "Just get us out of here. I don't like this place."

Britt stepped onto the flight deck and yawned. "I don't know what happened but I feel great."

"A good sleep will do that," kidded Marina as she piloted the ship away from Magnus. "Did you meet Kat?" she asked Rebecca curiously.

"Uh, yeah."

"So, Kat did get your tongue!" she teased.

"That's not funny."

"What am I missing?" Britt inquired as their strange behavior intrigued him.

"Not much," answered Marina. "Just be glad you're healed."

"But how?"

"Leave it alone, please," Rebecca requested.

Britt realized that whatever happened was sensitive and left the flight deck. He was amazed at how his ribs were healed and his jaw felt fine.

Rebecca finally gained the courage to ask, "What did Kat do to you?"

Marina was amused and answered, "She helped me to understand some things. At first, it was awkward. Now, she and I share some things."

"Did the kiss have anything to do with it?"

"I warned you about her kisses," teased Marina.

"You weren't kidding."

"Did you like it?" Marina continued to tease.

"Stop it! That's not right."

The two women burst into laughter and resumed the flight. Rebecca kept her revelations about their parents' deaths to herself.

"What's our plan?" inquired Rebecca.

"We're returning to the asteroid belt to resume our game of cat and mouse with Victor. His man-o'-war isn't there to protect him."

"I don't get it."

"What was it you always told me – it's my destiny?"

"Yeah, but this …"

Marina placed her hand on Rebecca's arm. "Relax. I know what I'm doing."

Rebecca noticed that Marina's touch was softer and reassuring. "You've changed, Marina," she commented.

"I hope so. I can't be a bitch all the time."

"Now, I am getting worried," joked Rebecca.

"When we get to the asteroid belt, you find us a good place to enter safely. I trust your navigation skills to keep us safe."

Rebecca eyed her suspiciously while Marina adjusted her seat back and slept. This new side of Marina was tough to get used to.

Chapter 10

Under Pressure

On board the *Orion*, Victor paced back and forth like a caged animal.

The two pilots glanced nervously at each other, concerned what he might do to them.

Victor stopped and eyed the transmitter on the control panel. He reached over Anton's shoulder and pressed the transmitter switch. Anton instinctively gave up his seat to Victor.

"Come in, *Neutrino*. This is the *Orion*," he requested into the transmitter. There was no response.

"Are we in range?" he asked Tibbs.

"Yes, sir. We know they are in range."

"*Neutrino*, respond now or we'll take action against you," he warned.

On board the *Neutrino*, Marina and Rebecca heard Victor's voice.

Marina toggled the overhead transmitter to 'receive' and back to 'on.' "Cut the crap, Victor. What do you want?" she replied impatiently.

Victor's temper rose and the veins over his temples swelled. The two pilots cringed and waited nervously for him to lash out at them. He regained his composure and responded, "I'm offering you one more chance to return my crystal and join me in ruling Yord."

Marina laughed mockingly and countered, "What makes you think I have it?"

Victor pounded his fist against the console and gritted his teeth. "My crystal is somewhere on that ship and I will do whatever it takes to get it back – with or without you," he warned.

"And I suppose you can read its revelations? You are full of surprises, Victor," she taunted.

Rebecca looked expectantly at Marina for some clue as to her plan. Marina smiled and replied, "I think Fiona has something to say about that. It seems that you and she had a parting of ways that she wasn't happy about it."

"She has nothing to say in this!" he shouted. "I have my own debt to settle with her."

Marina was pleased by his angry response and continued, "Then we'll both be waiting for you when we meet."

"If you turn her over to me, I will consider that as reparations for all the grief you caused me thus far."

"Oh, Victor, you are such an ass," replied Marina.

"I will find you!" he screamed. "You won't escape!"

"Yeah, yeah," mocked Marina and she toggled the transmitter off.

Victor was enraged. He pounded Tibbs in the back of the head several times and threw him across the flight deck. He noticed Anton's stare and shouted, "What are you looking at?"

Anton replied humbly, "Sir, do you think Fiona has really allied herself with Marina?"

"Why do you care?"

"Perhaps we can use that against them," he suggested.

"Shut up!" Victor ordered. "Fire at every asteroid out there until you drive them out into the open. Oh, and don't kill them if you know what's good for you." He stormed off the flight deck.

Anton shrugged his shoulders in disappointment and resumed his duties. Knowing Fiona's bad temper and envious nature, it would make sense to pit them against each other. Unfortunately, he didn't know Fiona was already dead.

Tibbs crawled back to his seat, still reeling from Victor's assault on him. Anton watched him pitifully and shook his head disappointedly at him.

***

Marina noticed the fatigue in Rebecca's eyes and suggested, "Why don't you get some rest? We're in no hurry to leave the belt."

"One day you'll make a great leader for our people," she remarked and departed.

Marina was stumped by her comment. "*Where the hell did that come from?*" she thought to herself. It bothered her that Rebecca and Britt both believed she would relent and take the throne when the time came. "*They both must be crazy.*" When she rubbed her eyes and dozed off in her seat, the strange dreams started again.

A man and woman stared at her through white mist. "Your destiny is nearly at hand, Marina," the woman informed her. "You must be strong."

Marina rushed at them and shouted, "Who are you? Why can't you leave me alone?"

The couple vanished as she drew near to them. Marina searched frantically through the mist but found no one. The man's voice startled her. "The truth will soon be at hand. Fear not for we are with you."

Marina grew frantic and fell to her knees. She felt a piercing pain in her head and cried out, "Why can't you leave me alone?"

"You are not alone," replied the woman's voice. "We will always be with you."

Marina shrieked and fell to the ground. Suddenly, she awoke in tears and was covered in sweat. "What the hell is going on with me?" she blurted.

Britt burst into the cabin. "Are you okay?" he asked.

Marina looked about the cabin as if she were lost. "I'm fine," she replied. "Just a bad dream."

The ship shuddered and startled them. The power flickered several times and dimmed. The ship was jarred again as large pieces of debris from the surrounding asteroids pounded the hull.

Rebecca had been drawn back to the flight deck by the impact of the assault. "What the hell is going on?"

Britt checked several of the indicators in the dim light and glanced at four of the faint flickering signals on the alarm panel. "They're taking pot shots at all the asteroids around us including ours."

"So they don't know we're here, right?"

Britt remarked sarcastically, "So long as we don't leave and the ship doesn't fall apart first."

"That's a relief," Marina quipped.

"Is it!" he sniped angrily. "If we can't get out of here, we're as good as dead.

Rebecca left the flight without a word to them. The ship lurched again, the impact knocking them down. Sparks flickered in the air, some landing on Marina from one of the control panels above her. Britt pulled her out of the way and ripped the power cables out of the top cover.

Marina turned off several circuit breakers on the rear panel but the ship rumbled again. She tumbled to the floor and slammed her head.

Britt noticed on the auxiliary control panel that someone just transported off the ship. He looked down at Marina and saw the fatigued expression on her face.

"Let me help you up," he offered apologetically and lifted her by her arm.

"I'm fine. Just get off my back right now."

"Well, I 'm glad you're fine but I think Rebecca just left the ship."

Marina pressed several buttons on the console and eyed the monitor. "What the hell for?" she asked urgently. Britt stared at her condescendingly.

They contemplated for a brief moment. "She must have boarded Victor's ship," Britt deduced.

"We've got to get her back here, fast!"

The two of them rushed from the flight deck down to the cargo bay.

***

Victor entered the flight deck and approached his pilots. "What's so important that you need to interrupt my meeting?" he inquired angrily.

Anton replied anxiously, "Sir, we've been boarded by a single individual down in corridor C."

One of the officers on the deck volunteered, "I'll send my men down there at once."

A ping sounded from the control console and quickly drew the pilot's attention. The monitor showed two red dots in a white circle on C deck. "Sir, two more individuals have boarded!" Anton announced excitedly.

Victor turned to the officers and waited for their response. They wisely exited the flight deck. He grinned deviously as he felt the end of their hunt was near. There's only one logical reason they'd risk transporting in an asteroid field. "We must have damaged their ship," he concluded smugly. "They've abandoned it."

Anton was relieved that something made Victor happy.

***

Rebecca peered out from the doorway of a supply room. The corridor was empty and the only sound was the hum of the engines from the propulsion room. She crept down the corridor to a stairwell. Stowed underneath were six cylinders of compressed gases with a pair of steel wheels on their bases. Rebecca eyed the cylinders and noticed that three were filled with oxygen and three with nitrogen. She carted each of the nitrogen cylinders down the hall to the supply room.

At the top of the stairs was the entrance to the navigation deck. Nearby was another corridor which led to the crew's quarters.

Rebecca approached the crew's quarters and peeked inside. No one was in sight. Opposite the compartment door was a 'weapons' cabinet secured with a digital lock. She entered the crew's quarters and set the oxygen cylinders aside.

Outside the crew's quarters, she drew her pulse pistol, adjusted the power setting to 'low' and heated the lock on the weapons locker.

Three soldiers sneaked toward her from the end of the corridor just as she melted through the lock. The soldiers fired several pulses of energy at her.

Rebecca hurriedly swung the door open and deflected their shots. She retreated into the crew's quarters and set the cylinders on their sides with the bases pointed into the corridor. She returned fire briefly so the soldiers would keep their distance.

"Surrender now and we'll spare your life," instructed one of the soldiers.

"Kiss my ass!" shouted Rebecca.

"Victor wants you and the other female alive. The traitor can die."

Rebecca considered his comment and realized that Marina and Britt must be on board as well. "We'll make sure all of you die with us," she replied and fired again.

More soldiers gathered in the corridor behind the stairs and hid in the doorways to avoid her gunfire. Rebecca knew they were going to rush her any moment. She set the switch on her pistol for 'high' and nudged the cylinders so their bases pointed at the corridor walls.

Marina and Britt heard the commotion and hid by the door inside the supply room. The two glanced curiously at the nitrogen cylinders and then at each other. Neither had any idea what purpose they served and thought nothing more of them.

"There are a lot of soldiers out there," Britt whispered.

"Too many," replied Marina. "But that never stopped us before, did it?"

Britt rolled his eyes in disbelief. He knew Marina was going to do something crazy again.

Marina opened the door with her pistol raised just as Rebecca fired a short pulse at the valve on the end of the cylinder and blew it off. The cylinder launched out of the quarters like a missile.

Marina stepped into the hall just as the cylinder ricocheted off the door jamb and smashed three soldiers against the wall.

"Holy shit!" Marina yelped, ducking back inside.

Britt pulled her aside and slammed the door closed. "Good call," he chastised.

"Ah, shut up," she muttered

Rebecca shot the valve off the second cylinder and launched it down the hall. The cylinder rang off the walls and tumbled wildly, striking several of the soldiers and injuring them severely. Two suffered broken arms and legs while others incurred head injuries. The remainder fled up the stairs to the navigation deck.

The corridor grew quiet except for the fading hissing of the oxygen from the cylinders. The near empty cylinders rolled across the hall and stopped against the wall with a thud.

The soldiers in the corridor were either dead or unconscious from their wounds. She stood the third cylinder upright and placed it next to the entrance to the crew's quarters. Next, she opened the 'weapons' cabinet in the corridor and reached inside for a grenade on the top shelf.

Three soldiers rushed down the stairs and aimed their rifles at her. One of them called out, "Don't move or you're dead."

Rebecca froze with the grenade out of sight. "I want to speak with Victor," she requested. "Tell him Red wants to make a deal. If not, then you will all start dying."

The soldiers laughed at her. "I think I'll start with her knee caps and work my way up," taunted one of them.

"Stand down, everyone," ordered an officer on the stairs. "Don't do anything rash," he told Rebecca. "I'll inform Victor."

Rebecca stepped out into the open with the grenade in her hand. The red light indicated that it was armed and only needed for her to press the button to detonate it.

The soldiers became concerned but held their ground. They aimed their weapons at Rebecca's head. She faked a toss of the grenade at them several times and frightened them. They jumped back each time and grew angrier.

Marina and Britt overheard them and opened the door slightly. "What the hell is she doing?" uttered Marina.

"Saving our asses." Britt pushed her back and whispered, "This time we do it my way."

"I can hardly wait," sniped Marina.

The officer returned and announced, "Victor is busy. What is it that you have to offer before my men kill you?"

"All I want is my friends' freedom," answered Rebecca. "If he lets them go, I'll surrender and no one gets hurt."

The soldiers laughed hysterically.

"Look, Marina doesn't know what powers she has nor does she know how to use them. Spare them," she pleaded.

The officer placed the barrel of his pistol against her forehead. "I doubt it," he replied disinterestedly. Rebecca held the grenade up to make sure he saw the red light illuminated. He broke a sweat but refused to back off. The soldiers watched anxiously and waited to see who gave in first.

Britt and Marina exited the supply room and sneaked up behind the soldiers with their pulse pistols drawn. Britt signaled Marina to remain quiet.

"What the hell do you think you're doing?" he asked the soldiers.

The startled soldier jumped and looked back at Britt. "Drop your weapons and put your hands up!" the soldier ordered them.

Marina smirked at Britt and fired two shots into the soldier's head. Rebecca seized the opportunity and grabbed the officer in front of her by the back of the neck. She rammed his head into the corner of the cabinet door. He hit the floor with a thud as blood seeped from a jagged gash in his forehead.

Britt grabbed the nearest soldier by the wrist. "I was hoping we could work this out," he remarked disappointedly.

"We have orders to kill you and take the Princess captive," the soldier informed him.

"And what about me?" asked Rebecca curiously.

"It's your choice but I prefer to kill you."

"That's what I like to hear," Rebecca quipped and fired at his knees.

Marina fired a shot into the soldier's face and killed him. "Me, too," she added giddily.

Britt turned red-faced and chastised the women, "Don't do that when I'm standing next to him!"

"Oops," Marina uttered sarcastically.

Britt bit his lip angrily and refrained from losing his temper.

Four more soldiers raced down the stairs and cut them off.

"Victor will be happy to see all of you now," the senior of the four soldiers remarked. "Drop your weapons now."

Rebecca held the grenade up and announced, "You will put your weapons down now or we all go BOOM!"

The soldiers were uncertain of what to do and hesitated. When they lowered their pistols, Rebecca lowered the grenade.

Marina yanked one of the silver balls from her wig, and tossed the ball to one soldier. "Here's a little something for you to remember me by," she taunted. The soldier caught the ball and eyed it curiously.

Rebecca retrieved a second grenade and hit the floor. Marina counted to three in her head.

At two, she and Britt dove to the floor. The other three soldiers raised their pistols to fire but the ball exploded in a bright flash. The soldier who held the flash grenade fell to the ground with a badly burnt arm and hand. The other soldiers, blinded by the flash, covered their eyes and cried out for help.

Rebecca set both grenades for two minutes and stowed one in the cabinet. As she closed the door, Marina grabbed her by the arm and yanked her down the hall. Britt guarded the stairwell and covered the women as they retreated to the supply room.

Rebecca broke away from Marina's grasp. She fired one shot at the oxygen cylinder in the doorway of the crew's quarters. The cylinder exploded, leaving a gaping hole in the floor. She rushed to the propulsion room at the end of the corridor and tossed the grenade inside. With little time to spare, she hurried back to the supply room, where Britt slammed the door behind her.

More soldiers appeared at the top of the stairwell and fired at the door. Britt took out the remote for their transporter and placed his finger on the 'return' button. A soldier waited inside the room with his pistol drawn. He grabbed Rebecca by the arm and held the barrel of his pistol against her head. "Drop your weapons now," he ordered, "or she dies."

Britt stowed the remote in his pocket and set his pistol on the floor. He glared at Marina and nodded for her to comply as well.

"Screw this!" she shouted and shot the man in the face. Rebecca was stunned by the closeness of the energy pulse to her face.

The soldier's jaw was a gaping crater of burnt flesh and bone as he fell to the ground.

"Marina!" cried Rebecca.

"Didn't I tell you about that?" Britt rebuked angrily. "One day, you're gonna' hurt someone real bad."

"I doubt it," Marina responded coldly. "I never miss."

"Yeah, except for …"

"Ah, shut up!" she groaned at him.

The door glowed red as the pulse fire from the soldiers struck the door continuously.

Britt took the remote from his pocket and activated the transporter. Rebecca fired at the valves on the nitrogen cylinders and blew them off, just as they transported off the ship. The bottles ricocheted off the walls and emptied their supply of frigid nitrogen into the air.

The second grenade exploded in the propulsion room and damaged one engine's cooling system. The two engine room mechanics died in the blast.

The weapons cabinet was destroyed by several explosions from the ordinates inside. A gaping hole in the wall where the cabinet once existed opened a pathway to the *Orion*'s Environmental Room where the air pressure and oxygen levels were maintained and set off a series of fire alarms.

The remaining soldiers in C corridor were now dead.

On board the *Neutrino*, Marina shoved Rebecca against the hull and screamed at her, "What the hell were you thinking?"

"Why did you come after me?" Rebecca countered.

"I asked you first," shouted Marina. "What is wrong with you?"

Britt became annoyed and sat down on the ground. "I can see this is going to take a while," he complained.

"Shut up!" shouted the two women in unison.

Marina suddenly burst into tears. "Talk to me, Rebecca," Marina pleaded. "What was that all about?"

Rebecca broke into tears, too. Britt was stunned by Marina's compassion. It was so unlike her.

"All these years, I've been doing the job you should have been doing," Rebecca reminded her. "It cost me the man I loved."

Marina suddenly felt embarrassed. She released her hold on Rebecca and backed away in shame.

"I've tried to do everything for our people that you needed to do as Princess until you were ready," she continued. "I can't do it anymore! I'm not their leader, you are."

"You didn't have to do it," Marina replied sheepishly.

"I had no choice. I did it for you, just as my parents sacrificed themselves for yours. It's our destiny."

"How do you know they sacrificed themselves?" Marina asked curiously.

"I just know."

Marina realized that Kat revealed something to Rebecca about their parents. "What did Kat show you?"

"Nothing," replied Rebecca defensively. "Nothing that concerns you."

"So why this?" inquired Marina with a confused look about her. "You could have died."

Rebecca replied somberly, "I have nothing left to live for if you won't take the throne. If I died saving you, then maybe you would have the decency to do the right thing and assume your role." She fell to her knees and cried, "I've failed."

Marina knelt next to her and hugged her. "You didn't fail," she explained. "We aren't done yet."

Rebecca looked up at her with teary eyes and asked, "Why did you risk your life for me, both of you?"

"Because I care about you," answered Marina. "As odd as it sounds, you are like a sister to me."

"I care, too, if anybody is interested," interjected Britt. Neither woman acknowledged him and he sighed in frustration.

"Come on, Rebecca," urged Marina as she helped her to her feet. "Get some rest before we make a run for it. I'm sure Victor is pissed over what we did to his ship."

Britt winked at Marina as she escorted Rebecca to one of the crew quarters. He left the cargo bay and went to the flight deck.

***

Four soldiers kicked the door open to the supply room and barged in. The freezing nitrogen immediately damaged their skin and hindered their breathing. One of the soldiers escaped the room and fell to the floor. His face was ashen from the freezing gas and his hands were stiff. He shivered and breathed irregularly. The others died quickly and fell to the floor.

Victor descended the stairs, accompanied by six of his men. Alarms sounded as the fire suppression system activated in the propulsion room. He stared at the dead soldiers on the floor of the corridor and became enraged. The wounded soldier looked at him pitifully. Victor drew his pistol and fired a pulse of energy into his head.

"How did they get on my ship and create this much destruction?" he shouted at his men. "Even worse, how did they get away?" he screamed in a rage.

"Sir, we dispatched men as soon as we detected their presence," replied one soldier.

Victor turned to him and placed his nose against the nose of the soldier. "Now that just wasn't good enough, was it?" he snarled as he drew his pulse pistol and fired a shot into the man's stomach. The soldier collapsed on the ground and quickly bled to death.

Victor faced his men and pointed the pistol at them. "I will not tolerate incompetence!" he shouted and fired another shot into a second soldier's chest. He, too, fell to the ground and died quickly.

Victor stormed down the corridor and kicked open the door to the propulsion room. He glanced quickly at the damaged cooling system and closed the door. "Summon the engineers and get that system repaired immediately!" he ordered the men and stormed angrily away.

When he entered the main quarters, three officers stood by anxiously awaiting information on the attack.

Victor passed them by and went immediately to the pilots. "Tell me you know where the intruders went," he demanded.

"Yes, sir, I do" replied Anton. "I've pinpointed the exact asteroid they are hiding in."

Victor turned to his three officers and instructed them, "I want ten men transported on board that ship. Is that clear?"

"Yes, sir," they replied in unison.

"And try not to screw this up or else ..." he warned them. The officers quickly left the flight deck and Victor leaned over Tibbs' shoulder. "I want those men on board in fifteen minutes," he ordered him. "Get us there now."

"But sir," interjected Tibbs.

Victor tensed up and clenched his fists.

Anton assured him that the deadline will be met. Victor punched Tibbs in the back of the head and left the flight deck.

"What is wrong with you?" shouted Anton. "I told you not to do that!"

"But we can't do this in fifteen minutes. There are too many obstructions."

"It doesn't matter! Tell him what he wants to hear or he's gonna' kill us."

Tibbs was confused but said no more.

Victor joined his men in the Transport Room and eyed each of them with the sharpness of an eagle. "If you fail me, I suggest you find another means of transportation back because I will kill you. Is that understood?"

"Sir, yes sir!" responded the men in unison.

One soldier asked, "Is it true we could die from interference between us and our targets?"

Victor bristled and approached the man. "It's true that you could die right here, right now, if I hear one more word out of you."

The man trembled and said nothing more.

Victor called to the flight deck via the intercom. "Are we ready to board?" he inquired.

The two pilots grew concerned. Tibbs mimicked Anton, "Tell him what he wants to hear."

Anton sneered at him and replied, "Almost, sir," he lied. "We have to clear an asteroid first to ensure the safety of the men."

"They won't escape, will they?" Victor asked anxiously.

"No way, sir."

Victor pondered briefly and ordered, "Blast the asteroid!"

"Yes, sir."

Victor bit his lip as he tried to contain his rage. He noticed that the men watched him expectantly. He shouted angrily at them, "Excuses! That's all I ever get are excuses! Maybe if I start holding you accountable for your incompetence with executions for treason then we won't have any more excuses."

Tibbs targeted the asteroid and set the fire control system to shoot at regular intervals. Once the large pulses of energy streamed from the cruiser, pieces of the huge asteroid scattered in random patterns.

The *Neutrino* shuddered as the asteroid was rocked by cannon fire. Marina and Britt started the ship's systems and engines for their escape.

Rebecca entered the pilots' cabin with a perplexed expression. "What's going on?" she asked anxiously.

"They're shooting at the asteroid." replied Marina. "They know we're here."

"I think they mean to board us," suggested Britt. "They're removing the interference so they can do it SAFELY." He glared at the two women as he emphasized his last word.

"Rebecca, take control of the ship," ordered Marina. "When I tell you, get us the hell out of here."

Marina and Britt left the flight deck, leaving Rebecca in control of the ship.

"Can you fix the power failure?" Marina asked.

"Maybe. You haven't thought this out very well, have you?" questioned Britt as he followed Marina back to the cargo bay.

Marina stopped and shoved him against the hull. "What is it with you?" she yelled angrily. "Do you have to question everything I do?"

Britt pushed her back against the door to the locker room. "Maybe I give a damn about you!" he replied just as angrily. "I sure don't know why, but I do."

Marina was lost for words and finally suggested, "Maybe you should act like it."

Britt embraced her and kissed her passionately. They held each other tightly, locked in a frozen moment in time until an alarm sounded and interrupted their passionate interlude.

"That's what I've been waiting for," whispered Marina. "What took you so long?"

Britt kissed her again. They seemed oblivious to the alarm but then Rebecca's voice over the intercom alerted them, "They've locked onto us! Get ready to be boarded."

Marina exhaled and grinned with delight. "Let's go kick some ass, shall we?"

"I'm right with you, Sweetheart."

Marina was pleased by his response. She drew her daggers and led the way.

Ten of Victor's soldiers appeared in the middle of the bay as Marina and Britt descended the stairs.

Marina shifted to an attack posture. Britt shoved her aside and fired several shots before the soldiers could fire back. Four were struck with lethal shots while the others returned fire.

Britt was struck several times in the chest and fell to the ground. Marina was shocked and overcome with rage for what they did to him. She lunged at the soldiers and fought desperately. She slashed at them and inflicted wounds, but they kicked her and punched her until she fell to the floor. One soldier stomped on her hands until she lost her hold on the daggers.

Rebecca barged into the bay with two pulse pistols and surprised the soldiers. Before they could fire, she gunned them down with repeated blasts.

Marina quivered and gasped on the floor. Rebecca rushed to her aid and cried, "This is the last time you'll do this to me, I swear." She wiped tears from her eyes.

Marina was touched by her concern. "I know," she whimpered. "Help me up."

When Rebecca lifted her to her feet, Marina surveyed the bodies and instructed her, "Set them in a circle with their backs to each other."

Rebecca was perplexed by her instructions but obeyed.

Marina staggered into the 'Flammable Stores Compartment' and dragged out a cylinder of hydrogen gas. She positioned the cylinder in the middle of the soldiers as Rebecca set the last corpse in place.

A voice emitted from one soldier's wrist transmitter, "Alpha Team, have you acquired the target? Come in, Alpha Team."

Marina glanced at Rebecca and raised the man's wrist close to her face. "This is Alpha Team leader," she replied with a gruff voice. "Target is acquired. Bring us back."

"Roger, Alpha Team."

Marina opened the valve on the cylinder and removed one of the silver balls from her wig. She tucked it under the collar of one of the corpses with the directional hole pointed at the valve on the cylinder. The mass of corpses vanished from the bay just as she backed away.

Rebecca was impressed with her ingenuity but said nothing as Marina hurried to Britt's side. She felt Marina's pain over Britt's injuries and thought about Cristos.

A brief pang in her lower abdomen nearly brought her to her knees. "Whoa!" she thought to herself and held her hand on her stomach. It was a cold reminder that she carried Cristos' child inside her. She felt somewhat guilty that she nearly ended their lives but she had to push Marina to step up or both their lives would be for naught. Perhaps now Marina would understand her burden and accept the role that she protected for her over all these years.

Marina stood up and faced Rebecca. "I'm tired of fighting," she uttered through tears. "I can't do this anymore."

"And you think I can?" Rebecca countered. "Let's finish this and make things right."

"What is 'right?' Killing Victor? Taking the throne?" questioned Marina. "Maybe death is right for all of us."

Britt stirred and sat up. "Maybe the right thing is to help ol' Britt to his feet," he remarked sarcastically, "and stop whining."

Marina was ecstatic by the sound of his voice. "Britt, you're alive!"

Britt patted his uniform and revealed that he wore a flak jacket. "You think I haven't learned from our fall out the window."

"You chicken shit!" shouted Marina mockingly. She rushed to him and hugged him. "And every time you were kicked and punched, I felt bad for you!"

"My ribs are finally healed. I don't want to relive that pain again."

The two stood up and held hands. They gazed at each other with love in their eyes for the first time.

"Shall we see how Victor likes his present?" Marina suggested.

"I think we need to get out of this asteroid first," Rebecca complained. "If I was Victor, I'd be thinking about blowing it up with us in it."

"She's right," Britt agreed. "I'll get on the power problem. You girls figure out where the hell we're going." He left the cargo bay by way of the corridor.

Rebecca helped Marina up the stairs and back to the flight deck.

"Now's the time for us to make our move," Marina explained. "By the time Victor recovers from the damage we inflicted, we'll have a head start and hopefully some speed."

"You put a lot of faith in other people doing their job," Rebecca commented.

Marina paused and glared at her. "Yes, I do," she snapped. "And I don't expect you or Britt to let me down."

"Consider this: There are hundreds of thousands of people around the sector that are counting on you to do your job, too. How about them?"

"Damn it, Rebecca! I get it already. Can you please leave it alone?"

Rebecca smiled at her. She knew she made her point. Marina groaned and continued to the flight deck ahead of her.

Marina heard Kat's voice in her head. Kat reminded her that they all have a future together and that they all cared about her. "I guess Kat's become my guardian angel," thought Marina, "or the devil on my shoulder."

"You could say that," Kat's voice responded.

Rebecca noticed the smile on Marina's face. "Something I should know about?"

Marina reached across and hugged her.

"Now you're scaring me, Marina!"

***

On board the *Orion*, Victor waited anxiously with three of his officers for his men to return. When they appeared in the middle of their Transport Bay, he knew it was a trap and immediately dove through the hatch into the corridor.

The flash grenade exploded and ignited the hydrogen. The blast was deafening and the sound of the hull bending from the force sent chills down Victor's spine. The three soldiers who once stood by him were incinerated with the corpses. Several crates burned and filled the compartment with smoke. The automatic fire-suppression system activated and sprayed foam down into the bay.

Victor's ears rang and his head throbbed from the force. His left leg was burnt by the flames that had shot through the hatch. "That friggin' bitch!" he screamed angrily. "I'm gonna' kill her!"

Two officers hurried down the corridor and helped him to his feet.

"Sir, we have no more troops," one officer mentioned as he secured the hatch.

Once Victor stood, he pushed them away and ordered, "Contact the *Scorpion* and have then send ten men."

"Only ten, sir?"

"You heard me! I'm going with them."

"As soon as we have contact, I'll requisition them," the officer assured him. He hurried down the corridor and returned to the flight deck.

Victor wiped sweat from his forehead and pounded the hull with his fist. The remaining officer backed away in fear. Victor hobbled to his quarters and bandaged his leg. Once finished, he changed into a clean uniform and returned to the flight deck.

***

Britt worked feverishly to repair damaged cables and patch the leaks to the ventilation and cooling systems. The deceased attackers' pulse rifles and pistols remained stacked on a pile next to the steps.

Marina and Rebecca piloted the *Neutrino* out of the asteroid's interior into the open space. "We only have half-speed, Rebecca," Marina complained nervously. "We have to do better than that."

Rebecca glanced at her calmly and reminded her, "Victor's speed is severely restricted, too. We damaged their propulsion system, remember?"

"I guess I owe you an apology. I thought your little trip was a suicide mission."

Rebecca hesitated then replied, "I didn't expect to return but it had to be done."

Marina eyed the monitor closely and noticed that the green blip, Victor's ship, trailed them but wasn't closing the distance between them. "What is it with everybody and this 'had to be done' or 'had to do it' crap?"

"What are you talking about?" asked Rebecca.

"A young girl gave me the same line of bull..., oh never mind."

Rebecca smiled and quipped, "A little girl, huh?"

Marina scowled and studied the long range sensors. She was pleased to see they were operating again. At least Britt had solved one of their problems. She grew irritated that she let Kara get into her head alongside Rebecca and Kat over her claim to the throne. She directed the sensors in various directions and plotted the coordinates of the asteroid belt they left behind.

"We should try to get back to Yord. I can gather whatever rebels are left to protect you," suggested Rebecca.

"No, we're going to draw Victor out to sector four."

Rebecca looked uncomfortable over Marina's decision. "But that's unexplored."

"I know. There's a portal beyond the belt that was set up for some odd reason and used but once."

Rebecca searched the database for any information on the portal and the distant sector. "Strange. There is some information on sector four in the Fleet's database."

Marina looked at her with a perplexed expression. "Why would they have data on that area?" she pondered aloud. "It's nowhere near the shipping lanes."

"Well, someone's database downloaded coordinates for several planets and their composite properties to the Fleet's computer."

"See if you can find out when the data was collected," Marina requested.

Rebecca scanned through several screens and searched for a time stamp.

The cabin door opened and Britt popped inside. "The cargo bay is repaired and sanitized. You should see a difference in the cooling system for the engines now, too."

Marina teased, "You can start on my quarters next."

"Yes, Mistress," Britt remarked sarcastically and left them.

"I'd better go humor him before he gets moody," Marina joked and left the flight deck.

Britt descended the stairs to the cargo bay. Marina followed looked down at him from atop the stairs and hollered, "Hey, wait a minute!"

Britt kept walking but responded sarcastically, "I have a cabin to clean." He entered the corridor to the crew's break room.

Marina hurried down the stairs and rushed after him. She grabbed his shoulder and spun him around.

"You want something?" he asked in an annoyed tone.

Marina stared into his eyes with a seductive gaze. "Yeah, don't ever leave me," she ordered him and kissed him passionately.

"How can I? Who would clean your ship?"

Marina opened the 'Data Processing Control System' panel and removed the backpack with the crystal in it. She took Britt by the hand and led him into the break room. They sat together on one of the bunks.

Britt watched her curiously as she removed the crystal from the backpack and gazed at it. He placed his arm around her and she cradled the crystal in her arms.

"Maybe the crystal can explain the mysteries that have clouded my life," she suggested.

"I think you have to have faith before you can understand anything about your destiny."

"Kat made me promise to destroy the crystal when we've defeated Victor. I wonder why?"

"Maybe you won't need its power anymore once you've taken the throne."

"Shut your mouth," she said with a coy smile and nestled against him. She closed her eyes and fell asleep. Britt tilted his head against hers and slept as well.

Marina was immersed in another nightmare. She piloted an alien cruiser while a blonde woman, much younger than her, watched. The stranger nodded in approval as Marina maneuvered the alien cruiser with ease. "You'll do fine," she said proudly.

Marina felt as though she had known the woman her whole life but couldn't recall her name. She felt at ease until the flight deck became clouded and chilly.

Suddenly Marina found herself standing in a snowstorm. In front of her were bodies encased in ice. Something compelled her to look more closely at the bodies. She brushed the snow off the ice and studied the faces of two bodies. They were the two recurring people in her dreams. The eyes opened and stared at her.

Marina screamed, horrified. Then she awoke, gasping for air. Britt held her arms and calmed her. Sweat poured down her forehead and cheeks as she stared wide-eyed at him.

"It's all right, Marina," he assured her. "I'm here with you."

Marina relaxed and hugged Britt tightly.

"Another bad dream?" he asked.

"Aren't they all?" she replied and returned the crystal to the backpack.

"Are you sure you're okay?" Britt asked with a concerned tone.

"Yeah, just fine." She got up and left the break room. Britt was bewildered by her recurring nightmares and followed her into the cargo bay. Marina looked at the backpack and stowed it in the 'Flammable Stores' room at the rear of the bay.

When she returned, she looked pale and somber. Britt attempted to hug her but she rebuffed him. "Please, Britt, not now."

"The crystal showed you something, didn't it?"

"Maybe."

"It's pushing you toward the throne and you don't want that, do you?"

Marina glared at him and cried, "It showed me the dead bodies of my parents, all right?"

"Wow. I'm really sorry." Britt picked up the plastic box with Fiona's head inside and suggested, "How about I get rid of this?"

"No!" she replied adamantly. "Just leave it right there."

Britt backed away with his hands in the air. "No problem," he replied defensively. "If that's what you want."

He lifted a plate in the floor and descended a ladder down to the propulsion compartment. He felt badly that Marina went off on him like that but hoped that some maintenance on the ship would take his mind off of her issues. It was obvious that her visions increased in frequency and the negative emotional impact on him was becoming more significant.

Marina unsealed the cover and lifted it off the box. Fiona's eye seemed to stare into her soul. "Maybe you're the lucky one," Marina remarked and resealed the box.

Rebecca piloted the *Neutrino* and kept a keen eye on the long range sensors for the *Scorpion*. So far, it was nowhere to be seen; only Victor's ship trailed them from a distance.

Marina entered the flight deck and sat in the co-pilot's seat. She placed it in a reclining position and leaned back. Her mind seemed to be elsewhere.

"We're almost out of the field," Rebecca informed her.

"What about the man-o'-war?" asked Marina.

"No sign of it."

"Then we'll take our chances with Victor."

Rebecca turned to Marina and studied her facial expression for a brief moment. "I still can't figure you out."

Marina turned toward Rebecca and responded, "And I can't figure you out either. You were the infamous Red who drove them crazy, yet you sit here so calmly."

"Just like you, I couldn't advertise my true identity, even to the other rebels."

"Just like me. A lifetime of hide and seek."

The two women chuckled.

"You do have a soft side to you, Marina. I really feared that you were dead inside and would never allow anyone into your life."

"I was dead," she replied. "You and Britt are responsible for the change in me."

"So, no more loner?"

"I'm getting there. Still a ways to go, though."

The power ramped up ten percent on the console. The women noticed and became excited.

"Britt must have found a way to repair the damage!" Rebecca exclaimed. "We're pulling away!"

"What would I do without that man," Marina remarked.

"He's rare," added Rebecca. "Hold on to him."

Marina considered her remark and left the cabin.

Chapter 11

The Chase

The *Orion* navigated perilously through the asteroid field. Without engine power to the left side of the ship, they constantly yawed to avoid collisions. This caused significant delays for them.

Victor pressed the button for the intercom and requested an update. A voice immediately responded, "We're replacing several of the components as quickly as we can. There's been significant damage, sir."

"Do I need to come down there?" Victor screamed.

"No, sir. We're rerouting some of the energy for the core-cooling systems to get some additional power during the repairs."

"Very well," relented Victor. "Keep me informed of your progress."

"Sir," interrupted Anton, "we have contact with the *Scorpion*. She's bypassed the asteroid field and will rendezvous with us shortly."

"Excellent."

"They are transporting ten of their troops on board our ship."

Victor nodded in satisfaction. Finally things were working in his favor.

***

Marina entered the cargo bay and peered down into the propulsion compartment. Britt worked tirelessly to secure a patch on a fractured section of pipe. He wore no shirt and sweated profusely.

Marina descended the ladder and stood behind him. She placed her hands on his shoulders and massaged them.

Britt ignored her and kept tightening the straps on the patch.

"What's wrong?" asked Marina. "Talk to me."

Britt finished securing the patch and turned to her. "It's you."

Marina felt badly for how she treated him and replied ruefully, "I'm sorry, Britt. I didn't mean to be such a hard-ass earlier."

"No, that's not it." He sat down on the floor of the small compartment and looked somberly at her. "You are the true heir to the throne. We can never be together because of that."

"So we're over, just like that?" she replied defensively.

"I swear, I will always be there to protect you but you won't use me to avoid your role as leader of your people."

Marina grew teary-eyed and sat next to him. "I won't take the throne," she affirmed. "I can never be that person."

Britt placed his hand on her cheek affectionately and urged her, "You must fulfill your duty. I will be there to support you in any way, I promise."

"That's not good enough," Marina replied coldly. "If there's any chance that I'll change my mind, you need to be more than my puppet."

Britt forced a smile and suggested, "Maybe we both have to reconsider our positions."

"Meaning?"

"Meaning..." Britt began and kissed her passionately.

Marina sighed with delight. "I think we finally found some common ground." She ran her hand along his chest and kissed him forcefully.

Britt maneuvered her onto his lap and pulled her body close to his. "Promise me you'll take the throne," he whispered.

"Not now," Marina replied and kissed him hungrily.

Rebecca's voice crackled from the intercom in the cargo bay, "Marina, we have company and it's not Victor!"

"Shit!" complained Marina. "I'd better get up there."

Britt groaned as Marina scurried up the ladder and vanished. He placed his hands on his hips and admired his patchwork on the pipe. Suddenly, the patch ruptured and the pipe broke free of its supports. Before Britt could react, the pipe struck him in the face and knocked him out. The cooling system for the ship's engines immediately lost flow and the temperature of the engines climbed. The safety system compensated for the rising temperatures by cutting back on power automatically.

Rebecca panicked as the ship slowed to fifty percent power and the *Scorpion* closed on them.

Marina burst onto the flight deck and quickly took her seat next to Rebecca. "What the hell happened?"

"The man-o'-war just appeared on the long-range scanners! We're losing power, too."

Marina took control of the ship and guided it away from the asteroid belt. Rebecca watched and wondered what she planned to do. Marina manipulated the sensors to seek out the portal she identified earlier.

Rebecca understood now where she was taking them. "What happens on the other side?" she asked.

Marina glanced at her somberly. "I guess we'll find out. Someone went through a lot of trouble to set up a portal out here, especially if no one uses it."

Rebecca monitored the *Scorpion* and the *Orion*. They're still following us."

"I figured as much." Marina toggled the intercom on and shouted, "Britt, what's going on? We're losing power!"

The *Neutrino* limped along at half speed while the *Scorpion* pursued from a distance. The *Orion* was still distant from them.

"Something's wrong. Britt should have responded."

"Get us through that portal any way you can," instructed Marina. "If they want to follow us, then let the fun begin."

"What if they fire at us?" Rebecca asked nervously. "We have no way of escaping them."

"Just get through the portal. I have to see what happened to Britt and our power." She hurried off the flight deck.

Panic set in as Marina feared Britt was injured or killed in an accident. That was the only explanation for the lack of response from him to her call.

Marina saw the vapors from the cooling system rising out of the propulsion compartment and immediately donned a mask with a small oxygen tank. She hurried down the ladder and found Britt lying motionless. She placed her mask on his face and pressed hard on his chest six times. She took the mask back and took several breaths, then placed it back on Britt. She lifted him to his feet and pushed him up the short ladder onto the cargo bay floor. As soon as she got out of the small compartment, she slammed the hatch shut and sealed it.

Marina continued her crude attempt at CPR on him and screamed, "Breathe, damn you!" She erupted in tears and pressed harder. His face was covered in blood with a jagged gash on his right cheekbone.

Marina cried and yanked him to a sitting position. "I won't let you die on me!" she shouted and punched him in the face. She dropped him flat and resumed her thrusts on his chest with the mask still over his mouth.

When Britt coughed and gasped, Marina ripped the oxygen mask off him and tossed the tank aside. She sat him up and hugged him. "Are you all right?" she asked with fear in her voice.

"Oh, shit!" he replied weakly. "My face is killing me."

Marina punched him again in the face and floored him. Tears streamed down her cheeks.

"What the hell was that for?" Britt asked dizzily.

"For scaring the shit out of me."

"I wasn't going anywhere. Why'd you hit me?"

"So you wouldn't forget," she replied angrily.

Britt rubbed his face and remarked, "Why do I feel like you hit me more than once?"

"You ass!" she shouted at him and then pleaded, "Can you do anything with the ship's cooling system?"

"No," he replied disappointedly. "The pipe is shot."

They looked at each other dejectedly.

All three ships emerged from the portal and continued into the unsettled region. The *Scorpion* drew closer and fired a series of red energy strobes. The *Neutrino* rocked as three of the pulses glanced off its hull.

Marina and Britt hurried back to the flight deck.

"It's about time you got back here," complained Rebecca. "I don't see our power increasing."

"Yeah, there's nothing we can do about it," answered Britt.

Marina took her seat next to Rebecca and studied the long-range sensors. "I got it, Rebecca," Marina said as she took over control of the ship. "If we can get close to one of those planets, the gravitational pull might force them to stay away."

"Yeah, but it'll pull us in."

One of the torpedoes struck the side of the *Neutrino* just behind the flight deck. The rear panels in the cabin exploded as sparks launched all over them. The impact sent Britt sprawling across the floor. Marina and Rebecca both struck their heads on the control panel and fell to the floor.

"On second thought, it's a good idea," blurted Rebecca.

Alarms sounded as a fire in the main corridor created a steady flow of smoke. Britt noticed the smoke seeping under the cabin door. Smoke billowed into the cabin. He left the flight deck and closed the door. The three 'fire-suppression system' panels had seven alarm indicators flashing and the entire system failed to operate because the explosion severed several wiring conduits.

Britt hurried down the corridor to the main panel and yanked it open. He manually opened three valves and closed the air supply to a solenoid valve.

Water and foam doused the walls and floor. Britt was soaked as he waited for the flames in other panels to extinguish.

"We're not gonna' make it!" cried Rebecca.

"Find a place for us to land this piece of junk," Marina directed her. "I'll think of something."

"There's a planet not far from here called Ithaca," Rebecca informed her. "The data base lists its position but the climate is cold and uninhabitable."

"I wonder how that information made it into the database if this is unexplored territory," Marina remarked sarcastically.

"Well, someone must have been there because the information didn't transmit itself."

Marina noticed the blood streaming from a cut on Rebecca's head and wiped it away from her eyes. "Aren't we a pair?" she kidded.

"What a way to die after everything we've been through," Rebecca remarked despondently. "I really believed that we were destined to accomplish something big."

"Maybe we were and we failed," Marina surmised dejectedly.

"Maybe you were right about this destiny crap all along," Rebecca whimpered.

Marina's thoughts were interrupted by a vision. She knelt by her parents in the ice. The ice cracked and broke part. The woman sat up and said, "This planet will set you free. Don't fear the cold and the ice. They are your friend."

Marina shook her head in an effort to grasp reality. She understood that they had to go to the frozen planet. "And maybe I was wrong," she said to Rebecca with renewed enthusiasm and patted her leg. "We're not done yet."

Rebecca wondered what Marina knew that changed her disposition so quickly.

***

Victor entered the flight deck and addressed the pilots, "Are we closing on them?"

"Yes, sir," replied Anton. "Their speed is significantly reduced."

"That's not good enough!" Victor shouted. "I want them stopped!"

Anton contacted the *Scorpion* and requested warning shots to stop the *Neutrino's* progress.

Tibbs complained, "Unless we have more power, we'll never catch them, sir."

Victor grew red-faced and clenched his fist. Anton whispered, "That was a mistake."

Victor grabbed Tibbs and threw him against the wall. "You friggin' moron! You haven't learned, have you?"

"But sir," he pleaded, "I didn't mean anything by it. I swear!"

Victor retrieved a dagger from his belt and cut the man's windpipe. The young man grasped at his throat and fell to his knees.

"If I hear even a peep out of you, I'll cut the rest of your throat," Victor warned him. He turned his attention to Anton and waited for a response.

Two officers removed Tibbs from the flight deck.

"Sir, if I may speak freely?" requested Anton.

"Go ahead but choose your words carefully."

"Sir, this Marina has proven to be quite a competitor."

Victor considered all the grief she caused him thus far and replied, "Yes she has. I've never met a woman so conniving."

"Even Fiona, sir?"

Victor felt his ire return and asked, "Why would you bring up her name?"

"I'm thinking: why not use Marina's anger against her?"

Victor considered Anton's suggestion and realized there was merit to it. He stood by the pilot with his hands on his hips and contemplated his next move. "Contact the *Neutrino*. I want to speak with Marina."

"Yes, sir." Anton immediately sent out a message by transmitter and attempted to establish a link to them.

***

The *Neutrino* rocked back and forth as strobe pulses from the *Scorpion* struck debris around them and exploded.

"We have to increase our speed or they'll cripple us!" Rebecca exclaimed in a panicked tone.

The ship rocked again and sparks flew from the rear panel. The lights flickered and dimmed.

"That's your cue, Britt," Marina informed him sarcastically.

"Just great," he muttered and left the flight deck.

"What can we eject off the ship, Marina?" Rebecca asked nervously.

"What the hell kind of question is that?"

"I mean, if we can dump some weight, we might be able to disrupt their targeting."

Marina operated three switches on the control console and attempted to eject the damaged engine. The light flickered dimly. Marina scanned over the alarm panel and noticed one marked 'Escape Pod Disabled.' She selected ESC PD and pressed 'eject.' Again the light flickered dimly.

"Damn it!" Marina uttered in frustration. She selected the disabled 'Engine Coolant System Left Side' and pressed 'eject.' Again the light flickered dimly.

The ship shuddered as another strobe pulse from the *Scorpion* glanced off the tail of the ship. Marina and Rebecca were jarred against the console and stunned.

Britt tumbled across the corridor away from the open breaker panel and lay dazed. Marina appeared from the flight deck and nearly fell over him. "I hope you're doing something to save our asses," she said disappointedly.

Britt groaned and stood up. "Yeah, I'm waiting for your next great plan," he taunted.

"Kiss my ass!" she shouted and disappeared into the passenger bay. The door slammed behind her.

Britt grit his teeth and snarled, "One day, I'm gonna' put her over my knee, so help me." He resumed inspecting the breakers in the panel. Two were tripped and non-essential so he turned them off.

Marina stood by a panel with nine large pistons mounted vertically inside. She studied the diagram on the panel door and opened four of the nine valves leading to the pistons. Above each piston was a lever to actuate the pistons manually. Next to the panel were six hand wheels to manually open and release the latching mechanisms on the pods, tanks and engines.

Rebecca shouted over the intercom, "The man-o'-war is closing on us. Somebody do something fast!"

Marina struggled with the hand wheel until the escape pod bay door opened. She yanked on the lever until the piston actuated and ejected the escape pod from beneath the ship. Marina then closed the bay door.

The pod fell clear of the bottom of the *Neutrino* and drifted behind it. The next blast from the *Scorpion* struck the pod, creating a brief explosion.

Marina anxiously opened the release latches for the left engine and yanked on the lever. This one was particularly difficult to maneuver. Finally, the lever transferred and the piston actuated much louder than the first. The damaged engine was ejected from the rear of the ship.

Marina focused on the hand wheel for the engine coolant tank but it was stuck. She took an axe from the Fire Equipment panel and fed the handle through the wheel. She leaned on it with every bit of strength she could muster. The wheel broke and she tumbled face-first to the floor. She lay dazed, her mouth busted open.

Britt reset the breakers and turned on the main feed. Power slowly restored to the ship and the control panel instrumentation illuminated brightly.

Rebecca anxiously pressed 'eject' for the left side engine coolant tanks and breathed a sigh of relief as the light extinguished.

Britt barged onto the flight deck and asked eagerly, "Any increase, Rebecca?"

Ten percent! It might be enough to pull away."

Two more blasts from the *Scorpion* struck the engine and the engine coolant tank behind the *Neutrino*. The debris exploded into a bright fireball and fizzled.

"Get us out of sight, quickly!" shouted Britt.

Rebecca navigated the ship toward the small planet of Ithaca.

***

On board the *Orion*, Victor and Anton watched the long-range sensors anxiously. The blip that represented the *Neutrino* was gone.

"What the hell just happened? Victor screamed.

"I don't know?" answered the pilot in a panic. "I think the *Scorpion* just blew them up!"

Victor sat down and activated the transmitter to the *Scorpion's* frequency. "Come in, *Scorpion*! This is Victor!" he shouted.

"Yes, Commander," replied the pilot. "This is the *Scorpion*."

"What the hell happened to that ship? You were told to fire strobes at them!"

"We, uh, don't know, Sir. It just vanished."

"Where's your Captain, soldier?"

Another voice came from the *Scorpion*. "This is McVeigh, Sir. What can I do for you?"

"You'd better find that ship because if it's gone, you are, too! Understand?"

"Yes, sir. We'll activate all sensors for a full scan."

"On second thought, don't do anything else. Stand down."

"Yes, sir."

Victor punched the control panel and covered his eyes in disgust. After contemplating his next move, he ordered Anton to proceed into the area where the *Neutrino* was last seen.

***

Britt took a seat next to Rebecca and looked relieved.

"Nice work," she complimented him.

"Normally I get punched or kicked or stabbed for doing a good job," he joked.

"Marina's gonna' make a hell of a Queen one day," she remarked confidently.

"Yeah, if we don't kill her first," kidded Britt again.

Marina hobbled up the stairs to the flight deck door and paused. The shattered door lay off to the side of the landing. She peeked inside and listened.

"So how did the two of you first meet?" Rebecca asked curiously.

"Marina yanked me off the top of a building. Fortunately we crashed on a fire escape. The next time, she shoved me out a second story window and used me for a cushion. Then she stabbed me, etc. etc. etc."

Rebecca's eyes widened with surprise. "And you still care for her after all that?"

"It seems that when you fall in love with someone, you only see the good in them."

"How did you know of her past?"

Britt recalled his days as a child. "My father was head of the King's Guard when Marina's parents ruled Yord. He spoke so profoundly of them and their accomplishments. I knew from the stories that Marina was alive somewhere and was the rightful heir to the throne. All I had to do was find her and I knew I could convince her that she had the support to rebuild her parents' alliance."

"But you served Victor. Why?"

"What else is a soldier to do? The Space Fleet is corrupt and that was before I knew that Victor was obsessed with conquering everyone, including the other militias."

"And yet, you left the militia to defend Marina? Wasn't that hard for you?"

"I have friends that will die for this cause as would I. More so than that, something about Marina steals my heart. I know she's worth it."

Marina became teary-eyed and sat on the floor. How could Britt love her after all she put him through? What kind of a monster had she become? She tortured herself with questions about her cold-hearted, uncaring nature and how anyone could want her to be their leader. Then she recalled how Kat embraced her and loved her. Maybe she wasn't really a monster, just lost.

Rebecca related how she and Cristos first met. She had just survived her first encounter with Fiona and was terrified. Five mercenaries died by her hand alone in that battle.

Britt noticed the far away expression in her eyes and asked, "How about your first meeting with Marina?"

Rebecca chuckled. "About ten years ago, my sister and I were trapped by a bunch of mercenaries. They beat my sister to death and were about to do the same to me. Marina stepped out of the trees and warned them to leave us alone. They refused and, well you know Marina, she killed them."

"So, she was a skilled fighter that far back?"

"Oh, yes," answered Rebecca. "She took me on board her ship and shot me up with adrenalin. Taught me to be tough and never fear anyone. I knew right away who she was but I couldn't understand why she wouldn't acknowledge her title. I've never met anyone so fearless against those odds. She is the type of leader that people would follow to the grave; committed, unwavering and hardened principles which, by the way, need a little work."

Britt placed a hand on Rebecca's shoulder sympathetically and explained, "Marina went through a volatile period in her childhood. There was so much that went unexplained about her parents' disappearance."

"Her parents weren't alone when they disappeared."

Britt looked at her curiously and replied, "No they weren't. Why do you ask?"

"My parents were with them when they disappeared."

"Then you have a stake in Marina's mystery dreams as well."

"I hope to find my answers with her."

"We'll keep trying until we get the closure you both seek."

"Thanks, Britt."

Marina faded into another premonition. The vision clouded her mind and then cleared. She found herself seated in the same alien ship that she dreamed of earlier next to the same young woman she presumed to be her mother. The woman maneuvered the cruiser through hundreds of other alien warships. A second ship like hers flew alongside of them. A young man's face, much like her father's, appeared on the monitor and smiled.

The two fighters wreaked havoc on their attackers with relentless aggression. The woman turned to Marina and explained, "This was our fate. This will be your fate as well. You cannot deny it."

Marina was frightened and asked, "Why is it my fate? Why me?"

"Your answers will become obvious soon enough. You will take my place and navigate the universe. People everywhere will know who you are."

Marina watched the short range scanners and was amazed at how the two ships worked together to repel the attacking force.

As she studied the ship's controls, they all seemed so familiar to her. "Who are you?" Marina asked.

"I am you. You are me. We are one." The woman leaned forward and kissed Marina's forehead and then vanished.

"Mother!" Marina shouted. The ship vanished and Marina felt as though she were falling.

The ship suddenly appeared on a snow-covered planet. The hatch was open and four bodies lay in the snow just outside the ship.

Marina screamed out, "No, it can't be!"

Britt left the flight deck and comforted her. He helped her to her feet and back to the flight deck.

Marina sat down and sobbed.

"The dreams are getting stronger, aren't they?" asked Rebecca.

Marina wiped the tears from her eyes. She didn't want to talk about the dream. "Where are we?"

"We're orbiting Ithaca," answered Rebecca.

"Scan the surface for anything that looks like a ship!"

"Come on, Marina," urged Britt. "You're not well."

Marina grew red-faced. "You two started all this fate and destiny crap!" she shouted. "Now shut up and follow my orders."

Britt and Rebecca glanced at each other uneasily. Rebecca initiated a surface scan and asked, "What happens if we find this ship?"

"Just let me know when you find it."

***

Two officers whispered to each other and worried about the consequences if the *Neutrino* was inadvertently destroyed. Victor entered the flight deck and anxiously stood by Anton. "Well?"

"The repairs to the propulsion system have been completed. We have full power."

"And what of the *Neutrino*?"

"Our scanners have found debris but not enough to indicate the ship was destroyed. I believe the ship ejected damaged sections to increase their speed."

"How could we not see that?" Victor asked pointedly.

"Well, sir, the explosion from the debris leaves a blur on the sensors for several seconds, thus blinding us. Once the sensors reset, they resume tracking."

Victor paced the flight deck and pondered aloud, "If they were alive, where could they possibly hide?"

"They're in unknown territory, which means they have no coordinates or charts to follow."

"Meaning what, you idiot?" screamed Victor.

The officers cringed. Victor glared at them and back at Anton.

"Meaning there are few places they could land and none are inhabitable," explained Anton.

"Could Ithaca be one of those places?" Victor asked curiously.

Anton entered several coordinates into the computer and waited. The monitor scrolled through a page of information. He read the information and replied, "Based on the time they disappeared from our sensors and scanners, Ithaca is the only likely place they could land and not be detected."

"Set a course for Ithaca and scan the surface for their ship. Notify the *Scorpion* to follow along."

"Yes, sir. Isn't Ithaca the place where …?"

Victor grabbed Anton by the neck and held his dagger against the man's jugular. Bring that up again and I'll make sure it's the last time."

Anton nodded in agreement and Victor released his hold on him. He stowed the knife and noticed a red line of blood formed on the pilot's neck. *"Why can't they just do as they're told?"* he thought to himself. *"They never learn!"*

Anton sent a message to the *Scorpion* and set a course for Ithaca.

Victor approached the officers. "I know they're out there!" he exclaimed, "And we're gonna' find them or blood will be spilled. Is that clear?"

The officers replied in unison, "Yes, sir!" They fled the flight deck immediately.

Victor attempted to contact the *Neutrino* once again. The transmitter beeped and Rebecca glanced at Marina for approval to respond.

"I'll take it," Marina said confidently.

Rebecca toggled the transmitter to 'receive' and waited for a response.

"Marina, this is Victor. I strongly suggest you surrender before I destroy your ship. You can't hide for long."

"I'm busy, Victor. Try something else."

"I have an offer for you. Perhaps we can meet in person to discuss the terms" he suggested.

Britt shook his head 'no' to Marina. She grinned sadistically and replied, "I don't have time for your nonsense. See ya."

Victor interjected before she could terminate the transmission. "But you'll find this so…ironic. Ithaca is the place where your parents met their demise."

Suddenly, Marina grew stone-faced and somber.

Victor ordered the pilot to program the transporter for ten of them to board Marina's ship as soon as they locked onto it. He continued, "What's wrong, Marina? Nothing to say?"

"That's bullshit. You know nothing about my parents."

"Did you ever wonder why no one ever found their bodies?"

Marina suddenly realized that they were murdered on Ithaca. Rebecca grabbed her arm and stared her down until Marina calmed.

"I can take you to them if you like," he continued. "All you have to do is read the crystal for me and join me in ruling Yord." Victor became excited as he was convinced she had no other choice. "I know your ship is badly damaged. I can help you if you help me."

Marina exploded and shouted, "Kiss my ass, you pathetic piece of shit!"

Britt covered his eyes in disbelief. Rebecca stood and placed her hands on Marina's cheeks. "Calm down," Rebecca urged. "He's playing into our hands. You don't want to lose him."

Marina realized that he could destroy them without anyone ever knowing the truth about her parents. "I think there are others with something to say about that," she replied. "I'll have to discuss it with them."

"Tell Fiona that ..." Victor started but Marina toggled the transmitter off before he could finish.

"We have him at a disadvantage," Marina declared. "He thinks Fiona is working with us so he has to watch his back."

"We can circle Ithaca and break away to the asteroid belt again," suggested Rebecca.

"No, we're going down to the surface but first, we have to find that ship."

"And then what?" inquired Rebecca curiously.

"Land as close to it as possible and I mean close."

Britt knelt next to Marina, looking concerned. Marina looked back at him and forced a smile. He placed his hand on her knee and nestled his head against her. She placed her arm around him affectionately as if they finally reached an understanding of each other.

"I'm so sorry for everything I put you two through," Marina said sadly. "I really was a total bitch."

"It's not too late to change, you know," Britt encouraged her. "You can start by not punching me in the face anymore."

Marina kissed his forehead. "I'm sorry about that. I lost control of my emotions."

"Britt's right," Rebecca added. "It's what we all do from here on out that will matter most of all." Then Rebecca noticed a blue shade on the monitor and was stunned. "I don't believe it!"

Britt and Marina leaned over her shoulder and peered at the monitor. "That's it! That's the ship!" shouted Marina.

"Based on its size, it could be a cruiser," suggested Britt. "The shape appears alien though."

"How did you know?" Rebecca asked Marina excitedly.

"It's hard to explain. Just get us down there fast."

Chapter 12

Retribution

Rebecca struggled to keep the ship steady as they entered the stormy atmosphere of Ithaca. Britt held onto a support rail at the rear of the flight deck.

Marina gripped the console tightly and eyed the monitor. "We need to land as close as possible to the ship," she reminded Rebecca.

"What's the importance of this ship?" Britt inquired.

"It may be our salvation," answered Marina eagerly.

Rebecca and Britt glanced uneasily at each other. Marina seemed determined so neither was anxious to question her.

Marina focused the short-range infra-red sensors around the frozen ship as they drew closer.

Rebecca noticed Marina's intense expression and asked, "What are you looking for?"

"Just get us down next to that ship. That's all that matters right now." She operated a targeting laser and followed it with the sensors. The monitor showed a red background with a light blue spot where the laser focused. Then one of the sensors displayed a dark spot in the ice. Marina maneuvered the scanning beam back and forth while focusing the sensors on the area.

Britt noticed the spot on the monitor and looked more closely. The sensor detected four shapes in the ice. "What is it, Marina?"

Marina ignored him and focused the infra-red sensors on the ship. A faint orange color appeared at the aft end.

"What do you think, Rebecca?" Marina asked.

"The ship was abandoned. The core is still active though."

"Any sign of life on board?" Britt asked.

"No. The ship's interior is at sub-zero," replied Rebecca. "The hatch must be open and the systems powered down."

"And the shapes?"

Marina turned to Britt somberly and answered, "I think those are the bodies of the crew."

Rebecca brought the ship down with a thud. The impact jarred the women against the control panel. Britt sprawled across the floor. Rebecca got up with an attitude. "Let's skip the detective drama now and get to the point," she demanded. "What are they doing all the way out here?"

"Perhaps that's where the data came from in the Fleet's database?" suggested Britt. "The non-secure server at Fleet headquarters logs all data from the flight recorders of every ship. It also makes that information available for all ships to access."

"Then, by someone's very presence out here, the Fleet server will automatically log that info into the data base," Rebecca explained.

"That's right," answered Britt. "But how would Victor know of Ithaca unless he was here before?"

"If that ship's central systems were disabled or shut down, no one would ever find it," replied Marina sarcastically. "Something about this really stinks."

"I sense that you're holding something back from us, Marina. What aren't you telling us?" asked Rebecca suspiciously.

Marina glared at each of them briefly and left the flight deck.

Britt shrugged his shoulders at Rebecca and followed Marina. Rebecca grumbled, "What a bitch she can be?"

An alarm sounded from the control panel. Rebecca looked up and saw the message window illuminate for 'Right Engine Temp Hi.' She checked indications and saw that the coolant pressure dropped to zero. "Damn!" she shouted and covered her face dejectedly. "We're screwed."

Marina and Britt descended the stairs into the cargo bay. She removed three survival suits and a portable floodlight from a survival locker. After inspecting the suits for sizes, she tossed one to Britt.

"What's this for?" he asked with a puzzled expression.

"How else are we going to reach the other ship?" We can't transport. With the alien ship's central systems shut down, there's no way to communicate with it and map our target."

Britt frowned as he looked over his suit. "It looks a little big for me. I guess the owners weren't small beings."

"You can always stay here," she suggested.

Rebecca barged through the door at the top of the stairs and interrupted, "I hope you have a plan to get off of this rock. This ship's not going anywhere. It's cooked."

Britt grew concerned and waited for her to explain. Marina donned the survival suit. "Are you sure about that?"

"The engine's coolant blew out from the nacelle. It's shot," Rebecca answered in a frustrated tone.

Marina tossed a suit onto the stairs for Rebecca. "Look, the alien ship is our way out of here. Victor will find us soon and he'll board this old crate."

"But that ship's buried against the mountainside in ice and snow!" uttered Rebecca as she dressed in the survival gear.

"What was it you told me about destiny?" Marina reminded her. "Have a little faith." She went to down the corridor and retrieved the crystal from the 'Data Processing Control System' panel.

Britt reluctantly donned his suit as well. Marina opened the hatch and led them through the gale force winds and blustery snow to the alien cruiser with only a small floodlight to guide them. They held onto each other tightly with one hand as they approached the open hatch of the ship. It was the only recognizable section of the ship as the remainder was embedded in the icy slope behind it. Once inside, Britt manually closed the hatch. Rebecca went to the flight deck and attempted to restore power to the ship.

Marina stared out of the ship at the surrounding ice until the hatch closed and she could see it no more. The lights came on as power was restored to the ship. An eerie mist filled the main quarters when the temperature rose and icicles melted. Britt knocked them to the ground as the snow turned to slush. They removed their hoods and gloves.

Marina appeared to be in a trance as she clutched the backpack to her chest. The crystal emitted a glow from under the flaps of the backpack. Britt watched her anxiously and wondered what she was experiencing. He placed his hand on her shoulder and rubbed it tenderly. Marina was startled but pleased by his attention to her. She took the crystal from the backpack and cradled it tightly against her.

"You want to talk about it?" he asked.

"Not yet. I'll need your help for just a little bit longer, though."

"For…?"

Marina ignored him and set the crystal on top of a cabinet. She searched each of the maintenance hatches in the floor until she found a motorized winch and a lengthy chain.

Britt helped her lift the winch and secure it above the hatch to an eyebolt.

Rebecca returned looking frustrated. "I restored the power but I can't operate anything else. This ship isn't anything like ours."

Marina replied, "You did well, Rebecca. Now, let me worry about that."

"What's up with you?" asked Britt suspiciously. "There's something you aren't telling us."

"Maybe there is, now get your hood on. We have work to do." Marina retrieved a blow torch and gas tank from the floor hatch and strapped it on her back. She also took a pickaxe and a hammer for Britt to use. "Britt, you'll help me pull the cable out. Rebecca, you'll operate the winch from in here. I'll signal with the floodlight for you to draw the cable in."

Once they secured their survival suits, Britt operated the remote controls for the hatch, located just inside the hatch. As the hatch opened, Rebecca took her position at the winch. Marina and Britt exited into the gusting winds. The main quarters quickly filled with snow as the temperature plummeted again.

Rebecca ran the cable out and watched the other two disappear in the blinding snow storm. She shuddered to think of all the things that could go wrong out there.

Marina knelt down and cleared the snow off a portion of ice. She saw a shadow that appeared to be a face. Britt knelt next to her and brushed away more snow until they exposed the whole figure.

Marina opened the valve on the tank and pressed the trigger on the torch. The flame shone like a blue sword. She cut around the body with the flame while Britt drove the pickaxe into the ice at the foot of the figure. He attached the cable to it while Marina finished cutting out the ice from around the body.

They signaled Rebecca to run the cable back in and returned to the ship. The cable went taut and hung up. Marina hurried out of the ship and used the torch to cut more of the ice from around the figure. The block cracked loudly and broke free. The winch dragged the frozen corpse to the ship where they lifted it inside the bay.

Marina and Britt returned to the site with the cable and worked until four frozen figures lay inside the main quarters of the ship.

Rebecca anxiously closed the hatch and the temperature rose back to a comfortable level. She removed her hood and announced determinedly, "We are done outside, I assume."

"Not yet," replied Marina. "Now we return to our ship."

Britt and Rebecca grew more confused than ever. Marina activated the 'Transport Control' panel at the rear of the main quarters and waited for the diagnostic codes to clear. When the 'transporter ready' light turned green, she removed her survival suit and programmed the transporter. The monitor showed an image of their ship. She moved a cursor to the cargo bay and set the timer for one minute.

"What are we going back for?" asked Rebecca as she and Britt removed their suits.

"Revenge. Resolution. Termination. Maybe something else," Marina answered cryptically. "I don't know."

"So psychotic. So you," taunted Rebecca.

They vanished in a brief flash of light and appeared on board the *Neutrino*.

"Check the scanners for Victor's ships, Rebecca," ordered Marina. "I have some things to prepare."

Rebecca ascended the stairs to the passenger deck.

"I need the explosives and the detonators you found earlier. Can you get them for me?" Marina requested.

Britt suspected that Marina would lay out a trap for Victor but wasn't quite sure how she would execute it. While he searched for the items, Marina placed the plastic box with Fiona's head on a table by the hatch. She studied the design of the hull opposite the hatch and thought.

Britt returned with a detonator, three fuses, primary igniters and explosive packages wired with a transmitter to receive their signal from their detonators. "Is this what you want?"

Marina was pleased to see the explosives and their devices. "It sure is. I'm preparing a little present for Victor when he arrives."

"I figured as much," replied Britt.

Marina mounted the explosives to the hull in a square configuration. Britt installed the fuses in each block and set the primary igniter last on the bottom right.

Marina programmed the detonator for three seconds and set it on top of the steel cabinet next to the hatch.

"Marina," called Rebecca over the intercom. "Victor's in range."

"Show time," quipped Marina. She and Britt ascended the stairs and headed to the flight deck.

***

"I've found them, sir. They've landed on the planet's surface," Anton announced excitedly.

"Inform the commander of the *Scorpion* that no one is to leave that planet without me."

Victor beamed with joy. He sensed that the hunt was nearly over. One way or another, he'll get what he wanted. "Contact the *Neutrino*," he ordered excitedly.

The transmitter pinged twice. Rebecca ignored it and summoned Marina on the intercom. "Victor's calling. How about some guidance here?" she requested.

Marina declared giddily, "Let the games begin." She and Britt entered the flight deck and joined Rebecca.

Anton attempted three more times to contact them without getting a response. Victor pushed him out of the way and sat down. "She'll reply shortly. I'm sure of it," he said confidently.

The transmitter pinged again. "Go ahead, Rebecca," Marina instructed. "It's time."

Rebecca smiled and toggled the transmitter to 'receive.' "Good morning, this is Rebel Air. How can we serve you?"

"Come now, Marina, don't you think this game has gone on long enough?"

"Are you lost, Victor?" taunted Rebecca. "It seems that you're a long way from the palace on Yord."

Marina and Britt chuckled at her humor.

Victor grew agitated and demanded, "Who is this? Where's Marina?"

"I'm right here, Victor, just waiting for our reunion. This time you're on my turf."

"The old Priestess told me that a woman I know would kill me. Now I have the opportunity to put both of you down and dispel that myth."

The women giggled as he still believed Fiona was working with them.

"Was it your ship that provided the coordinates for Ithaca in the database, Victor?" asked Marina. "It seems you know all about this place."

"Perhaps," he replied. "I have much to share with you but first, where is Fiona?"

"She's on cold standby right now. She can't wait for you to join her, though."

"I want to speak with her now," he ordered.

"You really miss that charred face, don't you?" mocked Marina.

Victor lost control and screamed, "You'll pay for your disrespect, you and your rebel friends!"

Rebecca pointed to the monitor. Victor's ships were hovering in the atmosphere above them. Marina nodded and continued her conversation. "Sorry, pal, but the rebels aren't my cause."

"But it was you who had the data chip all along. You fooled everyone including my men."

Marina was amused by his remark.

"You really aren't very bright, are you, Victor?" Rebecca interjected boldly.

"Does the arrogant wench have a name?"

"My name is Rebecca or 'Red' as you prefer to call me. It is I who led the rebels against you on Yord."

"So Marina really wasn't the rebel leader after all. This will make our little social so much sweeter. You, Fiona and Marina - a reunion for all ages."

"And it will be your last, I promise you," warned Rebecca, who then toggled the transmitter switch to the 'off' position. She gazed at Marina with a gleeful expression. "This could be fun. Victor and two hot women," she joked.

Britt rolled his eyes in annoyance and suggested they focus on Victor's coming assault.

Victor's eyes bulged and the veins on his temples flared. "Prepare to transport us on board that ship!" he screamed at Anton and stormed off.

He joined his new arrivals from the *Scorpion* in the transporter room and signaled the pilot to place them on board the *Neutrino*.

Marina instructed Rebecca, "When I give you the order, you must transport me back immediately. Any delay and I'll die with Victor. Now the two of you must leave."

Britt took her hands in his. "It doesn't have to be like this, Marina. I ..."

"This is what I want," she interrupted. "I ask you to respect that."

Britt hugged her and stood by Rebecca. Marina operated the transporter and sent them back to the alien cruiser. She sat down on one of the crates and thought about what would happen after her encounter with Victor.

Rebecca and Britt appeared on the alien cruiser and rushed to the flight deck. Rebecca attempted to scan Victor's ship for transporter activity but her lack of knowledge of the ship's systems left her frustrated.

"Don't forget me, Rebecca," Marina called over the transmitter. "I'm counting on you."

"Please be careful," Rebecca said sadly.

"Where's Britt?" Marina asked.

Britt shook his head 'no' to her.

"Don't know," Rebecca replied.

"Tell him... Tell him something nice if I don't make it back," Marina requested

"You will. Don't worry." The transmission ended.

"I'm going back, Rebecca," Britt declared. "She'll be outnumbered."

"I'll go, too."

"No, stay here in case this backfires on us." When Britt left the flight deck, Rebecca became worried as she realized they could die and she couldn't fly that ship. She'd die alone with her child and no one would ever know – just like her parents.

Marina wiped a tear from her eye and stood up. She held a dagger in one hand and a pulse pistol in another.

Victor and ten men appeared in the cargo bay in front of her. Marina was surprised to see so many but remained calm.

"Well, Marina, we meet again."

Marina pointed her pistol at Victor's head and warned the soldiers, "Stow your weapons or he dies."

Victor was amused and motioned for his men to stand down.

Rebecca finally was able to scan the *Neutrino* from the alien cruiser and realized Marina was outnumbered. "Damn it! They need backup." Rebecca took a remote device for the transporter and a pulse pistol from the locker in the corridor. She transported on board the *Neutrino* at the rear of the bay behind the soldiers.

Britt was already there and immediately pulled her back. He placed his hand over her mouth and held up a finger for her to be silent. He stood behind one of the soldiers and whispered, "She is the Princess and we will support her."

The soldier turned to Britt, who again motioned for silence. "All of you will return to your ship unless you want a war with the other militias," Britt continued. "Victor's time as our commander is over."

The soldier nodded and whispered to the others.

"Where is Fiona?" Victor inquired while unaware of Britt's presence. "I have a debt to settle with her."

Marina pointed to the box on the table. Victor opened it and was pleased at the sight of Fiona's head. He returned the box to the table and remarked, "How fitting. You've killed for me as she once did."

"Don't flatter yourself," she quipped sarcastically.

The soldiers transported back to their ship without Victor's knowledge. His gaze was fixed on Marina and what he stood to gain with her by his side.

"I'll offer you one more opportunity to join me in ruling Yord and much, much more. We could be unstoppable."

"If you are so powerful then why do you need me?"

"You will command the will of the people who support us and the crystal will lead us to victory over our enemies," he explained.

"I can do that myself. Why do I need you?"

Victor grew impatient. "Because I control the militias. They will do my bidding whenever I tell them, just like you and the red-headed wench will."

Rebecca became angry and clenched her fists.

"Oh, you shouldn't have said that," Britt retorted.

Victor was surprised to hear his voice and turned around. Rebecca stepped toward Victor and delivered a swift kick to his jaw. He fell to the floor and lay stunned. "Where are my men?" he demanded angrily as he searched for backup.

"They no longer answer to you," Britt informed him.

Victor rubbed his jaw and studied Rebecca for a moment. "Red I presume."

"Yes, I am. I've waited a long time for this."

"No!" shouted Marina. "He's mine. Return to the ship now."

Britt took Rebecca by the arm and backed away from them. Rebecca reluctantly activated the remote device and the two of them transported back to the alien cruiser.

Victor stood up and drew a pistol from his belt. "I see we're going to do this the hard way."

"Is there any other way?" replied Marina cynically. "Let's make this interesting, shall we?" She tossed her pistol on one of the crates and waited with her dagger for him to charge.

"We could do so much together, Marina. Think about it."

Marina kicked at his knife but he blocked her leg with his arm. He held her leg and clamped his other arm around her dagger. Marina struggled to get free but Victor held her tightly and rammed her into the hatch.

Marina head-butted him and briefly staggered him but he rammed her several times into the hull until she weakened. When he released his hold on her, he leveled her with a blow to the head. Marina lay dazed on the floor of the ship.

"Would you like to know about your parents, Marina?" he asked with a sadistic grin.

Marina pulled herself onto her knees. "What could you possibly know about them?" she inquired.

"It was I who sent them to their frozen deaths. They killed my parents and I killed yours in return. It seems we share some family history, wouldn't you say?"

Marina leaned with one hand against the steps for balance and seethed. "That's all I wanted to hear from you."

Victor took her pistol from the crate and pointed it at her. "I'm surprised you have nothing else to say."

Marina stood slowly and still held the stair rail for support. "There is one more issue we need to resolve, Victor."

"And what is that?" he asked with an amused expression.

Marina took the detonator off of the crate and pointed to the explosives on the hull. "As you sent my parents to an icy death, so I send you." She held up the detonator, pressed the button and tossed it to him.

Victor's eyes widened with fright as he caught the device.

"Now!" shouted Marina. She vanished and was transported to the alien cruiser just as the explosives detonated. The blast blew out a large section of the hull and slammed Victor against the hatch.

The gale force winds and swirling snow immediately filled the cargo bay. The temperature plummeted to sub-zero in seconds. The plastic box fell to the floor and spilled Fiona's head in the middle of the bay.

Victor froze to death within seconds. Soon after, his body became a block of ice and was knocked to the floor from the wind, shattering. His head broke off his torso and spun across the floor until it stopped next to Fiona's head. The two heads faced each other for their eternity of damnation.

Marina laid face-down on the floor of the alien cruiser. She heard the explosion and knew it was over. Victor and Fiona were out of her life forever.

The crackling sound of ice breaking apart startled her. She crawled to her knees and approached one of the frozen figures. The thought that Victor murdered her parents and left them in this frozen wasteland was mortifying. Marina nervously wiped the ice so she could see one of the faces. It was the woman in her dreams – her mother!

Marina shuddered in fear and stood up. She rubbed the ice on the next figure and saw the face of a young man – her father. She recognized him from the images she'd viewed on Orpheus-2. She fell to her knees and cried.

Britt and Rebecca arrived from the flight deck and joined her. Britt lifted her to her feet and held her as she sobbed. He looked down at the frozen figures and asked, "Is it them?"

Marina nodded and pulled away from him.

Rebecca knelt by the other two figures and rubbed the ice over their faces. Tears streamed down from her eyes as well.

The crystal glowed brightly and caught their attention. Marina took the crystal from the top of the cabinet and cradled it to her chest. She stood between the figures of her parents and prayed. The ice cracked and fell away from all four bodies. The preserved bodies stunned all of them. All but Marina's father had bloodstains and pulse gun wounds. *"That's strange,"* thought Marina. *"How did he die?"*

The eyes of Marina's mother opened and she spoke, "You must fulfill your destiny. We are one with you, Marina. Our love is strong."

Marina's father spoke next, "We will always be with you."

Marina stumbled backwards away from the remains. The crystal dimmed. "Did you hear that?" she exclaimed excitedly.

Britt and Rebecca looked at her with a confused expression. "Hear what?" asked Britt.

"They spoke to me! Didn't you hear them?"

Britt hugged her and whispered, "They've always been there for you. You just never listened before."

Rebecca knelt over the remains of her parents and prayed.

The bodies shriveled rapidly and became unrecognizable mushy piles.

Marina held out the crystal and waited for something to happen. She hoped that it would bring her parents back to life but the crystal was extinguished and remained so. She became angry and threw it against the hull of the ship. It shattered into thousands of fragments.

Rebecca jumped to her feet and shouted, "What the hell did you do that for?"

"I had to do it. I promised Kat."

"That's not why you did it," she challenged. "That crystal brought them together and now it's gone!"

"So are they. They are finally at peace and we need to move on."

Britt picked up several of the fragments and studied them. They were just shards of glass. He placed his arms around both women and suggested, "The power isn't in the crystal anymore. It doesn't matter."

Both women stared at him and waited for clarification.

Britt eyed Marina proudly and continued, "The power is in you. Now, it's up to you what you do with it."

Marina looked into his eyes like a frightened little girl. "Promise me that you won't ever leave me?" she pleaded.

"Only if you punch me again in my moment of need," he joked.

Marina turned to Rebecca. "And you, too. Please don't ever leave me."

Rebecca held Marina's hands and replied, "We're not going anywhere."

"So now what?" asked Britt.

The three of them stared at each other for a moment and smiled.

"We did it!" shouted Rebecca.

"Yes, we did!" replied Marina.

"I never had a doubt," added Britt.

The women stared at him in disbelief and then hugged him. They cherished the moment.

Britt backed away and looked at Marina for a moment. He took notice of the bumps and bruises on her face and arms. Her eyes were wet with tears and she was unsteady on her feet. "Young lady, you'd better get some rest," he suggested. "You're a mess."

"I'm fine," she replied stubbornly.

"Like hell you are. You have to slow down."

"Whoa, there!" shouted Rebecca. "Somebody better be able to fly this ship. I sure can't."

Marina entered the flight deck, followed by Britt and Rebecca. She sat down and studied the controls for a moment. Everything was just as she dreamed. "I can fly this ship," she assured them.

The transmitter beeped and startled them. They glanced at each other nervously. Marina pressed the switch and acknowledged the call.

"*Neutrino*, this is the *Orion*, are you there?" requested a man's voice in an urgent tone.

Britt held his hand out for the women to be silent. "This is Britt. Go ahead, *Neutrino*."

"This is Jarvis, Britt. The *Scorpion* has orders to destroy you if Victor doesn't return."

"But Victor's dead."

"Regardless, the *Scorpion* refuses to stand down. What can we do to help?"

Britt looked to Marina for direction. She reluctantly instructed Jarvis, "Contact Orpheus-2 from the other side of the portal and request help from Jeffries, the station commander. He'll know what to do."

"We will make great haste, Princess Marina," replied Jarvis. Marina was speechless. She had no idea how to react to that title.

Britt and Rebecca noticed and were quite amused. Marina elbowed him in the ribs. He clutched at his side and grumbled, "What's that for?"

"You know."

"Well, now that we bought some time, perhaps we can rest for a bit," suggested Rebecca. "I'm exhausted."

"The *Scorpion* won't find us buried this far in the snow, especially with the *Neutrino* so close to us. It'll still give off a heat signature until the systems shut down," Marina assured them. "They'll think it's just the wreckage of one ship so let's take advantage of it."

Rebecca went to the first cabin down the corridor and plopped on the bed. She was soon fast asleep.

Britt followed Marina to the next cabin down. She paused by the door and asked, "Would you mind leaving me a little space? I need to figure some things out."

"Of course, I will." Britt kissed her and watched as she closed the cabin door behind her. Not knowing what else to do, he covered the remains of the bodies with tarps and mopped the floor.

Marina sat on the edge of the bed and wondered if her mother was in this position many years ago: a free spirit who was suddenly thrust into the role of queen and forced to be responsible for her people and for herself. She wondered if she could come to see herself as a queen like her mother and worried if she'd be any good at it. People skills weren't on the top of her list of talents.

She lay back and thought about Dix and the courier business. Could she ever go back? Too many people know her real identity. Her secret life was over. *"And what about Britt?"* she thought. His hang-up with protocol could ruin what little relationship they had together.

She considered that Rebecca handled the fight for the people of Yord for ten years and now she's paid the price. She lost Cristos and she has the role of motherhood ahead of her without a father for her child. Marina craved a shot of adrenalin to take on her problems or a bottle of whiskey to make her forget. It's been a while since she had either. Maybe that was a good thing.

When Marina fell asleep, she dreamed of her mother and father. She wanted so badly to be held by them but they were too far away. She called to them but they didn't hear her. They faded away and she was left standing at the top of the steps in the palace. Tears streamed down her cheeks.

Britt slept in the third cabin after Marina's with the door open. He tried not to think too hard about things he couldn't control. The time was near when Marina would have to make her decision, once and for all. There would be no going back after that.

An alarm sounded throughout the ship. Rebecca hurried from her cabin to the flight deck and checked the monitors.

Britt and Marina emerged from their cabins and met in the hall. "They must have found us!" exclaimed Britt. "We have to get out of here fast!"

They hurried up to the flight deck and joined Rebecca. "What do you have?" asked Marina anxiously.

"Their scanners have locked onto us!"

"If we don't move now, they'll have a 'weapons lock' on us in a minute!" Britt announced.

Marina sat down and calmly took over the controls. Britt and Rebecca watched her anxiously as she started the engines.

"Do you really know how to operate this ship?" Rebecca asked nervously.

"Yeah, I do. My mother taught me in a dream."

"So this was our parents' last mission."

"It all makes sense," replied Marina. "Their plan succeeded against the Weevil but Victor screwed with the portals. That's how they became stranded out here, where no one would think to look."

Britt placed his hands on her shoulders and kissed the top of her head.

Marina activated a force field around the ship that blasted the snow and ice away. She promptly navigated the ship away from the wreck of the *Neutrino* and ascended into the atmosphere.

"Can we outrun them?" Britt inquired uneasily.

Marina looked surprised by his question. "Who's running? We're going after the bastards!"

"We can't take on a man-o'-war, Marina!" Rebecca uttered in a panicked tone.

Marina smiled deviously and increased their speed. The *Scorpion* fired several shots at them but never came close.

"Why don't you try diplomacy?" suggested Britt. "Give them a chance to surrender."

Marina bit her lip and reluctantly activated the transmitter. She waited impatiently as the alien cruiser circled the man-o'-war. "You know what my dad named this ship?" Marina quizzed them.

Britt and Rebecca had no idea and waited anxiously for her answer.

"They called it 'The Reaper.' It had one hell of a paint job, too from what I remember of the images Severin showed us."

The transmitter beeped. "Time to find out who is loyal and who isn't," she remarked with an amusing smile on her face.

A voice emitted from the transmitter with an air of arrogance, "This is Captain McVeigh, commander of the *Scorpion*. Who is this?"

Marina felt a rush of control come over her and responded, "This is your Queen. I order you to stand down and surrender or you will be dealt with as traitors to the kingdom."

McVeigh laughed and heckled her, "What kingdom? Where is Victor?"

"Victor and Fiona are spending eternity together in an icy grave. Now, stand down or you'll be dealt with severely."

"Then we have nothing more to discuss," he replied. "It's time for you to die."

Britt interceded and spoke, "McVeigh, this is Britt. Victor has been punished for his crimes. Stand down and let us return to Yord."

McVeigh laughed and replied, "Just because Victor's gone, it doesn't mean I'm going to roll over and cede my power to a white trash criminal. She belongs in prison with her friend Balthus."

Marina turned off the transmitter. "Now we do it my way," she announced and activated the weapons systems.

"You don't have to do this, Marina," urged Rebecca. "If this ship is as fast as you say, we can race past them and be gone."

Marina glared at her. "If you want respect, you have to earn it. If you want me to be queen, then I have to show that I can fight."

Britt and Rebecca's eyes lit up. "You're gonna' take the throne?" Rebecca asked anxiously.

"I'm thinking about it," Marina answered calmly. She fired six pulse torpedoes at the man-o'-war and followed them toward the ship.

"What the hell are you doing?" blurted Britt as he panicked. "We're gonna' explode with them."

Marina raced past the torpedoes just before impact and avoided any cannon fire from the *Scorpion*. Four of the torpedoes struck the ship while two were intercepted. A bright fiery blast appeared briefly at the forward weapons ports and extinguished, leaving a large crater in the front hull of the ship.

"Holy shit!" exclaimed Britt. "We just outraced our own torpedoes!"

"This ship is special," remarked Marina. "There's nothing faster than it in the galaxy."

Marina then launched four magnetic charges from the tail of the ship. Each charge was immediately drawn to the bottom hull of the ship and attached to it. A few seconds later, each charge exploded and ripped a gaping hole in the ship.

Random cannon fire left bursts of red energy around the *Reaper* but did no damage.

"That's enough, Marina," Britt said nervously. "They're finished."

"I'm not." She navigated around and approached the *Scorpion* from the front. She contacted McVeigh on the transmitter and asked cynically, "How does it feel, McVeigh, to see your mighty ship decimated by a common criminal – a female, no less?"

"Screw you, bitch!" he shouted. "We'll never surrender to you."

Marina placed a target lock on the control center of the ship and announced, "Here's a present for you, McVeigh. You can join Victor and Fiona in hell!" She laughed sadistically and terminated the transmission. She continued toward the *Scorpion* and waited patiently until she was in range.

On board the *Scorpion*, the officers on the deck grew uneasy and pleaded with McVeigh to surrender. When he refused, they executed him. One of the officers immediately contacted Marina. "This is Quinton. Please hold your fire! We surrender."

Just as Marina was about to flex her finger and fire, Quinton's voice rang out. Disappointedly, Marina inquired, "Where's McVeigh? Why the change of heart?"

"McVeigh is dead. We're standing down and surrendering to you, Princess Marina. Our ship is incapacitated. Can you help us?"

"We'll be in touch shortly." Marina ended the transmission.

Rebecca noticed that another ship approached from a distance. Rebecca scanned for their frequency and replied, "It's a Fleet warship!"

The transmitter beeped, much to Marina's annoyance. "Identify yourself," she requested.

"This is Commander Sheena Brice of the *S.F. Argos*. Is this Marina, daughter of Will and Shanna?"

Marina was impressed with the words. "Yes, it is."

"And what of Victor and Fiona?"

"They have paid for their treasonous acts," announced Marina proudly as she enjoyed her new role.

"Then the alliance stands by you. I will recall our forces to pay you homage on Yord."

Marina was stunned at the idea of returning to Yord. She hesitated as a cold chill swept over her. "Thank you, Commander Brice. Can you render assistance to the man-o'-war? They have surrendered and request our aid."

"Of course. It's a pleasure to finally serve under you, your Highness."

"Thank you, Commander."

Britt and Rebecca were amused by her behavior. Marina switched the transmitter off and glared at them. "What?" she asked irritably.

"You seem quite at home being in charge of your own military," teased Rebecca.

"Yeah, and I almost destroyed some of it, too."

Britt rubbed her shoulders and assured her, "You'll get better at this. After all, you did wait before pressing the trigger. Normally you shoot first and enjoy the consequences."

They laughed and set a course for Yord.

Chapter 13

Loose Ends

Marina set the navigation system on 'auto-pilot' for Yord. Rebecca rested in her quarters while Marina and Britt shared hers.

Rebecca pondered whether or not Marina would accept her role as Princess and then Queen. It would be foolish to assume she would. When they reached Yord, she would play the diplomat with the people and see what happens.

The baby stirred inside her and she turned her thoughts to motherhood. Memories of Cristos and the battles they fought filled her head. Whenever she gave up hope, he was there to remind her that one day there would be peace.

Marina lay in bed with Britt and gazed at him. She rubbed her hand across his chest and nestled against him. "Still considering your options, I see."

Britt was lost in his thoughts but replied, "We have difficult decisions to make. I'm trying to come to terms with them."

Marina stroked his cheek affectionately. "And what if we don't make them? What if we just keep things the way they are?"

Britt sighed in frustration and sat up on the end of the bed. "You still don't get it. Things can never be the way they were. You have a responsibility to rule or leave. I have a responsibility to protect you if you rule and if not, I don't know what that means. To me, you will always be the Princess I gave up my friends and my rank for."

Marina sat up and turned his face to hers. "I know what you gave up for me and I am grateful. I now understand what Rebecca gave up for me and for that, too, I am grateful. I didn't ask for this but I am trying to understand how I fit into all this."

Britt placed his arm around her and tilted his head against hers. "You don't fit into it. You take it by storm and do what comes natural. When you do, I'll be there beside you."

Marina smiled and kissed him passionately. They lay back down on the bed and made love.

***

Marina awoke and went to the flight deck. She found a device that recorded the ship's travels and events. She noted that the *Reaper* spent a lot of time over a three year period on a distant planet called Andros-3. She wondered what was on that planet that required so many trips. The details focused on attacks made by the ship on various enemies and the amount of damage inflicted. Perhaps one day she would find out from the historians.

The auto-pilot system beeped and alarmed briefly. Marina glanced at it and acknowledged the alarm. The ship entered Yord's atmosphere and the system swapped to 'manual' navigation. Marina's nerves tingled and she became edgy as she fretted what to do. Maybe she would drop Britt and Rebecca off and then disappear someplace far away like Andros-3.

Rebecca entered the flight deck. She was showered and already dressed in clean clothes.

"I see you found your way around the ship pretty well," teased Marina.

"It has all the comforts of home. It's as if someone lived on it."

Marina considered her words and recalled that her father lived alone for a while during the Great War when the kingdom was overrun and friends fled with her to escape capture. She remembered that her mother endured great pains to find her. That's when she recalled the stories of her father fighting the aliens on his own from a distant planet. He wreaked havoc for quite some time before being reunited with Marina and her mother. A tear streamed down her cheek.

"Are you okay?" asked Rebecca.

"Yeah, just some memories coming back to me."

"Me, too. I'm also worried about having this baby. I'm afraid I won't be a good mother."

Marina hugged her and assured her, "You'll be a great mother. You took care of me all this time and I'm a handful."

"You were a real brat," joked Rebecca. "But we made a hell of a team."

Marina thought about what Rebecca just said. It was past tense. "*We 'made' a hell of a team.*" Did it have to end? Thoughts raced through her head as she landed the ship in front of the palace.

Rebecca smiled and said, "Wish me luck. We'll meet again." She kissed Marina and left the flight deck.

Marina was shocked. Rebecca didn't expect her to take her role. She just walked away like it was over.

Marina activated the external cameras on the ship and studied the surrounding area. The palace was a dilapidated mess. The gates lay covered in rust and dirt on the palace grounds. People gathered outside the *Reaper* and watched curiously.

Britt was strangely absent and that worried Marina. She shut down the ship's engines and systems. It was time for her to make her decision.

Outside the ship people gathered and waited anxiously. Many remembered the vivid tales of Marina's parents and the *Reaper* with its ghostly flowing white tails streaming behind screaming skulls on the ship's black surface. It was quite an attraction for everyone.

The hatch opened and Rebecca stepped out. The crowd was massive now as people already heard the news and returned in large numbers to hear her speak. They became quiet as Rebecca raised her arms for attention.

"Victor lives no more!" she announced triumphantly. "The militia rules us no more!"

The crowd cheered for several moments then silenced.

"We have recovered the bodies of our long lost king and queen along with my parents who fought by their side. All were victims of Victor's treachery."

The crowd was stunned by her news.

Marina leaned against the hull just inside the hatch and listened to her speak. She looked distraught. Britt approached and stood behind her.

"Where were you?" she asked nervously.

"I spoke with the militias. They know the alliance has their flash drive back and are happy to pledge their support to you if you choose to accept your role."

Marina was surprised by his news. "And they listened to you just like that?"

Britt replied giddily, "Seems the 1st militia needs a leader and they like my style."

She wasn't thrilled and banged her head against the hull in frustration. "So you're going back to the militia?"

"I wouldn't say that. There's a lot we need to talk about. Right now, I'm here for you," he assured her and massaged her shoulders. Outside Rebecca related the details of their ordeal.

Marina pushed him away and paced the floor. "What am I doing here?" she said frantically. "This isn't me!"

"Who is the real you?" asked Britt. "I want to know."

Marina suddenly felt ill. She grew dizzy and had a premonition. She stood over her parents' bodies inside the ship. They opened their eyes and spoke to her, "This is who we are. This is who you are."

Marina quivered in fear. Britt understood what was happening and held her tightly. The premonition continued.

Marina's father pleaded, "Do this for us, Marina. We sacrificed everything for you."

Marina's mother added, "We will always be with you."

Marina gasped for breath and the premonition ended. She grew impatient and exclaimed, "Damn it!"

Britt was concerned and asked, "Are you okay?"

Marina frowned at him and approached the hatch. She turned back to him and became teary-eyed. She removed the wig with the dreadlocks and tossed it in the corner. She untied her hair and her long dark locks fell over her shoulder. "Are you happy now?"

"It's a start. Are you?"

"I guess I'll learn."

"For what it's worth, you're beautiful, Marina."

Marina threw her arms around him and kissed him passionately. "I'll never wear that wig again," she whispered. "That part of me just died."

"And what part of you is left for me?" he teased.

Marina smiled and turned back to the hatch. She peered out at Rebecca.

Rebecca studied the familiar faces in the crowd. Fleet officers lined the left side of the grounds. Militia officers lined the right side.

"Many have died so that I can stand before you today without fear to announce the news you've all been waiting for," she said proudly.

Marina took Britt's hand and led him outside the ship. They stood next to Rebecca.

"What are you doing?" she asked Marina with a surprised expression.

"I hope you didn't think I'd go away that easily, did you?"

Rebecca beamed with pride at her.

"So what am I supposed to do, give a speech or something?" Marina joked.

"Maybe a smile for starters. Just don't shoot anybody," she ribbed.

The crowd murmured curiously and wondered who Rebecca's friends were.

Rebecca sensed Marina's nervousness. "I'll help you through this," she offered.

Britt whispered, "Just relax. It'll be fine."

Marina squeezed his hand tightly.

Rebecca announced, "Standing here before you is Princess Marina, daughter of our King and Queen who has returned to claim the throne which is rightfully hers."

After a brief pause, the crowd broke into a cheer. The cheer grew louder and became a roar.

"What the hell are you doing?" Marina asked frantically.

"I'm helping you," replied Rebecca giddily and pushed her forward.

The crowd became quiet and anxiously waited for Marina to speak. She looked nervously over the crowd and gulped. "I have been away a long time," she started uneasily. "Rebecca has been here to lead the fight against Victor and Fiona." She hesitated and gulped again.

"You're doing fine," whispered Britt.

Marina glanced at him uneasily and continued, "As such, I would like Rebecca to be my liaison between myself and my people to help us rebuild our world and our alliance into something bigger and better than my parents created."

"I gladly accept that offer," Rebecca quickly affirmed.

"Thank you," whispered Marina. The two hugged.

The crowd cheered again ecstatically.

Marina's confidence grew and she relaxed. "I could never have defeated Victor and Fiona without the help of Rebecca and Britt," she announced and glanced at him with a smile. "Britt helped us prevent a war between the militias and the Fleet which could have destroyed all of us. I'd like for Britt to stay on as my liaison between the militias, the Fleet and myself."

Britt stepped forward and announced, "I, too, gladly accept your Highness' offer."

The people cheered again.

"There are others that helped me to be the person you see here today. They know who they are. Thank you."

Seven men wearing cloaks and bearing arms moved to the front of the crowd. They lowered their hoods and raised their crossbows in support of Marina. One of them shouted, "Well done, Rebecca."

Marina noticed and kidded, "Boyfriends of yours?"

Rebecca blushed and said, "You really are a ..."

"I know - a bitch. The story of my life."

Three militia officers saluted and nodded to Britt. Britt and Marina returned their salute.

Marina embraced Rebecca and Britt as the crowd cheered. Officers from the Space Fleet stepped to the front and saluted. Marina returned their salute. She stepped down to them and asked, "Would one of you be Commander Brice?"

A tall, brunette female, about twenty-five years old, smiled at her. "Yes, ma'am. It's an honor to meet you."

"Did you know Commander Severin on Orpheus-2?" Marina asked.

"Yes, ma'am. That was my older sister."

Marina was stunned. She took the woman's hands in hers. "I'm so sorry. She did so much for my parents and for me. If you ever need my help, I'd be honored to comply."

Commander Brice hesitated and replied, "If you could make things like they were before, that would be the greatest thing you can do. Your parents built a wonderful empire."

Marina was flattered. "I'll do my best," she promised.

Kara and her grandparents pushed through the crowd and reached her. Kara shouted excitedly, "Marina!"

Marina hugged her tightly and whispered, "Victor paid for what he did to our parents."

Kara kissed her cheek and hugged her back tightly. Britt and Rebecca were amused as Marina blushed.

Clem and Dora clapped for her and smiled approvingly.

"I knew you wouldn't let me down," she said excitedly. "You're my hero!"

Marina responded humbly, "No, Rebecca is the real hero. I wouldn't be here today if it wasn't for her."

Rebecca was pleased by her comment. "So where do we go from here?"

Marina sighed. "I guess we have a kingdom to rebuild."

"We?"

"Yes, Rebecca, 'we.' Remember, this was your idea."

Rebecca gave her a playful push.

Marina turned to Britt. "And you, you big oaf…"

"What?"

"It's your job to keep me happy or else."

Britt feigned concern and looked away. Marina pulled him to her side and placed her arm around him. She held Kara's hand as well, glancing at her young friend with a smile.

The crowd continued to cheer.

Kat's image appeared inside Marina's head. "You did well, Marina. I am proud of you." The image ended.

Marina scanned the crowd and saw Dix standing with Kat. "What the hell is that all about?" she thought to herself. "I think I've been set up for this."

Dix smiled at her and Kat blew a kiss to her.

Britt noticed and asked, "Something I should know about?"

"Ask Rebecca."

Rebecca was startled and replied, "No, ask Marina."

"You wouldn't believe it," Marina finally answered and turned back toward the ship.

"Where are you going?" Rebecca inquired.

"Princess needs her sleep. You have the floor, Ms. Liaison." She grabbed Britt by the arm and pulled him inside with her.

Rebecca stood with hands on her hips and thought, "She'll always be a bitch." She chuckled and summoned several of the officers to meet with her.

Inside the ship, Marina warned Britt, "You have duties to fulfill." She loosened her bodice seductively and pulled him close to her. "Are you up to the challenge?"

Britt responded eagerly, "For you, always."

"For some reason, I think my problems are only just beginning," Marina joked.

"Am I a problem?"

"I hope not."

After a long passionate kiss, they entered the cabin and closed the hatch.

About the Author

Michael, a lifelong resident of the Philadelphia area, has developed his creativity from his Mideast tours as a Weapons Crewchief with the 111th FG for 22 years; as a controls technician in a local nuclear plant; and several years of field work in the US and Europe as a nuclear field engineer with a B.S. in Technical and Industrial Administration from Widener University and other Associates degrees.

With the success of the Fractured Time Trilogy and Space Frontiers Series, the Pain Series is Michael's current project beginning with *Princess Pain*.

Now writing screenplays based on his novels, Michael's dream is to see his stories on the big screen. Visit *www.fracturedtime.com* for more details on his appearances and projects.

Also from BlackWyrm...

A CROP OF CIRCLES

by Gerald Duff

A craft from deep space has been forced to land in an Illinois cornfield, and only a twelve-year old boy named Torbert can see it for what it truly is. The meth cookers next door, the drug dealers in East Saint Louis, and even Torbert's own family have no idea what's been forced to Earth to await a way home.
[Science Fiction Humor, ages 14+]

by Ian Harac

An FBI agent goes to the land of Oz to solve a Munchkin's murder, but finds an interdimensional conspiracy. Along the way, he encounters a bicycling turtle, a talking broom, retro-tech, flying monkeys with machine guns, and numerous other oddities.
[Snarky SciFi Thriller, 14+]

THE STARCROSSED

by William I. Levy

What are the odds of meeting your soulmate sixty light years away from home on the very first expedition to another star system?

Not as good as the chance of getting killed by a military conspiracy, renegade scientists, or a demonic entity from beyond time. But Barret and Paum have found something special. And they're not going to let a little thing like Armageddon stand in the way. Hopefully.

[Sci-Fi Action Romance, ages 18+]

BLEEDING EDGE

by Ramsey Lundock

Cybernetic pirates, self-driving cars, streetwise hackers, wired-up bodyguards, transplanted minds, psychic youngsters, and more.

This collection of cyberpunk short stories by Ramsey "Tome Wyrm" Lundock presents many common themes in a new light. When a dehumanizing society, high technology, and violence collide, can the human heart ever win?

[Cyberpunk Short Stories, ages 14+]

Nakba

The Civilizing War, Volume I
by Jason Walters

All that stands between a newly imperial Earth and the rest of the solar system is a loose coalition of Maasai tribesmen, cloned feminists, shape-shifting humannequins, and vengeful Berbers led by the least likely hero in human history: a young woman with Down syndrome and a bad attitude.
[Science Fiction, ages 14+]

MEDIC

by Ian Harac

After the apocalypse, nothing is left but mad robots, madder life forms, and desperate survivors. Doctor MacIntyre, a self-aware ambulance, acts as a freelance medic offering help to those who need it. In this violent, desperate world, MacIntyre can rely on nothing but his wits, his uneasy allies... and a few missile racks he had installed, just in case. He battles violent fanatics, would-be conquerors, and a force that would snuff out any hope of a future.
[Snarky Apocalyptic Sci-Fi 14+]

www.ingramcontent.com/pod-product-compliance
Lightning Source LLC
Chambersburg PA
CBHW070446260626
47161CB00004B/1214